Natalie didn't resist. But not resisting was a far cry from wanting.

Devin *wanted*. Not just the slender beauty he found in her. But what he'd seen in her this past week and more. The distinct lines she drew around herself while still utterly respecting his own. The resiliency of her. The empathy.

And there was her mouth, barely a whisper from his. "Up to you," he managed, if barely.

Your choice.

She understood that—understood further that he knew what it meant to her.

Every bit of him was alive and aware and *present*. He knew the exact moment she realized how low her hand had dropped, as it tightened slightly around the curve of his buttock.

"Oh," she said. And then he fell just a little bit in love, because instead of growing flustered and snatching her hand away, she let it linger.

Books by Doranna Durgin

Harlequin Nocturne

**Sentinels: Tiger Bound* #142
**Sentinels: Kodiak Chained* #150
  Taming the Demon #160

Silhouette Nocturne

**Sentinels: Jaguar Night* #64
**Sentinels: Lion Heart* #70
**Sentinels: Wolf Hunt* #80

**The Sentinels

DORANNA DURGIN

spent her childhood filling notebooks first with stories and art, and then with novels. After obtaining a degree in wild-life illustration and environmental education, she spent a number of years deep in the Appalachian Mountains. When she emerged, it was as a writer who found herself irrevocably tied to the natural world and its creatures—and with a new touchstone to the rugged spirit that helped settle the area, which she instills in her characters.

Doranna's first fantasy novel received the 1995 Compton Crook/Stephen Tall Award for best first book in the fantasy, science fiction and horror genres; she now has fifteen novels in eclectic genres, including paranormal romance, on the shelves. When she's not writing, Doranna builds web pages, enjoys photography and works with horses and dogs. You can find a complete list of her titles at www.doranna.net.

TAMING THE DEMON
DORANNA DURGIN

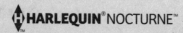

Recycling programs
for this product may
not exist in your area.

ISBN-13: 978-0-373-88570-1

TAMING THE DEMON

Printed in U.S.A.

Dear Reader,

This book wasn't actually supposed to be set in various fictional parts of Albuquerque, New Mexico, at all. But one of the fun things about moving into a new area is discovering it. Even from one high desert home to another, only five hours away...an entirely different culture, entirely different origins.

Still, the rich potential of exploring it in fiction only percolated in my hindbrain for the first months of settling in—at least until the day I rode my horse out along the local acquecia (the generations-old canal system running through the Rio Grande valley) and discovered, tucked away in the middle of nowhere, a rather grand old southwestern home. *This,* I realized, *is where Devin and Natalie will come to know each other.*

And so I found a way to honor my new home while exploring Devin and Natalie's story, and an excuse to look at each new facet of it with an inquisitive eye. This is a place Natalie and Devin each love, and it turned out to be a perfect place for them to fall in love, too. I hope you enjoy it!

Doranna Durgin

This book could be dedicated only to Nancy,
who welcomed me to this New Mexico home as only
a sister could.

Chapter 1

Sharp steel whispered in Devin's mind. Once ancient copper, then bronze, finally iron...now finely honed steel that took and held a sharp edge, never rusting, never dulling.

Then again, no demon blade had ever needed sharpening, whatever its form and substance.

This blade—the one attached to Devin, a merciless presence within his mind and soul—nudged him through the night, riding him endlessly. *Patrol the streets, protect the innocent.*

Never mind that the demon trapped within would prefer to be doing anything but.

And so Devin now drifted along the ugly end of a short strip mall in southwest Albuquerque, following the grudging guidance of the geas-compelled—and cursed—demon. He didn't see anything in the sporadically lit parking area, didn't hear anything…but the blade knew. Someone here meant harm to an innocent.

Currently the demon manifested itself as a small lock-blade pocket knife, a default form that suited them both. And in this cold night, it served as a pocket warmer as well, keeping his hands in leather half-finger gloves warmer than they had any right to be, even warming his body beneath the black leather jacket. A plain old lock-blade knife…

Truth was, he never knew what he'd find when he reached for it, just that he'd find something.

And that he was ready for anything.

I must have heard wrong. Or written down the wrong address. Or misunderstood *something*. Even if she knew she hadn't.

But this just couldn't be right.

Natalie Chambers hesitated at the narrow alley between buildings in the strip mall. Surely there should be better lighting here. This was the southwest quarter of Albuquerque, after all. A place of tightly placed and colorful shops, bars over the windows, gang tags at the corners and copious stout fencing. She'd expected to find direct lighting here at this parking lot of ancient asphalt and stark white adobe structures.

A glance overhead pinpointed the burned-out bulb. Great. According to the notes she could no longer read, the small architectural office she sought should be…

Right here. Right between the two stores. Right in this alley.

She jammed the paper into the pocket of her slacks and pulled her vintage peacoat more tightly around her turtleneck as the breeze lifted the thick waves of her hair and brought out a shiver along her arms.

Then again, maybe the shiver wasn't all about the cold. Maybe it was about standing here in this run-down shopping strip going on midnight, with no sign of any architect's office and no sign of any welcoming window light and her "uh-oh" alarms suggesting that if she planned to call Compton and double-check the address, she should do it from the car.

With the doors locked.

But if she secretly hoped her boss would suggest it could wait until morning, she knew he wouldn't. He didn't jerk her around on a whim, but he did expect her to respond when occasion arose. And it was a good job, an *amazing* job, her freakin' dream job after years of pulling herself back together in the aftermath of one incredibly wrong road taken.

She fumbled in her flapped coat pocket, hunting the phone even as she turned for the car. "Note to self," she muttered. "Add mini-flashlight to key chain."

"Too late for that, sweet ass." The man's voice came from the darkness; the phone squirted from her startled fingers back into her pocket. She fumbled for it, digging past keys and tissues and a baby tin of curiously strong mints even as she backed away from the voice, searching for the man in the shadows.

And ran smack into the solid presence of another body, his wash of garlic breath across her ear, strong hands clamping down on her upper arms and squeezing them to her sides.

Fear raced through her belly, weakening her knees. "Sorry, boys," she said through gritted teeth, hand still groping for that phone, knowing if she could flip it open and hit the autodial for Compton's household…if he could hear what was happening… "This particular sweet ass is busy tonight."

"Just give us the documents." The first figure emerged from the alley, grew close and large—very large—and resolved into a rugged man with tattoos across his heavily used face. "Then we can make this fast. Otherwise…" He shrugged. "We get to have fun."

Fear escalated. This man wasn't posturing. He wasn't trying to impress her. He was without soul, without heart…and he would eat her alive if it served him.

Or maybe even just for the fun of it.

"I—" she said, and the word got stuck in her throat. "I don't have any—" Still just a whisper, it was enough; if his smile had been frightening, the scowl was now terrifying. She blurted, "I haven't found the office yet!"

The hands tightened, digging in painfully even through the thick wool of the coat, numbing her fingers. Tattoo Head shrugged, looking beyond her to his accomplice. "We'll come with you," he decided.

But I don't know where I'm going seemed like exactly the wrong thing to say. *Get screwed* wasn't going to go over so well, either. But these men weren't going to let her go once they had the documents, either. No, they'd take the papers, and then…

They'd have fun.

Not with me. She went utterly limp in the hands that held her, slipping down while he cursed and bent to catch at her coat.

With a courage-bolstering cry, she sprang up, the top of her head connecting with some part of his face—something that cracked and gave—as she rammed her elbows back and slammed her heels at his shins and turned herself into a whirling dervish of resistance, taking the man so very by surprise that he staggered back, tripping over the parking curb. Natalie went down, too, stumbling to her hands and knees, but only for a moment—and she was already running by the time she regained her feet.

It didn't stop Tattoo Head from snagging her, cruelly wrenching her arm back so she cried out again, this time from surprise and pain and *oh, yes,* fear again. "Stupid bitch," he growled. And when she opened her mouth to scream, the loudest, the most attention-getting sound she could muster, he backhanded her with such casual force that she would have gone flying had he not still held her.

Scream! her deep inner survivalist self cried to her. *Fight! Kick! Gouge his eyes out!*

Dazed, she hung limply in his grip, her vision full of dark shadows and blurry edges, her face one big throb of pain.

"Get up," Tattoo Head growled at his partner, his voice no less impatient. "Get the car."

"Too late for that."

Hold on. That was a third voice. A third man. One who meant to interrupt…one who somehow sounded yet more dangerous than the first two put together. And though fear and violence still combined to keep Natalie's knees loose and useless, that small deep inner voice said *They'll keep each other busy, and then you run.*

But Tattoo Head stiffened, just ever so slightly. "This isn't your problem."

Maybe it was the tension that laced his voice. Maybe it was his words, hanging heavy in the air, slowing the moment. Natalie lifted her head, blinking her dazed vision into something sharper. Blinked again, disbelieving. As if there was really a man striding out of the parking lot, all full of a predator's power, lithe strides with just the right amount of prowl. Not arrogant, not even with that movement and those long strong legs and broad shoulders beneath a formfitting leather jacket, dark hair unruly, brows dark and lowered, gaze too intense for the darkness…

But a man who knew what he was. *Danger.*

"Walk away," Tattoo Head said, shifting his grip ever so slightly. Natalie felt strength trickle back into her knees, limbs coming alive with hope. "This isn't your problem."

"You'd think not," the man said, a strange acknowledgment there, maybe even a hint of apology. "And yet, here I am."

Tattoo Head's partner finally made it to his feet, coming up beside Natalie—reaching into his jacket. "No,"

Tattoo Head snapped. "Take him down—and don't bring the cops in on us."

A gun. The man had been reaching for a gun. But now he made a disgruntled noise, spat blood at Natalie's feet with a look that said she'd pay for every drop, and reached for the back of his belt instead, freeing a small stub that whipped out into a telescoping, weighted security baton.

If her approaching rescuer had any weapon at all, she couldn't see it. Unless…

Is that a pocket knife?

One of the really small ones?

She swallowed. Hard.

Something flashed suddenly in his hand, hard and white hot, sunlight gleaming off bright metal in the midnight darkness. Natalie squinted against it and Tattoo Head raised a hand to shield his eyes. And then she could see again, but she didn't believe it. Not really. Because where had that thing come from? That *sword*? What else could you call it, all long and thin and pointy, with a guard of elaborate whorled metal.

He held it as though his hand was perfectly at home with it. And he gave Tattoo Head and his partner a strangely regretful look. "Well," he said. "Looks like you get to die."

Because of what they'd seen?

But I saw it, too.

New plan. Run from the rescuer, too.

But for the moment she was still solidly snared, and even as Tattoo Head reached for his own weapon, he dragged her back—heading for the car that she just knew she'd never leave alive. She made herself heavy, she dragged her heels, she skinned her palms. Her slacks tore. He didn't appear to notice any of it. She grabbed a parking curb and held it; he jerked her and she cried out, losing flesh and breaking fingernails.

But neither of them looked away from the two men—Tattoo Head's partner and the interloper closing on one another—the partner cocky, the interloper…

No posturing, just grim resignation. No sign of fear—not even though the baton could take him down with one well-placed blow, could disarm him, break his wrist bones, his hand…his arm. Could kill him, if it landed just so, whipping dangerously through the air to pop against his head.

And who knew how to use a *sword* these days, anyway? A refugee from the Renfair so recently in town?

This man, that's who. This man who held his body in an easy guard, the sword in position to cover all four vulnerable quarters, his shoulders turned to present as little target as possible. Not as though he thought about it, not as though he arranged himself, but as though he just simply *knew.* The long, slim blade moved precisely, fending off the baton's feints with little effort. Patient. Until the attacker grew anxious, hovered perceptibly on the edge of some great attack—even Natalie could see that much—and then charged, whipping the baton into a game of brute strength.

A quick flick of the sword, a binding motion, and the baton flew away. In the same motion, the man—*her res-*

cuer—stepped forward, straightened his arm…impaled his erstwhile opponent with a meaty impact. Natalie flinched, startled by a mind's eye flash of old memory, *metal and death and looming strike*—

Tattoo Head snarled a startled curse, and before Natalie could do anything more than gasp warning, lifted his own weapon and flung it—a knife, big but dark and all but invisible in the darkness, flipping end over end and still somehow even as the man yanked his sword from the big lump of dead person on the asphalt, he ducked wildly aside and *didn't* take that blade in the chest or the throat or the central part of his body where it had been aimed.

He took it in his upper arm instead, staggering backward a step, and then he ignored it completely, that handle sticking out of his arm like the world's biggest sliver and *oh, hell,* how could he *not* grab it and yank it away. How could he heft his own sword, no good from fifteen feet away now except then came that *flash*—and with it the scent of hot steel and the light running down metal in coursing rivulets. Natalie's jaw dropped and she damned well didn't have to be told *duck* as she saw the knife suddenly in his hand, held so lightly, so expertly. She scrunched herself into a tight little ball and as the knife caught every bit of available light, spinning air toward astonished Tattoo Head.

And *this* knife found its mark.

Natalie jerked herself free the moment she heard the impact, rolling away. Tattoo Head fell heavily just beside her, and she scooted another several feet. *Rescue yourself, girl. That's what you know. And that means it's time to run—*

But somehow, that silvered blade was back in her rescuer's hand, though he'd never closed the space between himself and Tattoo Head. Two men down, and looking pretty dead. One man still standing, his weapon…disappeared. A big knife handle sticking out of his arm. His stance wavering.

Run away, girl. To the car. To the phone. To call Compton.

Okay, to lock the doors first.

He made a disgruntled noise, kneeling awkwardly beside the first man, pressing what was left of his blade— back to a pocket knife, it was—against the man's flesh.

An acrid scent wafted across the space between them on a breeze Natalie no longer found cold. *Run away.* But her legs weren't obeying and her body trembled, weak with relief instead of fear and her eyes stayed riveted on the dead man, on the way his flesh seemed to crumble or maybe that was just the darkness and her freak factor. She blinked hard and no, she knew crumbling when she saw it. She'd built her share of sand castles; she'd watched them soften and melt and tumble grain by grain back to the ground until there was…

Nothing.

No body.

No blood.

No man who had first laid his hands on her.

Too late to run away. Time to throw up.

But the man who'd come out of the parking lot to rescue her took it all in stride, and she didn't think that was quite fair. The whole night wasn't fair, come to that. Especially not if he was going to come over here and dissolve Tattoo Head away right *next* to her—she scooted away in anticipation, but he'd stopped. On his knees, hands propped on his thighs, he finally seemed to notice the big freakin' knife sticking out of his arm—and with that same expression of resignation but no hesitation, he reached for it…yanked it out.

It must have hurt like hell, to judge from that gritty little sound he made, the way his eyes squeezed closed and his jaw opened, as if he'd managed to take himself by surprise. And then she felt it, the warm drops of rain, heard the sudden steady pulse of fluid against the asphalt.

"Oh," she said. "Hey. Whoa. You, uh—"

By then he'd opened his eyes. "Ah, *hell*."

Yeah. Arterial blood, spurting hard and fast with every beat of his heart. Blood rain. He'd bleed out fast, without help. Maybe he'd bleed out anyway.

Natalie didn't bother to glance around. No one here to help but her. That's the way it was.

Yeah, way too late to run away.

Chapter 2

Just about…

Now.

Natalie Chambers had been a good assistant. An unexpectedly good assistant. It would be a shame to lose her.

Her proficiency…now, that had been an unexpected benefit, given that he'd hired her with no regard to her skills at all. Sawyer Compton's interest had started not with Natalie Chambers, but with Ajay Dudek, her ex-fiancé. The one who had once run with Devin James's brother, Leo—or perhaps it had been the other way around. It didn't matter.

Either way, the hunt had started with the deceased Leo James…and moved to Devin James, the man who now wielded the blade. But Compton was a patient man, satisfied to work through the dead brother's friends, following that trail for sources he could exploit, people he could use. It didn't matter that Natalie Chambers had, as it turned out, never actually known Devin James—she'd still known the men who'd befriended and then rejected him. She'd been part of that crowd, part of that life.

Once.

Now she thought she was cleaned up, a decent woman looking for a decent life. But she couldn't outrun those connections. Natalie to Ajay to Leo James. And that meant she had precious insight into the James boys, and that had made her someone to use.

Sawyer Compton knew how to use.

He knew how to own, too. How to acquire.

Everything served a purpose. *His* purpose. And right now, Natalie was serving him well. Theoretically, she'd survive. But if not…that would work, too; he'd already extracted what information he could from her. Breaking in a new personal assistant would be inconvenient, but of course he was prepared.

The crude muscle he'd sent to deal with her—just the right place, just the right time—they served him well, also.

If likely for the last time.

Compton tapped his fingers on his quiescent phone. She should be calling by now. He began to think James had failed him. Not that he intended her death. But it was always possible he'd overestimated the younger James brother. Because—a glance at his watch—yes. His timing was right.

Just about…
Now.

The pavement loomed hard and dark and so very ready to smack Devin in the face.

So much for any thought of ending this night with dawn pushing the horizon, an old movie as flickering backdrop to elusive sleep and a cold beer sitting once more unopened on an otherwise empty fridge shelf.

Devin snorted a dark, short little laugh at his own skewed notion of the good life and realized instantly what a mistake that had been—his strength spurting out on the ground, the pain deep and his vision getting gray, his body going shocky—and mostly, the look on her face.

Didn't matter what she'd seen. No bodies, no witnesses…she wouldn't go to the police. Not with *this* story. But it mattered if he wasted energy in wry self-awareness and passed out. Or if his sardonic amusement sent her over the edge—wavy curls tumbling around her face but not obscuring eyes blue and bright and aghast, hand groping in the pocket of her stylish peacoat. *Phone.* She was going for a phone.

Suddenly he wasn't the least bit amused at all. "No," he bit out at her, slapping a hand over the blood-slick leather of his arm, trying to staunch the wound—to give the blade time to work. *The wild road.* Dammit, he hadn't even finished cleaning up. *"Don't."*

She shot him not fear, but a sudden resentful glare. So much for gratitude. And she came up with the cell phone, and he didn't have a choice—didn't give himself time to think. One last surge of speed and cruel strength, and he wrested the device from her hand with his bloody fingers, slamming it to the ground. It spun into two pieces and he slammed the butt end of the knife onto the biggest—never wondering where the knife came from, not anymore—and he knew damned well the wild road showed in his face as she recoiled from him in the darkness.

He winced, checking himself—holding up a hand in apology—reaching as though she might actually take it, which didn't seem too damned likely. Not with her expression frozen—fear and dismay and even a hint of anger—and not with the blood now beating a steady tattoo against the inside of the leather coat, warm and wet and gliding down his arm to spatter to the pavement.

He had the fleeting thought that she was about to run.

An even more fleeting thought, laced with surprise and a startling little slap of fear, jarred a startled "Oh, *hell*" from him: even a demon blade couldn't heal what was already dead.

And *then* the pavement came up and smacked him in the face.

Metal and death and looming strike—
But that had been years ago. Another time, another place. Natalie inhaled sharply, bringing herself back to the now.

"Oh, *hell*." He'd said it again, annoyed and surprised and still fighting the inevitable, and then he'd gone down. Out before he hit the ground, no attempt to soften the landing.

The knife lay glimmering on the pavement just outside loosely curled fingers. Lethal. Inexplicable.

Natalie reached for it—but with her fingers trembling a mere hairsbreadth away, changed her mind. *No.* Not this knife.

With a curse, she left it. She yanked her scarf away from her neck—fine alpaca wool, a rare luxury—and wrapped it around the man's arm with sore fingers, jerking a tight half hitch at each turn until she ran out of scarf altogether. She wiped her hands on the gaily tasseled ends and turned to the dead man—finding the baton he'd used so effectively and collapsing it, stuffing it into her pocket even as she dug out his wallet.

Only after she'd grabbed the cash and pulled the driver's license did she realize how quickly, how stupidly, she'd slid right back into old ways. Ways that had been hers for only a brief time, but even then they'd become so ingrained....

They'd taken her all over again.

And so had the familiar heart-racing, stomach-sickening rush.

She wanted to throw the wallet across the parking lot.

She didn't. She forced herself to return it. *But not the money.* If things went bad here, really bad, she might need it. *And not the driver's license.* Because she wanted to know who this man had been. Not respect so much as caution. She'd hire someone....

She shoved the wallet back into place, still shaking,

and stumbled more than stepped away from her erstwhile attacker, half tripping over the man who'd saved
her. The gleaming pocket knife skittered from his fin-
gertips and up against the dead man.

That's not right. She'd barely brushed him.

And if she'd glanced away at just the right time, she
wouldn't have seen the tattooed man crumble away.

"Oh," she said out loud. "That is just. Not. *Right.*"

And there she stood, in a dark parking lot with two
dead men who had disappeared, their killer and her
phone in pieces and her boss waiting for her report that
she'd met his special architectural designer with her
usual crisp efficiency and now had his equally special
plans in hand.

The sharp breeze gusted through her, a visceral slap
of nature. She needed a phone, that's what. She needed
to call Compton. The what-to-do-next decision…that
wasn't really hers to make. Not when she was on his
clock. A good job? Yes. A dream job? *Yes.* But there
were rules to it, too.

And still, when she looked at the dark figure sprawled
on the ground, his fingers twitching ever so slightly toward a knife that was no longer there, she couldn't help
but think of the expression on his face just before he
fell. More than just annoyance and more than just last-
ditch defiance, but…

Fear.

And there *wasn't* any calling Compton, was there?
Not without walking dark blocks to find the nearest public phone. The nearest *working* public phone.

It got easier, then—decision made, mere moments gone by in spite of the struggle of it all. She reached him in a few swift strides, crouching to put one quiet hand on his shoulder—and if her scarf seemed patchily sodden, the blood no longer dripped rivulets off his fingers, black in the mercury light that filtered in from the streetlamps. "Hey—" she started to say.

He surged up, grabbing her no less cruelly than when wrenching away her phone. The ferocity of it warred with confusion and then sudden understanding, although by then he'd made it back up to his knees—but just barely, before he slumped over, propping himself on one shaking arm against pavement. Releasing her.

The knife was in his hand.

"I'm sorry," he said. "I couldn't let you— You're okay?"

He couldn't let her call the cops. Of course not. He'd killed two men. He'd made them *disappear.* By what stretch of the imagination would he *want* cops here?

"Okay?" she asked, and her alto had more husk in it than usual. "You must be kidding. Either I saw what I saw, or I think I saw it—and which of those things could be okay?"

He tipped his head up. Light eyes, she thought, and hair short enough to stay out of his face even in disarray. Enough illumination to show her his briefest reaction to her words, but not quite to fully define it. "Physically," he said. "You?"

She'd hurt like hell tomorrow. Bruises, scrapes…

bodily payback. But relatively speaking? "I'm okay," she told him.

"Car?"

"I—" Without thinking, she slipped her hand into her pocket to touch the keys. "Yes. But you need to go to the hosp—"

He turned that ferocious look on her again. "Help me *my* way," he said. "Or leave me alone."

"You could die!" she snapped, exasperated beyond herself, feeling herself tipping askew—toward doing what was right for him at the expense of what was right for her.

Rescue yourself. Because look what being here had already done to her—what it had brought out in her. She realized how tightly she'd clenched her hand closed around the keys, and took a deliberate and slow breath, feeling every notch and edge of the metal against her palm. Focusing on it and taking back control of herself. "Yeah," she said. "I do things my way, now. For me. You can make your own choices. But thanks. You know. For the help."

He laughed faintly as she turned away. "Smart," he said, a little breathless. "Smart woman."

She really expected him to stop her. She thought she'd hear his voice as she headed for the car, keys withdrawn from her pocket and ready for the lock. *I changed my mind* or even *oh, hell!* again.

But no. Nothing other than his audible breathing—the

pain in it, and the struggle. A strange kind of vigil, as if he was, somehow, still watching out for her.

Right up until the moment she got into the car and drove away.

Devin laughed again.

Yeah, probably not the thing to do with the single marginally friendly face of this dark night closing the little hybrid's door behind her to pull smoothly out of the lot, barely a mutter of engine along the way.

And still. Just for the grit of her, he laughed. She'd gotten the message, all right—and she'd sent her own back. He could make choices for himself, but not for her. *Smart woman.* Nervy. Completely overpowered by the men who'd come after her, and she'd still kept her head. Fought as hard as she could. Hadn't even panicked when the blade drank down its first victim, sending a narrow spear of electric pain down Devin's spine along with the lingering trickle of relief and pleasure that he'd come to dread.

Because one day he might just look forward to it, and then the battle would be lost.

She hadn't panicked…but she'd come close. He'd seen it in eyes darkened by fear and deep night; he'd seen it in an unexpected face of high Slavic cheekbones and a narrow jaw. And then her mouth had gone firm and her fists had gone clenched and she'd just plain walked away.

He laughed one last time, a mere huff of exhalation, and shook his head. Good for her. He'd follow in her footsteps, if he had an ounce of sense—before the vultures found him.

Too bad his old pickup sat three blocks down. Too far, he thought. He got to his knees, pushed up to one foot, and knew it for sure.

She'd stopped the bleeding—or she'd stopped it enough. He hadn't died; he wouldn't die. But if the blade offered up gifts, wrapped in gilt and chains, it didn't offer up miracles. It would save his life; it would save his arm. It would shorten healing.

It wouldn't give him the means to saunter three blocks to the truck, drive himself home and lock the doors safely behind him while he slept himself to stability.

The back corner of the nearby alley was looking better all the time. Out of the wind, out of sight…he might make it through what was to come. His flesh hadn't yet quite figured out what had happened—but the blood loss had left his vision fading in and out, his body slipping into cold, clammy shock…strength elusive. The cold pressed in on him and only the bright heat of an innocuous pocket blade pushed him forward.

Until the pale hybrid hatchback zipped silently up beside him, traversing the sidewalk and ignoring a median to get there, gliding to a stop only a foot away. The door opened; warmth wafted out. "Get in," she said, full of conflicting urgency and doubt.

Shock made him stupid. *Something* made him stupid, staring as she bent over the passenger seat to catch his eye, the fear back on her face and fully accompanied by annoyance.

"Come on," she said. "Get *in*." She extended her hand, an impatient gesture. "God, you're about to pass out again, aren't you? Can you just *get in the car* first?"

Cheekbones and angry-frantic eyes and such a line of jaw—

Something hit his face. A tiny stuffed animal, bouncing to the pavement. "Right now!" she said, as she might speak to a reluctant dog. "Unless you want those guys to get here first, because they're *looking,* do you get me? And do you think I'd be back here for anything less?"

Looking. Of course. For their friends.

Not to be found. But they'd find Devin.

Her voice lashed at him. The blade burned in his pocket, a fiery prod. His arm gave the first whisper of the pain that would soon envelop it. But he heard her urgency, and he reached for her outstretched hand. A heave of effort, a hard yank...heavy footfalls in the background, a rough voice calling someone's name—

He wasn't quite in the car when she floored it, an eerily silent and swift acceleration that closed the door on his ankle. He dragged his foot into the car and the door clicked loosely into place; they hit a curb and shot out into the street, and all the while his face mashed into her shoulder and then slipped downward to softer flesh.

"I don't think so," she said sharply and shoved him back, deftly navigating out of the clustered shops until she hit the through street; the gas motor kicked in. "Dammit, you're bleeding—" and she reached behind his seat and fumbled to pull out an old blanket. "Don't get it on my car. Now where are we going?"

He stared at the blanket. Definitely made of stupid.

She made an exasperated noise, yanking the car over to the curb—bold driving in scant nighttime traffic. A belated punch at the hazard lights on the center console and she turned to him, reclaiming the worn blanket, curling it around his arm and tucking it in. "We're not going to the hospital," she said, "but if you die in the car, I'm heading straight there and pretending we were on the way all along. And we are *not* going to my place. God, my boss—" She stopped herself, took a breath and ignored his bemusement as she snapped his seat belt into place. "So it's up to you. And I wouldn't faint again. You'll find yourself on a river bench, if you wake up again at all."

He felt that sloppy grin on his face—knew it was there by her startled reaction. "Be still my heart," he said, and passed out again anyway.

Chapter 3

Devin came out of the darkness explosively, shredded awake by the searing claws of a demon's healing touch—flame and agony. *Consequences.* He realized only vaguely that she was searching through his front pocket; he surged up, smacked his head and grappled for freedom—hitting the hard curving console, hitting soft flesh, finally scrabbling his way to the latch and exploding out onto the ground.

Husky alto words slapped a distant corner of his mind, succinct and sharp; her car door slammed. He found just enough sanity to remember where he'd been—to recognize where he was.

From the parking lot to his own postage stamp of a front yard, scratchy dry winter grass and bare patches. His own home. Sanctuary.

Without bothering to check the raw noise in his throat, he scrambled to his feet—or close enough—and threw himself at the front door. Because inside was the cold shower, the only faint relief the night offered. Flames scored his body, incinerating thoughts before they could complete themselves—incinerating sanity.

The door didn't open. Robust metal security door, pretending to be decorative; solid wood door beyond.

"Try the *keys*," said that voice, honey and whiskey, and it came with a jingle of metal. "Did you think I was groping you for kicks?"

Meaningless words. He slid back against the aging stucco—slid down it, the brief surge of strength gone and all his focus on the heat—bent over his arm, clamping down on it—hunting for the honest pain now buried beneath the cost of being what he was.

"There!" she cried, flinging the screen door back and pushing the inner door open. "The house, for what good it'll do you!"

He rolled to his feet and pushed past her, headed for the tiny home's single bathroom and shower—yanking at leather along the way, unable to fathom why the jacket wouldn't come off.

There she was again, fumbling at the material around his arm and tugging the jacket off. "There!" she said again, tossing it aside, beyond any comprehension—patronizing the clearly crazy man.

And wasn't she just so very right...

He stumbled, clinging to a wall—smearing blood along the length of it even as he went after his shirt.

Mindless, instinctive—thinking of nothing more than cold water on flames and only dimly realizing that she'd helped with the jacket, gloves and then the shirt, pulling it over his head, freeing the sopping sleeve from his arm as he finally careened off the bathroom door and into the shower—cool tile against his feet, familiar faucets beneath his hands, cold water cranked all the way up.

Only when she cried out in dismay did he realize she'd come that far, had probably kept him from bashing his head against the tile, and had now gotten caught under the icy spray.

Brief sanity washed over him along with the water. Fires not quenched, but no longer white hot. He came back to himself enough to watch the fresh flow of blood stain the water, dilute red swirls heading down the drain in the bright light she'd somehow switched on along the way.

She stepped back from him, flinging back ash-blond hair gone brown and curly with water, tossing his sodden shirt into the corner of the big square shower. She snatched a towel from the wall rack and blotted her jacket and her shirt and her face, and she said tightly, "I need to use your phone. See if you can be crazy on your own for a while."

His breath hissed through his teeth at a rising wave of incendiary payback. *No problem.*

Natalie fled the bathroom.

This was some other person's night. Maybe some other person's life, and she'd accidentally stepped into it. This wasn't *her* life. Even in the worst of her past, this hadn't been her life.

It sure as hell wasn't about to become it.

She stopped short in the living room, her eyes no longer accustomed to darkness, and finally located the light switch. A strong draft of cold winter air reminded her that they'd come in hard and fast, the doors open behind them. With calm purpose, she went out to close up her car, and then returned to close the doors behind her.

Not that she intended to stay. But she damn sure intended to use the phone before she went anywhere.

Wet clothes had her shivering. She wrapped the towel around her neck, breathing deeply of it…calming another step. What was he even thinking, to stand under that cold water, injured and shocky and still losing blood?

Then again, what had *she* been thinking, to strip a stranger down to bare gleaming chest, stained with blood and the dark scattered hair arrowing straight down his belly and who even had abs like that? In real life?

Another deep breath and she realized quite suddenly that the towel carried his scent—that she had absorbed it without thinking. And that wasn't right either, far too intimate—as though he had somehow invaded her space instead of the other way around.

She pulled the towel away and dropped it on the couch.

No good. The scent clung to her wet wool coat.

She took a deep breath, pretending not to notice, and deliberately—slowly—flexed her sore fingers. Fist and flex. *Awareness*. And then, controlled and deliberate, she pulled his wallet from her flapped coat pocket and tossed it on the low table in front of the couch. She dropped the keys on top of it. Maybe he'd figure out that she'd groped his back pockets to get the wallet—with his license, name and address—and his front pockets to get the keys, and maybe *she'd* figure out that she'd caught that scent of him long before she'd ever gotten mixed up with his towel.

That and the scent of blood, raw and heavy.

She glanced around the living room—tiny, with a well-used couch and pillows lumped at one end and fallen to the floor there, a no-nonsense floor lamp within reach at the end, a small television sitting on long, low shelves of neatly filed DVDs. No phone, so she glanced down the hall—the bathroom, and one other room that had to be his bedroom. In the other direction, a tiny kitchen—appliances simple but modern, cabinets scarce but all gleaming, refinished wood, and an open pass-through to the living room...on which sat a flat, wireless phone. A few steps and it was hers.

And still the water ran.

Sawyer Compton's voice came to Natalie's ear over the cell phone just as surrealistically as the rest of the evening. "As long as you're all right," he said, surprisingly solicitous. For if not a cold man, he was indeed a man with exacting expectations. A man whose business priorities had created his successes, as well as a certain personal isolation.

A man not given to sentiment.

So although he added a few words acknowledging issues with the architect's address, Natalie barely absorbed them, still stumbling with the import of her own news—her fumbling words: *I was attacked. A man helped me. He was hurt and I saw him home, but I'll return as soon as possible.*

For her own little home was a large casita on the generous grounds of her employer's property.

Compton said, "About your new friend—" and Natalie inadvertently interrupted him. *Friend.* Try *crazy stranger.* The sound she made might have been laughter, or maybe denial—she wasn't sure, and she bit her lip on it. Interrupting wasn't part of her job.

Compton let it pass. "Please convey my gratitude. If he needs medical attention, of course I'll pay for it. And I know you're tired…but I'd feel better if you could stay long enough to make sure he gets what help he needs."

She almost took the phone away from her ear to stare at it, sitcom style. Had she even called the right number? "That could take a while."

"Understandably. But I assume you have tomorrow's schedule on my desk, as well as your own necessary tasks. If there's anything flagged for the day, I'll see that it gets done. I'm concerned for you, Natalie. I feel quite responsible."

She probably should have said it was all part of the job, but that wouldn't have been the truth. Nothing in her job description included nights like this one, even with her loosely defined girl Friday duties.

He didn't wait for it. Wise man. "If you can, see if he'll come by tomorrow. Anytime. There are few enough heroes in the world today. I'd like to acknowledge this one."

She held her breath, ever so briefly—caught up in the notion of this *hero* descending on the Compton estate.

For Devin James was all raw grit…and Compton's home was all sophisticated, lavish Southwest finery— tiles and fountains and soaring pueblo architecture, flat sloped roofs draining to canals, stout viga beams carrying the ceiling and protruding through the exterior walls, *latillas* ceiling accents—a home with a hundred years of history surrounded by rich bosk land and supplemented with *acequias*. Alfalfa still grew in its fields; elms and cottonwoods sheltered the house and lined the canals, creating layers of impenetrable privacy.

One might catch a glimpse of the property from the nearest of the curving, interlaced streets in the area—or if persistent, realize that the lone mailbox at the dead-end street sat at the end of a gated footpath—but the only vehicle approach came from the canal access road itself.

A home from another time and place, tucked away and kept away, and housing a man of such means to keep it as it was.

"Natalie?" he said, brusque tone more familiar. "You'll do that?"

"Yes," she said, if a little faintly. "I'll try."

"Good. Call me if you need anything. And, Natalie—"

"Sir?" For that's how it was between them. *Yes, sir* and *no, sir* and on the rare occasion, *I'll do my best, sir.*

The unexpected warmth had returned. "I'm glad you weren't hurt."

"Thank you," she said, but he'd already cut the connection.

A breathy memory pushed the edges of her mind, images crystallizing there—Devin James stalking out of the darkness, his eyes just a little bit mad, his intent written in every line of his body, anger simmering hard just below the surface no matter how calm his words. The swift efficiency of his motion in attack…the inexplicable responses to two men dead and his own blood splattering the pavement. *Echoes of a night not so many years ago…*

And the fear now surfacing in his expression, just long enough for her to be sure she'd seen it before he pushed it—and her—away.

Natalie shuddered, breaking free of that preternatural clarity of memory—and realized that the shower had gone quiet.

And here she still stood.

She hadn't meant to be in his house when he climbed out of that shower, never mind standing at the edge of his kitchen with errant familiarity.

Then again, she wasn't sure she could have walked away. Not twice. Not without knowing he was truly all right—and not after seeing that he was so truly not.

He came down the hall, shirtless and dripping, exposed by the overhead light—diluted blood still sheeting his arm but no longer spurting; the stab wound deep and gaping but narrow. Water sparkled across his chest and darkened the small tattoo just to the right of center; he'd gotten his shoes off but his jeans, darkened and slopping heavily against his legs, dripped a path across the flecked Berber carpet.

He didn't respond to her presence; he used a hand to sluice water from his face, hair scruffed into an inadvertently trendy style, and his expression—

She flexed her fingers, remembered to breathe. *Driven and haunted and striking.* Nose a little strong, mouth defined, eyes…arresting, gray-blue and deep beneath dark brows. They were her first impression of him, and still the strongest—and if he'd said little so far, she felt the world was hidden behind the expression there.

A mad, mad world.

He found the towel on the couch and stumbled for it, scrubbing it over his chest and face and stiffening then. Inhaling.

Realizing he hadn't been the last one to use it.

Then, he found her.

"You shouldn't—" he said, and his eyes widened slightly. He gave his head a short, sharp shake. "I can't," he said, and tried again, eyes going wide with the effort of it. And finally, "I won't hurt you," as he wrenched himself back a few steps and looked as though he could barely stop himself from doing just that.

"You won't," she said, grim at that, and found the pepper spray in her pocket after all. Finally.

He dropped the towel on the floor—stained and blood-streaked now—his eyes gone dark and wide.

"Oh, my God," she said, just realizing it. "You're

high. That's why none of this makes any sense! You're *on* something! Meth? I hope to hell not PCP—" If so, he'd never even feel her puny pepper spray.

He sucked in air, let his head drop back. A man hunting for control. "Not," he said, through gritted teeth, "drugs." And then he looked at her once more, speaking so clearly and directly that the words hit her ears with the same preternatural clarity of those recent memories. "I won't," he said, *"hurt you."*

And then he dropped to his knees and clamped his arms around his head and howled the anguish of a man possessed.

Chapter 4

Natalie startled back, a few stumbling steps—and she ran for it. Right up against the door set at the back corner of the kitchen, fumbling at the dead bolt lock there—and taking long enough at it to have second thoughts.

Don't even consider it. Just do the smart thing.

But this wasn't a case of weighing what someone else wanted against what was best for her. He hadn't, in fact, *asked* her to do a thing. He'd only asked her *not* to call the police.

Everything else, her choice.

She recalled with fearful clarity the decisive sanity of him as he'd stalked out of the darkness to take on two armed men with a pocket knife. *Sword. No, pocket knife.*

What he'd *done* was insane, maybe.

But he hadn't been drugged. *Wasn't* drugged. So

maybe there was no point trying to understand. Maybe she should simply respond to a man in pain.

She eased out toward the living room.

The blade scratched along the outside edges of Devin's mind, gusting flames through his thoughts and his body and setting his arm purely to fire. He lost himself to that, flinging himself down the short hall and back again, a mindless creature with only a faint, frightened awareness. *It's never been like this before.*

Devin no longer wondered if his transformation would happen—if it would be necessary.

Because it was happening now. Tonight. A first breakthrough between what he was and what he would become.

It was easy enough to remember when his brother, Leo, had started down this road. When his forays with the blade had become less about protecting those who needed it and more about the power rush.

Neither of them had realized what they'd stumbled over, that first night—two brothers out walking, both still in school, both nothing but average smart-ass adolescent boys, lives so damned simple, goals so damned short-term. Avoiding schoolwork, fishing the Rio Grande, out-hiking the Sandia mountain bears and earning enough money for that old junker sports car. And oh, yeah. Girls. Leo with his first worshipful steady, Devin still a painful virgin but not planning on staying that way one moment longer than necessary.

It turned out it wasn't the Sandia wilderness bears

they had to worry about, coming off the strenuous La Luz trail at the northeast edge of Albuquerque, two cocky teens out later than they should have been.

The man who'd jumped them...

Hadn't been sane. Hadn't been hard to defeat. And if Devin hadn't understood it then, he understood it now—that the blade had taken that man down the wild road, and he had, finally, desperately, chosen his own way out.

And when it was over, Leo stood with the blade in his hand, and then the world changed.

Leo had fumbled through every step of it—learning that the blade would draw him into trouble—that it demanded it. That it was happy to slake on the blood of those who needed justice.

The brothers, however, had made their own rules. About intervening, about which moments to choose. Leo had controlled the blade.

Until suddenly he hadn't. Until those he gathered around him had dark hearts, and Devin's voice got lost in the manly posturing and chest-beating and hunting, Leo's expression wild and haunted and never quite present.

One day Leo had gone for innocent blood—God, the luck of it, for that damned punk to come bouncing off the two of them in that dark alley—and when Devin had tried to stop him, Leo had gone for him.

But Devin had known the blade, too. And he had known Leo.

Even if that hadn't really been Leo any longer.

Brother dead in the alley...brother gone to the hungry

blade. *The slap of metal against flesh as the blade came to him, claiming him...bonding with him.*

"Stop," she said, a voice so distant to his awareness that it barely echoed through to him—a hand on his arm. A curse. *Damn, you're hot.* A hand withdrawn... in retreat.

But more words, murmured, as she returned—and this time slapped wet, cold material over his shoulders. The towel, dripping heavily.

Cooling. Barely breaking through, but—

There. A moment of reality. Her hand on his arm, her hand at his face. Her voice, fully realized. "Better?"

He nodded, if barely. Flames curled instantly around his thoughts, reclaiming him.

"No!" she said, and tugged the towel tighter against the back of his neck, all pale blue eyes and curving mouth, chin set stubbornly. "I saw you in there! Don't leave—"

He grabbed her hands—fine bone and slender fingers, soft skin...a reality to counter his own. But fear flickered in her eyes and he drew a ragged breath and released her, this woman who knew nothing of him. "I won't hurt you," he said—said again?—voice rough in his throat.

She looked at her liberated hands, and then reached again for his. "Okay," she said. "Hang on to me, then."

Too late, though, with the fire licking around his thoughts, curling up to consume them. "Too late," he said out loud, and gave himself up to it, a mindless thing flinging himself down the hall and back again, down the hall and back again, outrunning that which he carried inside.

But he no longer walked alone.

Natalie woke with a crick in her neck and an ache in her ribs. When she dislodged the lumpy pillow beneath her, she found bruises and little shooting paybacks of pain laced throughout her body, her hands sore and scraped.

Because…right. The night before. The strange, strange night before. Hard to believe it had happened at all.

Hard to believe it was still happening.

Because the pillow in her hand wasn't hers. The couch on which she'd folded her body wasn't hers. Her eyes snapped open, confirming it; the ceiling over her head wasn't the least bit hers.

The rest of the house settled in silence—an early morning kind of silence, when the rest of the world hadn't quite woken yet, either, and the cold blanketed the ground—a January cold, forever promising desert snow and never quite delivering it. The furnace kicked on, but Natalie knew better than to hope for any true heat. She'd turned the thermostat down on an inspiration, and when it seemed to help, that's where it had stayed.

Not that she'd ever understood what held Devin James in its grip. Then again, she'd stopped understanding why she stayed, too. She just made sure it was a choice, each and every moment.

Carefully, heeding her stiffened body, she sat. And

winced anew—this time at what she could see of the hallway wall, smeared with endless layers of watery blood—the result of one man's endless, staggering, wet journey down the hallway with a wound that should have killed him but somehow bled less and less as the night passed.

No sign of him now.

Natalie eased her feet to the floor and stood, stretching out the stiffness. Here, where she'd been dragged. Here, where she'd fallen. She had no recollection of falling asleep—or of pushing off the loafers she now found and slipped on. *Where is he?*

She peered down the hall, finding the back half just as gory as the front...looking around and realizing that the home, as small as it was, as simply appointed as it was, had been tended in every detail.

This paint was fresh; the simple carpet had bounce beneath her feet. The windows were tight against the morning wind; the kitchen gleamed with updated appliances and fixtures, modern Southwest touches here and there. The house might be smack in the middle of an older neighborhood of less-than-modest homes, but behind the security door and dead bolts it was downright cozy.

Natalie shivered. Well. Maybe if she turned the heat back up.

A noise from the bedroom interrupted the current surreality and replaced it with a reminder of the previous. Cautiously—feeling like an intruder, and at the same time worried that she'd somehow fallen asleep at the worst possible time and now Devin James lay in a pool of his own blood—she peeked into the bedroom.

It was the largest room in the small house, made airy by huge south windows and a French door opening to a covered side porch, and filled with unassuming masculine things. A pair of running shoes, sweats thrown over the back of a chair, heavy furniture of solid old wood, a bed large enough for a man of height and substance to sprawl over.

And there, finally. Against the wall in a muddle, a smear of blood tracing the downward slide and on his skin…*goose bumps*. Across his arms, across his chest. A paled face, his eyelids looking bruised—and believe it or not, that was even a shiver. After a night of burning up, he finally shivered in this cold like any normal man.

Natalie swept a thin down comforter from the bed and dropped it around his shoulders. "You look better," she said.

"Do I?" He frowned. "I'm not sure I… Who are…?"

"From last night," she said. "It was dark, mostly. You saved me in the—"

He jerked his head, a single impatient movement. "I remember. I meant…*who?*"

An actual introduction. "Natalie Chambers," she said, and automatically held out her hand—only for an instant, before she gave it a how-stupid-are-you look and withdrew it. "Mr. James."

"Devin," he said, and frowned. "My wallet. That's how you found this place."

"Your wallet," she agreed. "And now that we're communicating—look, I don't understand what happened last night and I'm not sure I want to. But your arm... Let me take you somewhere."

He shifted, pressing his back against the wall, and lifted his arm to get a look at the wound. "Stitches," he said, which seemed to her to be the least of it. No one's flesh should gape so casually unattended. "I can..." He frowned, and his gaze wandered, eyes clear in the morning light.

"Hey," she said.

He tried. He took a sharp breath, pulled himself back. "I need to..."

She raised a hand to prod him—but something about the tension in his body stopped her. This wasn't last night, when he was so beside himself that she could push him for a response. Now he was just enough *here* to show her some of what he'd been in that parking lot. So she crouched beside him, abruptly, and she said shortly, "Count your toes, then."

And cringed. Not words she'd thought about ahead of time.

He looked back to her, for the moment refocused... honest bafflement.

"Your toes," she said, wincing just a little. She hadn't really meant to say that. "When you start to lose it like that. I don't know what's going on, but...you can hang on to the real things. And what's more real than toes?"

"Count," he said. "My toes."

"Not just like that. Think of them when you do it. What does each one look like and what is it feeling at that moment, separate of the other toes. Not just a lump of toe-things on the end of your foot, but—" She stopped herself, briefly hid her face behind her hands and stood. "Never mind. Listen, I work for a man named Sawyer Compton. Maybe you've heard of him. I was on the clock last night when—" No, she wasn't going to say she got lost, because she hadn't. She'd gone to the address the architect had given her on the phone. "Anyway, thanks. And Mr. Compton would like to say thank you, as well—though he's asked me to make sure you get help as you need it, first."

"Toes," he said, sounding a little surprised this time—and looking down at his bare feet. "What the hell."

"Stitches," she said, patiently. "Or *something.*"

He got, quite suddenly, to his feet. "Something," he agreed, and reached for the hoodie draped with the sweatpants, not bothering with a shirt beneath. "You should go."

Absurdly, hurt twinged in her chest. "But—"

"You *should,*" he said. "But my truck is still where I found you, and I need a ride. So if you could…" He trailed off again, hand on the hoodie zipper—and she was about to give him a verbal nudge when his eyes widened slightly and he took another of those sharp, sudden breaths, and looked directly at her. "Toes," he said, and grinned, and thus transformed himself.

Natalie stared—and then she took a hasty step back, in case he hadn't already seen the blush suffusing her features from inside and out. She straightened her shoulders. "Is it the hospital, then? Maybe the urgent-care clinic on Rio Bravo?"

He shook his head, a decisive motion. Not the man who had stalked out of the darkness and not the man who had spent the night trapped in some agonizing reaction she still didn't understand. "I've got a place," he said. "But my truck is still on Broadway."

"Mr. Compton—"

"I do what I do," he said, interrupting her without any apparent regret, a glimmer of that hard exterior back in play. "I don't need to talk to your boss about it."

One look at his mouth gone from rakish grin to hard line, his eyes regarding her with flat decision behind them, and she decided…*not now.*

It didn't mean *not later.*

Devin almost remembered the sand-colored hybrid sitting in his driveway. He definitely remembered the blood-soaked blanket he found in the foot well of the passenger side; he tossed it to the side of his house and said, "I'll replace that."

"No," she said faintly, watching him as if she'd forgotten about the blanket altogether and now wished it hadn't been sitting in her car all night. "Please don't think twice about it."

Interesting woman. So polite, so carefully and quietly spoken. And yet the night before, she'd had that grit behind her. She'd fought back; she'd acted with a certain quick efficiency that spoke of habits ingrained. Old or current, he didn't know.

And she'd stayed with him. Not that he'd wanted it, with his mind and body searing against the growing influence of the blade. But she'd done it, and she'd fought back then, too—against things she didn't even understand.

She still fought back. Still trying to reconcile the situation in which she found herself, emotions just barely peeking out and then sublimating again. Trying to find the right steps on a path for which no one could have prepared her.

He levered himself into the car, the injured arm tucked to his side, hot and heavy and useless. No longer bleeding but still gaping, still burning with the unnatural attention the blade gave it. He didn't have much longer to get it stitched.

He realized, suddenly, that she'd started the car with the press of a button, and waited—for how long, he didn't know—for his direction. And he knew it because she took a deep breath and said, "Okay, then. Where's this *place* of yours? I'll take you there."

"My truck—"

She laughed. Truly amused, a light sound of sunlight and briefly open heart. She tucked her hair behind her ear—ash-brown and blond, curls left unruly with the night's dousing and faintly olive-toned skin devoid of makeup but blushing up nicely on her neck when she realized his regard. "I'm not taking you to your truck. You can't possibly think you're safe to drive. Toes or no toes."

He wanted to scowl and demand and take the wheel himself.

Problem was, she was right.

Not to mention, she was still, indeed, fighting back. Her own way.

He muttered a curse. "Enrique's," he said. "It's off Isleta. South of that giant spray-foam roadrunner." He raised a challenging eyebrow. "In an alley."

"I've been in alleys before last night," she said. "No doubt I'll be alleys again. And I've always thought that's got to be the biggest roadrunner *ever.*"

"Not," he murmured, conceding that particular skirmish, "as big as the freakish pecan outside that Tularosa pecan farm."

"They had to put the Roswell UFO somewhere," she told him, backing silently out of the short driveway. "So, dress it up as a giant pecan and stick it outside Tularosa."

Okay, he couldn't help it. To be sitting in this silent-running car with a uniquely beautiful stranger in the wake of a uniquely horrifying night, cracking wise about the giant pecan...

As if there was no such thing as a demon blade. As if his life wasn't set along an irrevocable path of destruction, as possessed as he was. As if this were a normal morning on a normal crunchy-cold Albuquerque January morning. He let down his guard, just for that instant, and laughed.

It startled her, then wrung a wry smile from her—not that it lasted long. As she navigated the quick series of turns that took her back out to University, she slanted him a look. "I wasn't sure, last night, what you would do. With me, I mean. After what I saw."

He shifted his arm, a careful grip on his elbow, and snorted in disbelief. "Because maybe I'd go to all that trouble to save you just to kill you?" Soft fleece brushed hot skin.

She hesitated at a stop sign, long enough to look him straight on. Eyes bluer than his own, a little darker. Arching brows that held the perfect quirk of the cynic—but behind it, he saw wariness. "Who knows?" she said. "I still have no idea why you went to all that trouble at all. You could have done what everyone else would have done—grabbed a phone and kept your distance."

"Maybe I don't have a cell phone."

She didn't dignify that with a response. He kept his own silence, wishing for the luxury of painkillers and not even knowing what the blade would do with them. It tended to soak such things up for its own—or spit them back at him.

And even if he'd had a handy phone in that parking lot, the blade wouldn't have let him use it.

The blade wanted things done its own way.

"Question is," she said, "what do you do now?"

"Question is," he said right back, "why did you come back? Why didn't you just go call for help?"

She responded without hesitation. "Maybe I no longer had a cell phone."

He laughed. It held none of the easy humor of the earlier moment. But appreciation for her ability to bite back—yeah. For sure. So many people ran from what they saw in him. And they'd never truly even *seen* it. Not like she had.

"Besides," she said, "you know as well as I do that by the time I found a working public phone—"

He looked away from the cheekbones, from the slight flush there; from the wide and sculpted mouth and the particular way it formed her words. "Yeah," he said, thinking about the impending reinforcements of the night before. "Probably."

She held her silence a few long moments, navigating the Prius. Then she said, "You're good at that. Evasion."

This time he looked away—haunted, for that moment, by a glimpse of what it would be like to simply *tell* someone. And then he said, "Yeah. I am."

Chapter 5

Enrique saw him coming. Sometimes Devin thought the man could smell the blood, holed up in that little office and surrounded by the thick scents of sweat and muscle rub and the peculiar eau de gym mat.

Typical trainer, Enrique. Tough on his guys, all heart beneath, running his little boxing gym for the love of it and, yeah, to give the kids a place where someone would kick their asses if they crossed the line and slap their backs when they tried to walk it. Knew how to drive a man on, knew when to back off...

Knew how to put his guys back together.

And, when a dazed younger Devin had wandered in, hunting a safe place to blow off steam, he'd seen some of what lay beneath the James brothers. Not everything, because only a handful of people still alive knew everything—or thought they did. Enrique had respected it, directed it...accepted it. And gained enough trust to become a confidant when the blade took Leo...and then changed him.

Now he came out of the little office with its plain plywood walls and jammed his fists on his hips, paperwork and all, to give Devin the little I-see-you lift of his chin. "Aiee, *hijo*," he said. "What have you done now?"

Devin stood a little taller. "Brought company, Rick." Not that he hadn't felt her move just a little bit closer in wary acknowledgment of all the testosterone in the air—fists against leather, bodies thumping down to the mats, flesh smacking flesh.

Enrique lifted one hand to make a little circling motion at Devin's arm. "And again?"

Devin glanced at the sweatshirt, found faint seepage through gray material. "Damn," he said. "Made that one easy for you." Not that Enrique and his highly tuned eye would miss even the slightest guarding of any injury, but...it was all part of the dance.

Enrique grunted. He'd been a featherweight as a fighter, and nothing in the years had changed that— still spare, still fast. And he'd gotten out young—he still had his ears, his brow and his lightning wit. His nose had taken a few good licks along the way—but not, as he made clear with a glance at Natalie, his good taste.

He didn't linger there. "Now you tell me no doctors, no antibiotics, no worry..." His hand spun out the familiar litany of words. "Just sew, Enrique. Am I right?"

He glanced again at Natalie. "Above all, no police. Does she know?"

"Are you protecting me?" Natalie said, surprise in that realization as she glanced from Enrique to Devin and back again. "From what?"

"From not knowing." Impervious to the annoyance, Enrique jerked his head at the office, leading the way—a bowlegged walk with a hitch.

Devin hesitated, glancing at Natalie. Ever hidden beneath that peacoat, but never striking him as a person of physical substance and now…even less so. Now looking as though she might have hit her limit. "You might want to stay here."

The skin went tight around her eyes, the corners of her mouth—she gave the gym denizens a meaningful glance.

"They're good guys," Devin told her.

"They're average," Enrique grunted. "But they won't bother one of Devin's."

Yeah, that was the right thing to say. *One of Devin's.* He expected the flash of annoyance; he wasn't disappointed.

"You want a rolled magazine to bite on?" Enrique suggested with some bite of his own, rummaging through a drawer that had squeaked on the way open.

"Girlie magazine?" Devin asked, winking at Natalie, watching her eyes widen slightly. "Or some boxing rag that your guys have been pawing through?"

She shook her head at him, beyond words. This whole thing, beyond words…

He offered up a wry grin, a one-shouldered shrug, and followed Enrique into the office.

Natalie didn't linger long at the door.

Long enough to see a broad expanse of shoulder, the harsh overhead light tracing strength she hadn't truly noticed the evening before. She'd half expected additional tattoos, but his skin was patterned only by the shape of bone and muscle as he sat on the desk, presenting her with a clean profile—jaw stubborn, nose strong, eyes that flashed from brooding to carefree and back again too quickly for Natalie to find her balance with either. Quiet, at the moment. Patient…an air of resignation.

Beside him sat a pile of bandages and a few matter-of-fact bottles, clear and brown plastic. When Enrique came back into view, Natalie barely had time to register what he was doing before he slopped the contents onto a rough cloth and began scrubbing.

She closed her eyes; she turned her head away. She wasn't fast enough to miss the tension that suddenly shot through Devin's back or the pain on his face, eyes closed and jaw clenched and mouth tight with defiance of it.

She didn't stay by the door.

After all, no matter what Enrique thought, she wasn't one of *Devin's*. She wasn't one of *anybody's*. But she did still work for Sawyer Compton. "I'm going to make a local call," she told Enrique, happy enough when he didn't break his concentration to do more than grunt a response. "I see the phone."

Sitting on a bar-height table beside a tattered phone

book and most of the morning paper, it was an old-style phone with a rotary dial and the phone cord tangled in so many knots it wasn't functionally more than six inches long. Half the men in the gym stopped working out to watch her stride for it…but they also left her alone.

One of Devin's. Right. She could well believe that no one here would mess with Devin James. Maybe he threw a mean punch, maybe not. But he had that white hot flash of a mutable blade, and just because Natalie hadn't been able to bring herself to ask about it—to say the words out loud—didn't mean she hadn't seen what she'd seen.

Echoes of memory and fear…

She pushed away distractions, focusing on the battered phone and Compton's private number.

"Natalie," he said, recognizing her voice immediately. "Are you coming? Is *he* coming?"

She hadn't realized the intensity of his interest. "I'm working on it," she said, aware of his disappointment. Not just in the circumstances, but in her. "He's finally getting some care," she told him. "And he's a little reclusive."

"I imagine he is," Compton said, an edge to his voice.

"Is there something I should know?" Natalie asked. She couldn't help but glance over at that open doorway, even though from this angle she could see nothing. Compton might have a personal assistant, but he remained his own primary resource—and he'd had plenty of time to dig around in Devin James's background.

"Nothing to worry about," Compton said, in such a

perfunctory tone that Natalie relaxed. Classic Compton. Whatever he had in mind, concerns about her safety were so far off his radar that it hadn't even occurred to him to mention it.

She might eventually find out what that was; she might not.

Compton's voice went short. "Keep working on him. I'll expect to see you both here as soon as possible." And he hung up.

Natalie replaced the handset in the cradle with the faintest of smiles. Last night, Compton had been worried and solicitous—and she hadn't known what to do with that man. *This* man, she knew. And she knew how to do her job.

She flipped through the insubstantial paper, scanning the headlines.

If anyone had noticed the activity the night before, they hadn't called it in. Or if they'd called it in, the police hadn't put it out on their blotter or the paper hadn't cared. Under other circumstances, she might have suspected Compton's hand—he'd never said anything, but she'd long ago noticed his ability to squelch certain stories. But he hadn't had nearly enough advance time to work on this one.

The bad guys might turn up on someone's missing persons list…but they weren't going to turn up, not literally. Natalie's hand crept to her pocket, where Tattoo Head's license waited. She didn't know who the others were, but…

This family, if there was one, deserved some clo-sure. Somehow.

Like with the skip tracer in Compton's contact files.

She set the newspaper aside and returned to the of-fice, peeked in...went unnoticed.

"Should I even bother to say you should be taking medicine for this wound?" Enrique was saying, tying a complicated knot and snipping the suture ends. A sheen of sweat covered Devin's back; he didn't appear to be listening. "I guess we see if now your luck runs out. This is a bad one, *hijo.*"

"Yeah," Devin muttered, barely audible at that. Lips not moving, jaw tight. He sighed as Enrique blotted his arm with the antiseptic-soaked cloth—a rough cloth, but a surprisingly careful touch. "It'll do. Thanks, Rick. I owe you."

Enrique snorted as he gathered the suturing supplies, but his expression—concealed from Devin as he turned away to the cabinet from which they'd come—hardly matched. Plenty of worry there. A long-term worry, Natalie thought. "You watch it, then. For the swelling, the redness. And you left a lot of blood somewhere last night, *hijo*—I can see it in your color. So stay away from the streets a night or two. That's what you owe me."

"Ahh, Rick," Devin said, and flashed a sudden and unrepentant grin. "Gotta roam. You know that."

"I know your brother said the same, once, and he and those boys—" Enrique's lips thinned; he replaced the bottles where they belonged, tossed suture packets...set the dirty cloth aside.

To judge by the look on Devin's face, this was an old conversation, and not a welcome one. He met it with resignation. "They were hardly boys."

Enrique glanced back at him. "So you say. I say a man acts like a man. Back then, if your brother had acted as a man...he would not be dead now. And you— this *diablo*—"

Definite weariness on Devin's face—pain of an entirely different sort. He briefly squeezed his eyes closed. "I didn't have any choice."

Enrique closed the cabinet door and put his back to it, crossing his arms over his thin chest in scowling belligerence. "No choice at all. Exactly my point. No brother does that to another." And when Devin jerked his head up to look at Enrique, expression stricken, Enrique shook his head. "You see? *That* is what I mean. It's not what you did to him, *hijo*. It is what he did to you."

Natalie held her breath, suddenly aware that she was eavesdropping on something more raw, more profound, than she'd ever expected or intended—and that she really, really didn't want to get caught. Her lungs burned in the silence; she allowed herself a shallow draught of air as the two men locked gazes—Enrique's dark, perceptive eye, unflinching—and Devin's grayed blue layered with more than pain. Grief and guilt.

Devin looked away first.

Enrique turned from him without a word, yanking open a low cabinet drawer and rummaging therein— coming up with a hack-sleeved heather-gray T-shirt. He balled it up and threw it at Devin without looking.

"Cover yourself," he said. "Be a gentleman with your friend."

Devin caught the shirt one-handed. "She—" he started, and then stopped, shaking his head. "Just someone I ran into last night," he said. "When things got messy. I didn't—" He frowned, jamming his head through the shirt and then one arm, and following more gingerly with the next. "I don't—" He shook his head. "It's no big deal. She's dropping me off at my truck. Just seemed best to get this over with, before it started scarring up at the ends."

"The proud flesh." Enrique nodded. "Not much to do with it once that starts. We learned that with Leo fast enough."

And if she still wanted no part of this conversation, Natalie nonetheless found herself drawn in. Enough to hear Enrique say, as he reached to jerk down the back of the shirt—brusque, even, but somehow with the echoes of the gesture a father might use with his son— "It's good that it's no big deal. She seems like a nice young woman. Best you don't mess with her life."

Devin looked away. *"Dammit."*

Enrique's expression softened for the first time since this conversation had started. "That's the way of it, *hijo.* With what you carry."

"Yeah," Devin said. Now he just looked tired. He picked up his sweatshirt and pushed off the desk to his feet. "Thanks, Rick. I'll be careful."

He headed for the door so limber, so fast—Natalie found herself caught flat-footed. Only one thing to do—

take a quick step forward, almost colliding with him as he yanked the door the rest of the way open and headed out.

"Oh, hey!" she said, doing a quick two-step back again. "You're done?" *And look, it's happening again.* How long had it been since she had fallen so easily into lying?

Years.

Enrique was right. She was a nice young woman now. And she didn't need Devin James messing with her life.

Devin had almost forgotten she was there. Forgotten *about* her, no. Forgotten her presence the night before…

Far from it.

And this morning. If anything of this past day reigned crystal clear in his mind, it was the moment this morning when the blade tried to curl back through his mind and she'd brought him back. Given him that silly little trick. *Count your toes….*

And if anything reigned crystal clear in his mind, it was that every time she'd touched him—all through the fiery tumult of the night—he'd found just that instant of respite, of focus.

It hadn't been enough, of course. Nothing was enough—nothing *could* be enough, if the blade had finally broken through his boundaries of self.

But it was more than he'd had before.

"You okay?" she asked him, looking up into his face—direct and unabashed. "Your color isn't—"

Enrique snorted. "Every time," he said. "Sits through the stitching like a man, walks out the door and—"

"Once," Devin said sharply. "Just *once.* And I—"

Natalie's interruption came with haste. "Now," she said, with some purpose, "will you come with me to see Mr. Compton?"

For a moment, he didn't know what she was talking about. A blink, a frown…a quick search of her features and the determination there. His gaze slid down her cheekbones, came to rest on her mouth…lingered there, while his thoughts blurred around the edges.

It was some moments later that he felt Enrique's hand on his arm—fingers closing at his elbow, a firm but understanding grip. "Whoever you want to see," he said, "it should be later. Now he should rest."

Devin shook himself free. "I'm fine," he said, suddenly annoyed at the entire situation. Mothered by an aging boxer, pushed to meet Natalie's demanding boss—tethered to it all by weakness.

He should have been able to drive home the night before; he should have been able to get himself to Enrique on the bus. *Dammit.*

"I'm *fine,"* he said again, though no one had argued. He shook off Enrique's hand, stalked away from Natalie's expectant eyes and aimed himself at the grimy glass gym door. Enrique's Spanish curse at his back meant nothing; Natalie's noise of dismay meant nothing.

The guys in workout mode between Devin and the door faded back and out of the way.

He stalked out into the bright sunshine and started

walking, cat-footed in the black high-topped martial arts shoes he'd pulled this morning instead of wet sneakers. The cold hit him like a cruel slap, and he tipped his head back to soak it in, absurdly glad to feel it at all. Enough to laugh at himself, there on the sidewalk, his arms open to receive the cold and sunshine—to garner a strange look or two along the way.

Well, that was okay, too. All part of the game.

For however long it lasted.

He wasn't surprised to hear hasty steps on the sidewalk coming up behind him. "You're following pretty closely for a woman who drove away so easily last night," he observed, not turning around.

Even if he'd just realized he'd turned in the wrong direction, and would need to cut over at the next cross walk in order to reach the right ABQ Ride bus stop. As if to drive the point home, one of the striking, red-and-white, double-length buses roared past.

"Hey," she said, a little breathless. "I came *back*."

"Right. You make your own choices." If he shivered a little, he took a deep breath and enjoyed that, too. "Or so you say."

"Hey!"

Now he stopped, so abruptly she ran into him and bounced back a step or two—and then another, as he took a step toward her, ignoring the faint alarm and definite surprise on her face. "Tell your boss no thanks. I've got things to do."

Such as not wasting time with a man who thought his money meant people did as he bid them, whether they worked for him or not. Devin knew it well enough—just as he knew enough about Natalie's influential and affluent boss. He was the last man who could gain even a mere whiff of the blade's existence—because he was the first man who would scheme to take advantage of it.

Obvious enough, in the way he'd sent Natalie out into the dark of a difficult neighborhood, and in the way he'd pushed her to get Devin's cooperation in spite of the absurdly inconvenient circumstances.

Maybe the man was grateful. *Probably* the man was grateful. An assistant like Natalie would be hard to find. But only a man used to controlling others would insist on this morning, this day…this *now*.

"Hey," Natalie said, lifting her head and setting her stance—holding her ground. Sidewalk traffic flowed around her—mostly Pueblo and Latino in this neighborhood, making Natalie's the out-of-place face. "I make my own *personal* choices, damn right. But when it comes to work, yes—I do as Mr. Compton asks. That's the *point*."

"Uh-huh." He cocked his head, considering her. The flash of blue eye in sunlight, the indignation in her mouth and the way the curve of her full upper lip flattened out. "You good with that?"

It flustered her. "It's a *job*. Sawyer Compton is a good man who does good things for this city. Maybe you *should* stop by—you might learn something."

He watched her for a long moment, catching the tiny signs of rising temper. Thinking again of the night before, how she'd held together—fought back as she could, and fought smart. Stayed cool.

Not a skirmish virgin.

He gave her a sudden grin, one that took her back just as much as his sudden turnaround. It suited him. He didn't underestimate this one, no. He didn't take her lightly. And he needed her just as off-balance as he was. So he grinned—the I-don't-really-have-any-thing-to-lose-anymore grin—catching the surprise in her eyes. "Maybe," he said, shrugging the shoulder that was willing to do it just before he turned away again. "Or maybe not."

She didn't follow him this time—but her low voice reached his ears. "I saw all that, you know. Probably you wish I hadn't. But I did."

He stopped. He didn't turn around.

She came up behind him—right behind him, her voice in his ear. "The knife that turned into a sword. Dead men, gone. And you—you should be dead. You know it. I know it."

That ache…that was his jaw. His teeth clenching. His fists, so tight his nails cut into the flesh of his palms. "That," he said flatly, "is crazy talk."

"Maybe," she said, but her expression said she was more sure of it than that. "But it's still what I saw. And it's what I'll tell my boss—unless you want to come and choose your own story."

He took a deep breath through those clenched teeth. Now the cold just felt…cold. Sleeveless old gray T-shirt under a gray hoodie with the stained fleece gone stiff where it had dried. "Black," he said, as much to him-self as to her.

"Excuse me?" She sounded wary, which was wise enough.

"The shirt. This day needed black." Like the black that curled around his soul, taking advantage of precarious balance lost.

He hadn't expected blackmail. Not from her. He'd somehow stupidly thought, after the raw intensity of this past night, after the excruciating vulnerability had come and gone, that she'd understand. That she'd respect it.

That she'd realize no one else could know about the blade.

As if the very mention made the blade come to life, flame hissed along his skin, raised the hair on the back of his neck…sent his thoughts bouncing along scattered paths. Natalie's voice rested briefly against his ears, meaning nothing. The blade tugged at reality, replacing it with a hint of dark laughter—

And suddenly her eyes were there. Right in front of him. Her hands on his face, pulling his head down just enough to meet her gaze—sharp blue concern, mouth parted just enough for her teeth to catch her lower lip.

Right away, she realized he'd come back to the here and now. She dropped her hands and said dryly, "Toes."

He scrubbed a hand over his face. "Only works if you think of it *before*." He scrubbed a hand over his face. Of course he wouldn't be able to simply walk away from the previous night, just like that—from the first true taste of the wild road. And while what he needed most was rest, what he could afford to do least was let his mind wander.

She might well have read his mind. "Come with me,"

she said. "And he won't be able to say no when I have to take you back home. Leave him hanging, and he'll just keep asking." She hesitated. "If the toe thing really helped, I have some other things I can show you."

"Do you?" he said. *Weak.* He knew it, and she knew it—he wasn't going to walk away. He'd barely stopped himself from following her touch; he still felt the lack of it. Clarity, and awareness—and a gentler warmth that supplanted both the chill and the unnatural heat. "I can't help but wonder why."

"Good," she said, and turned back for the gym—for the tiny little parking alley alongside the gym where he'd had her tuck the Prius away. She tossed her next words over her shoulder, as if she was suddenly quite confident enough that he'd be following behind. "It'll give you something to think about."

And yeah, look at that. There he was, following behind.

Compton ignored the man waiting for his attention as he set the phone on the desk and pushed it slightly—precisely—to the side of an otherwise clear desk. The small room adjacent to his estate office held several desks and a massive custom-made work station—and there, Natalie organized his time and his day, while at the same time never touching those files he hadn't given her clearance to touch.

He'd given her plenty of chance to break those rules; if she'd been tempted, it hadn't shown.

And so he trusted her now. And while he'd heard her

reluctance on the phone, he'd also heard her acquiescence. She'd find a way to make it happen.

Unlike her ex-fiancé, who was both infinitely temptable and not nearly as reliable. Not that he didn't try. He simply didn't have it in him. Not the edge; not the determination. Ahh, if Compton had only gotten his hands on Natalie a few years earlier…

Definitely before her ex-fiancé had engineered the circumstances of Leo James's death, hoping for the blade…failing. It wasn't possible to predict what a blade would do during transition—sometimes it accepted the first new hand that snatched it up; sometimes it didn't.

Maybe Natalie had even glimpsed some aspect of the blade that night—research told him that this blade, shared by two brothers, had a taste for flash. A major, with all the extra power that came with it. A blade that thought much of itself, with reason.

Damned thing liked to show off, is what it came down to.

Maybe when it came down to it, that was one reason he wanted this particular blade so very badly.

Then again, he wanted them all.

"Ajay," he said, barely glancing at the man who still waited by the door—older than Natalie, coarser in every way, and her ex-fiancé…well aware that Compton had taken him on for his own means. Quite probably hoping to engineer himself back into her life, even if Compton had made clear that she was not to know Ajay Dudek was even in the area, never mind connected to her employer.

So Ajay's name was all Compton had to say by way of

admonishment. The man hesitated—an awkward flash of resentment he lacked the skills to cover—and inclined his head, acknowledging unspoken orders. He'd leave, now—and he'd take certain of his team members with him.

After all, Compton knew how to compartmentalize his activities. And this particular man yet had a role to play in Natalie's life, whether she realized it or not.

Chapter 6

Natalie had learned long ago that the drive to Compton's estate wasn't nearly as far as people expected it to be. And it wasn't to the posh housing on the exposed western slopes of the Sandia Mountains, which they also generally expected.

No, the whittled-down old de Salas property now nestled between the old *acequias* of the Spanish land grants clustered in the Rio Grande bosk, all long since broken into tiny agricultural pieces. That the pieces followed the *acequias*—the canals—gave Compton his utter privacy.

Even Devin drew back from distraction to give Natalie a surprised glance when she pulled off the old El Camino Real highway—a grand name for a tight little two-lane road, even if it *had* been the first true highway of a country not yet born—and onto the narrow side street splitting an alfalfa field and sheep watched over by their glaring ram.

The speed bumps slowed them—broad humps of badly raised pavement, impossible to navigate gracefully even below the speed limit. They curved past an adobe hut of questionable soundness, a grandly decorated gate with all the bright colors and flowered dignity of old Spain, and a cluster of bright blue plastic barrels with fighting cock occupants.

He sat straighter when she quite suddenly made the turn down the wide sand-clay maintenance path of a main feeder canal, heading deep into the trees of the bosk—and straighter yet when she whipped the car through a tight turn into an unpaved driveway, winter-dead honeysuckle and creeper vines brushing the windows and snagging the antenna.

They slowed to navigate the gravel, and the estate home grounds opened up around them: thick browned grass, winter birds scattering through the bushes, high pampas grasses and trees lining the property, and the grounds themselves vast and groomed, a cluster of buildings toward the back third of the property.

"Well, huh," Devin said.

And it was pretty much all he said, even as she parked—beside her own casita, a guest building as large as his own house—and led him toward the house.

She found she didn't have much to say. Not with the trickle of second thoughts, the sudden trepidation that the moment these two men met…

Might just not be a good thing after all.

"What, no manservant?" Devin asked, as she opened one of the massive double doors beneath the long covered portal of the house front. Beautiful Pueblo style married with some of the old Mediterranean ways, painstakingly restored and maintained.

Natalie said, "Mr. Compton is a very private man. No one comes here unexpected or uninvited."

"I'm supposed to feel flattered," he observed, not sounding it.

What he felt, clearly, was unwell, and Natalie flinched from it—and from the truth of the words he'd so recently said to her.

Stop it. Of course Compton made a huge number of the decisions in her day—he was making those decisions for himself; she merely saw them through.

This one, she thought, was one she might well have made differently. Given a choice.

Too late for that.

She'd keep this short; she'd see him home. And she'd take the opportunity to get answers from him about what had happened the night before—to those men, to Devin himself. To her, if it came to that. And then it would be over.

The second story ran in a mezzanine around three walls, leaving room for a soaring cathedral ceiling with a *latilla* rondel. Compton knew how to make a grand entrance—and knew when. "Natalie. Thank you."

He had a rich voice—a cultured voice. Mellifluous enough to deserve a stage, intimate enough to command it. A man of his early fifties, he had a trainer-sculpted body, hair gone early to a bright silvery sheen and piercing blue eyes.

For all he demanded, he also rewarded. Until today—until this moment—Natalie had thought herself in the perfect situation.

Devin, on the other hand, didn't seem to be overly impressed. "Nice place," he said, without glancing at it beyond a cursory check of doorways and corners and shadows.

"Mr. James. I'm pleased to thank you in person." Compton had his smooth persona on, no doubt about that.

Devin didn't seem much impressed by that, either. "I'm glad I could help. But I actually had plans for today, so…"

Compton ignored the blunt nature of those words. "I should think you would want to rest after last night. I understand you were hurt."

Devin stiffened slightly—not, she thought, at the suggestion of weakness, but because he simply didn't want anyone to know how quickly he'd gone from bleeding out to healing up. And indeed, he said, "Barely," and shrugged as if that would make it so.

"Then I won't waste your time." Compton strode smoothly for the staircase, trotting down the slightly curving length of it to emerge at the back of the room. Natalie took a step to meet him, realized that Devin intended to wait, and hesitated.

She did not feel so full of choices any longer.

She felt, in fact, caught up in an oddly disjointed war of responsibility. Of loyalty.

But that was absurd.

Maybe that's why she did take that final step forward as Compton arrived before them. Trying to create a buffer between them—for just which of them, she wasn't sure. Compton, who had not seen this man fight the night before and who now pushed at him, trying to define him by his reactions as he always did. Or Devin, who could not possibly be prepared for Compton's ruthless nature and who still, in fact, wavered in the wake of the night they'd spent.

"Mr. James," Compton said. "There are those who would bring me down, and they're especially…let's call it *annoyed*…at the moment. This makes them rash." He stopped, watching for Devin's reaction—analyzing his every twitch of mouth, his faintest shift of weight, and doing it without any attempt to pretend that he wasn't.

Devin didn't give him much. He watched Natalie, not Sawyer Compton. She felt the flush of it on her cheeks.

"The point," said Compton, just a little bit more loudly, "is that I don't think the attack on Natalie was a coincidence."

"No," Devin said, surprising her. "Neither do I."

"What?" She turned a startled look on him—couldn't quite figure out why she felt betrayed.

Maybe because this was just *a little bit important*. And he hadn't said a thing about it.

Now he looked at Compton. "However she ended up at a dead-end address, those men were targeting her.

They weren't drunk or on drugs, and they weren't run-of-the-mill dumbasses."

"So, then," Compton said, brows raised. "I've chosen well."

He—*what?*

Devin looked at Natalie. "Call me a cab, will you? I'll go wait on the street."

She stiffened in protest. Out in the cold, with only the sweatshirt, still pale from blood loss, his hand jammed into his pocket to hide the way the arm pained him? "Devin—"

"All right," Compton said. "No games. I can respect that. I want you to work for me, Mr. James. I want you to stay by Natalie's side these next weeks, while I conclude the particular business in which I'm involved."

Devin glanced at her. "You *should* get someone. But someone who isn't me. I'm not pro, I'm streets."

"You're effective," Compton pointed out.

More than you've guessed, Natalie thought at him, and realized for the first time that she had no intention of telling Compton that two men had died the night before.

"It's not a good idea," Devin said, with evident amusement at Compton's persistence.

Not a good idea? Why *not* a good idea? Because of what she'd seen? What she knew? Because she'd been in his inner sanctum and seen him hurt and seen him just a little bit crazy?

Because what if she *wanted* the kind of protection he could offer?

She wasn't a fool. If someone wanted to reach Saw-

yer Compton through her, she wanted that someone to
have to go through a man like Devin James.

She'd been on the street, too. She knew what it took
to survive.

She wasn't expecting him to look straight at her, his
gaze serious, to say, "I'm not what you need. You know
that."

No. She damned well didn't.

"Maybe you should think about it," Compton said,
unreadable.

A flash of annoyance crossed Devin's features, a brief
lowering of his brow. "I'm glad I was able to help," he
said. "But you should—"

And he faltered. Not physically, despite the obvious
strain, but his face showing brief struggle—a twitch of
his lip, a narrowing of his eye, one shoulder jerking back
in the faintest of movements.

Natalie felt it in him. She *knew.* One night of watching him fight it at its worse, and she knew.

She moved without thinking, closing the space between them to put a hand on Devin's arm. He sucked in
a breath, closing his eyes—she thought he leaned into
her touch.

In a moment his gaze found Compton's again. "You
should find yourself another man."

She couldn't begin to understand the faint smile on
Compton's face. He said, "Natalie, it's been a difficult
time for you. Why don't you take Mr. James home, and
then take the rest of the day off. I suggest you spend the

time here, of course, where we know it's safe, but it's entirely up to you."

"I—" Natalie struggled to process all the surprises in those words. She gave Devin a dazed look of her own; he lifted one shoulder in a shrug.

A ride home. A day off. Fine.

Good.

Because suddenly she'd seen too much, and she knew too much without knowing nearly enough—and now she wanted answers.

She mustered her professional smile, the one that came with all the slightly formal manners she'd layered over her past. "Of course, Mr. Compton," she said. "I'd be glad to. And thank you." She waited for Devin to offer a hard little nod of acknowledgment to Compton, and let him precede her out the door.

She should have known it wouldn't be that easy.

The moment the door snicked closed behind him, he turned on her—a fast move that startled her up against the other side of the double door; he pushed up close, shattering any illusion of personal space. She gasped as he jammed a hand behind her neck—tangling in her hair, curving to encompass the side and back of her head, his thumb brushing her ear.

Not gentle.

Personal.

"What," he said, not so very far away at all, brooding eyes full of demand and close enough to show the smudgy layered strokes of blue and gray iris, "was that?"

And his hand tightened ever so slightly at the back of her head.

She could have slammed a fist into his injured arm. She could have jerked a knee up into his crotch. For all of that, she could have rammed her head into his nose.

But she did none of those things, and she didn't look over to the entry security camera; she had no doubt Devin knew they were being watched. She narrowed her eyes and bit her lip, pulling in air—scents of stress and soap and something cinnamon. With tight control, she said, "You're welcome."

He held her gaze a moment longer, his own eyes narrowing. And then, abruptly, he laughed. That guileless expression, backed up with its borderline boyish grin. He laughed and he said, "Yeah, okay," and then to her astonishment, he leaned in those last inches and kissed her forehead. "Guess we'll see."

And then he left her there, the cold air rushing in around her like a slap of reality, and helped himself to the passenger seat of her car.

Getting in the warm car was a mistake; sitting down was a mistake. The flush of heat rippled up Devin's arm like a living thing, sinking talons into every stitch of puckered, healing skin.

Kissing her—that hadn't been a mistake. Soft skin under his lips, the surprise on her face, blue eyes opened wide.

Impulse. Not always a bad thing.

Because that nothing-to-lose feeling…sometimes it gave you little moments of *win*.

He grinned then, as she started the car and pointedly waited for him to buckle up, and he grinned as he did it.

"Oh, *what?*" she asked, putting the car into gear and whipping it around the circular drive in front of the house, all eerie silent engine in the stark slanting winter sunshine.

He let the grin linger.

She rolled her eyes and pulled out onto the canal, and then onto the street—but she turned in the opposite direction from which they'd come. "I need gas," she said shortly, in response to his glance. And then, as he gave the hybrid's space-age dashboard an incredulous look, she added, "It happens!"

The blade warmed in Devin's pocket, tugging at him with the burn of a limb waking up from frostbite. He inhaled sharply, his eyes widening briefly—a man trying to stay awake.

Or in this case, a man trying to stay himself.

A pale SUV spat out of the road behind her, shooting out abruptly into light traffic.

"Natalie," he said, his voice no more than low.

"Assholes happen," she said. But she frowned into the rearview again.

A glance at the passenger-side view showed him that the SUV crowded them from behind. Crowded them *close*. A big vehicle, full-size gas-hogging glory, suitable for farm work.

Or, given its gleam and styling, for hauling any basic urban team that thought much of itself.

"What are they—" Natalie's hands tightened on the wheel, and Devin took the cue to brace himself.

Tap. From behind, a polite sort of kiss to the back of the car.

Natalie cursed—a short, harsh word that didn't suit her careful exterior. "Oh," she said. "I don't *think* so." The Prius leaped forward, shooting up past the speed limit.

"Pull over!" Devin turned in the seat, looking over his shoulder. "You can't outrun these guys!"

As if to prove it, the SUV came back up on their bumper for a less polite smack of metal on metal, high bumper against the back hatch and an audible crunch this time. Natalie cursed again. "I'll pull over *my* way, thank you very much!"

He cast her an incredulous look. "Don't tell me this is about doing it your way—"

"No," she said, grim but steady as she shifted her grip on the wheel, and he should have seen it coming. "This is about doing it *right*." And she yanked them in a sudden turn across traffic.

Devin swore. Loudly. He grabbed the handle over the door, holding his injured arm close to his body where it punished him anyway. "Natalie, what the fu—"

"Wait for it," she said, voice raised over the rattle of the new road—narrow and rough and erratically curving. She glanced in her rearview, slowing as the SUV navigated its clumsier turn with a screech of rubber and asphalt—and then hitting the gas when it again loomed large behind.

"Natalie—"

"*Wait* for it!" Down the road, way faster than the speed limit, past the Pigs For Sale sign and goats exploring a fence loophole and—

"Chickens!" Devin shouted at her, too late—they blew by a flurry of cackle and feathers. And then suddenly he had other things to worry about. "Speed bump, Natalie, *speed bump*—"

The car surged forward, the SUV right behind it. Not subtle, not hanging back, and now they were trapped—

The yellow painted lines of the speed bump filled the road from edge to edge; the sloppy, unevenly humped nature of the thing clarified as they closed on it. *"Speed-fucking-bump!"* Devin shouted at her, all too futile and all too late, bracing himself against the floor and the door, solidifying his hold on the overhead handle as Natalie's knuckles tightened on the wheel.

She whipped right, so abruptly he lurched into the curved center console; his vision went gray and brightly sparked as his arm hit the thing.

From behind came a tremendous bang and scrape, locked brakes and tires ripping across pavement. Natalie braked almost as suddenly, craning around in her seat.

Devin opened watering eyes, scrubbed them clear with hasty fingers. "What—"

Natalie jabbed a thumb back. "Speed-fucking-bump," she said matter-of-factly, challenge behind the slight raise of her chin, three-quarter profile showing that slight bump at the bridge of her nose. "*My* way."

He figured it out, then. Realized they'd swerved onto the edge of someone's lawn, missing most of the misshapen speed bump and somehow missing the homeowner's fence, too. And realized that their pursuit had been too close to see that speed bump coming, and sure as hell hadn't realized its worn, uneven nature—but that Natalie had known about it from the start.

The SUV sat skewed across the road, deployed air bags visible, passengers stunned.

Devin grinned. Fiercely. "Sweet," he told her, and sprung the seat belt loose, unlatching the door in swift follow-through.

"Wait—what're you—" Panic flickered across her face, erasing the satisfaction. "Let's just *go*."

He shook his head, short and sharp, and slid out of the car. "We don't learn anything that way."

"But you—" Her voice grew filtered as he stood and glared down the SUV, finding the blade in his hand without conscious awareness of having reached for it— no longer just the pen knife, but an agate-handled tactical knife, solid in his hand. Her car door open and she stood tucked inside the shelter of it. "You can't! You're still—they could have *guns*—you have no idea what they're after—"

"Exactly." He stalked for the SUV, the blade held down and away; the energy of it surged up his arm, swirling a tight weave of molten light—a net, clamping down around his arm and setting hooks of light and

Doranna Durgin   85

pain. *Bold.* Bolder than it had been, crawling up along his flesh to find his thoughts, inflaming them with vengeance.

The blade grew to a saber, beautifully balanced, aching to sing. The pavement slapped hard against his feet, and the rest of the world—the fields, the fences, the livestock—went hazy and unimportant. Only those men in the vehicle before him—men who had chased Natalie, men who had threatened her, men who could never be allowed to do it again—only they mattered.

Their bloody-nosed expressions sharpened, cycling from confusion to high alarm. One fumbled with a gun, briefly sighting down on Devin through the windshield—but his buddy smacked it away, snarling a few words at him.

The man didn't stick around to argue. He bailed—and by then Devin had made his swift way to the driver's side; when the door started to open he instantly kicked it shut again. The man gaped at him—down at the sword, at the bloodstained sweatshirt. But it was what he saw in Devin's eyes that triggered the flood of response—hands up, gesturing and warding at the same time. Big guy, no neck, no hair, *tough* written all over him, fear in his eyes. "No harm, no harm," he said, words tripping over each other. "We weren't going to—"

Devin slammed the closed window with the saber guard; the glass shattered, crumbling away; the rest of the world crumbled away in the periphery, and the blade sang of righteous hunger, pushing against the notch of the man's throat and jaw. "I didn't come to talk."

Blood trickled down that beefy neck, mingling with sweat; the man's breath puffed hot panic.

Another's words reached him, so faint. He shrugged them off. He shrugged off the faint struggle remaining in the back of his own mind—a voice from a different time and a different man. He pressed—

Natalie's blue peacoat, Natalie's gleaming ash-blond hair, Natalie's blue eyes wide and frightened—all slamming up against him, shoving him away from the car; all suddenly in startling focus.

Not that it stopped him. Not that it *would* have stopped him—if he of the beefy neck hadn't scrambled out from behind the wheel and across the seat, spilling out the other side of the car to his escape—a staggering, jolting run that soon steadied out into pumping arms and legs and distance between them.

Not that it stopped him yet—not with the rage of metal burning up his arm, pushing, *pushing* him—

But for Natalie.

She shoved him another few staggering steps back to pivot against the stalled SUV, and her hands shook where they fisted up in his sweatshirt. It was instinctive to lash back at her, hand around the sword hilt and the guard heading right for her face—cheekbones and nose, her wide, beautiful mouth flattened in fear.

But she didn't flinch; she pushed against him, finding his gaze—holding on to that, too, while he just barely pulled the blow, hovering at the edge of it....

Hovering...yes...no...yes...

"No," she said, a low and ragged voice. "I *see* you.

I saw you last night. This isn't you. This is what happened *after*."

His arm trembled; he searched her eyes while the flames licked in around his mind, grasping at him, little sparking hooks of pain driving rage.

Her breath fluttered against his mouth. The breeze stirred her hair. And suddenly there were birds rustling in the massive old creeper vines draping the fence lines and a jet flying in low overhead and dogs barking both near and far.

His arm sagged; his body still sang with tension. He wanted to close his eyes—to escape what he saw in hers. He had to swallow down his breath, short and harsh, to say, "This is *exactly* what I am."

She shook her head. "No," she said. "This is what you are when you lose yourself."

The shock of that startled the blade into submission—into the knife, a lock blade snicking closed in his hand. With his other he grabbed her—as quick as that, the sweet feel of her neck curving into the back of her head, just as he'd done back at the house only this time—

This time, she believed it.

This time, so close, the brush of her hair against his skin, the thread of her life in his hand. "Either you don't know what the hell you're talking about," he said, sparing her none of the raw pain, "or you know too damned much."

He pushed her away. Not gentle. Not kind. And pretending so damned hard that his legs weren't wobbling weak beneath him as he returned to the car.

He wasn't expecting her footsteps behind him—light and calm and purposeful, right up behind him at the open passenger side, wondering if he dared get in at all.

He damned sure wasn't expecting her hand to settle quietly on his back, tightening his skin at the touch. She said, "Maybe a little of both." And then she took a deep, audible breath, and she said, "I don't want another bodyguard, I want you. And I think you need me, too."

Chapter 7

Sawyer Compton closed the file drawer with more force than necessary, drawing a startled look from Natalie as she bent over her desk, flipping through the pages of her resource book.

She was damned attractive this morning, her current expression notwithstanding—pinched around the corners of her lovely mouth, an anxious set to the faint worry between her brows, her slow exhalation obvious.

She thought she'd hidden her past from him, and that she hid her reactions now, but he always knew when she struggled. The flex of her fingers, so deliberate. The distinct pause before she reacted at all. The way her manner was ever so slightly formal when she did.

Regrettable, that she'd had to experience the attack several evenings earlier, so similar to that which had driven her away from Ajay Dudek and eventually into Compton's world.

Regrettable, but so very worth it.

Or Compton had thought so. From the way Devin had responded to her in the entry of this very house—possessive, in a way he himself probably hadn't realized—he'd been so certain that a second threat to Natalie would prove a final touch.

About the possessiveness, Compton was still certain—he still felt the sting of it.

It doesn't matter. Let James think he had a chance with her. It served Compton's purpose, and *that's* what mattered. And then James would be dead, just like his brother, and Natalie—if she survived—would still be Compton's.

And Compton would have the blade.

Except that Devin James hadn't called.

Compton paced to the window, looking out on the estate, tucked away as it was for a winter of hard hoarfrosts and scant snow in the crisp, dry air. A familiar sight, soothing in its exacting nature—making way for the clarity of what he felt beneath it all—a tingle of avarice, a deep thrum of *want,* a bass undertone of entitlement.

Unlike James, he knew what he was; he didn't fight it. And that allowed him to integrate all the better…to conceal himself among those who were lesser.

But James was not *lesser.* And so he had to be handled carefully, indeed. Sending Natalie back to him now, even on the best of pretexts, might well be enough to alert him. A fine line…

In his peripheral vision, Natalie looked up from the resource book—a thing of her own making, because while she used a tablet at his behest, she preferred the loose leaf with its collection of business cards, clippings, laminated yellow page entries and neatly transcribed notes. "Sir?" she asked, tucking back a wayward strand from her temple, the rest of her hair barely tamed by the twist in which she'd trapped it. "Is there something I can do?"

Why, yes. As you look particularly fine today, my dear, I would very much like you to bend over that desk.

Maybe one day. But right now, he'd look to the long view. "I've pulled back on the Alley of Life restaurant project," he said, referring to the controversial introduction of community gardens in Albuquerque's narrow urban allies. "I'm almost certain these threats stem from the latest developments there—and it's obvious you've been associated with that project, given your invaluable assistance." He hesitated just long enough for her shock, the faint shake of her head in denial.... She hadn't said anything, but he knew she loved this project.

Just as he knew the threats had nothing to do with it.

"Unfortunately," he told her, not quite giving her time to protest, "I don't have the luxury of postponing my involvement indefinitely. I had hoped to find a suitable bodyguard by now." In fact, he'd conducted five token interviews.

"I'm afraid I've been wondering if it might be necessary for you to take a paid sabbatical," he added. Because he knew Natalie…take away the work on which she so thrived, and she might go straight to James on her own. He could hardly come up with a more convincing ploy to draw James in than Natalie in sincere distress.

He'd known she'd be shocked—and that she'd quickly hide it. "I'm sure that's not necessary—"

"Are you?" he asked, cutting her off—reminding her who was in control here, if so subtly. "Because I can only interrupt my business for just so long, Natalie."

"That's not what I meant." She shook her head. "Maybe if I stop by his place again—"

Compton gave her a gentle smile. "Natalie, Devin James knows his own mind."

"He was hurt," she said. "I should have checked back in on him. But I was so sure…" Wistfulness touched that mouth; she looked away, as if she could hide it from him.

Possessiveness flared; he couldn't stop himself from saying, "It may be that we simply asked too much of him."

"You don't say."

Compton jerked at the unfamiliar voice—deep and a little rusty and belonging to the man who now lounged in the doorway, his hands jammed into black vest pockets, gray hoodie beneath. Worn jeans, sloppy black high-top sneakers, sunglasses hanging from a slanted breast pocket in the vest…and a self-assured expression.

Not much like the man he'd been several days ago, standing in the entry and so obviously struggling.

Damn.

If Compton had realized the blade's strength, the man's strength, he wouldn't have played things so cool.

He would have sacrificed Natalie to get the blade, then and there.

Too late now. This man, healed, had all the strength and self-assurance that his brother had never grown into. And he had damned well made it past a dozen layers of security to be here at all.

"Devin!" Natalie said, and if she stared at him in utter confusion, nearly as aware of the security around this estate as Compton was, it came only after a flash of delight.

Compton suppressed hot anger, knowing far too well it would only stir things best left alone for now. "Mr. James," he said. "I can't imagine what you hope to gain by this unorthodox entrance."

James shrugged. "Call it a test," he said, lazy with the words. He offered up a half grin, and if it earned a little smile from Natalie, it only stoked Compton's ire.

Compton pushed his resentment even deeper. "And we're supposed to ask what kind of test? Although there is, of course, that tempting option of having you escorted out."

"You know what kind of test," James said. "And there's no one available to escort me out."

"You didn't—" Natalie breathed.

He looked genuinely startled, and then genuinely offended. "No," he said. "I didn't." He withdrew a half-finger glove-clad hand from his pocket, bringing with it a tangle of cable tie restraints, and gave her the driest of looks.

Compton felt compelled to take a step forward and

break the moment. Even then, when James glanced at him, it was dismissively enough to rankle. "Don't tell me you didn't have me checked out," he said. "Average misspent youth, average promise, living off the grid... That's the official story, isn't it?" When Compton didn't respond, he snorted again. "*Tell* me you had me checked out. Because I sure looked into you."

"Ah," Compton said. "Charming mature gentleman of substantial means with diverse interests throughout the Southwest."

Devin rolled a shoulder, hands jammed back in his pockets...at amazing ease, given the circumstances. "I didn't use a dating service," he said dryly. "But I know you've been busy. My guess is that she doesn't know the half of it."

"Hey," Natalie said, standing straighter.

"You seem to have left some things out of your own résumé," Compton said. "The year of misspent youth turned to darker things, for instance. Your boxing mentor... You credit him with coming through that time, do you not?"

Give him credit, James didn't let it discomfit him—not the reference to his brother, not the allusion to the effect of the blade.

"Kickboxing is more my thing," he said. "But then, you know that."

Natalie threw her hands up, a muted gesture. "You two going to be at this awhile?"

Damned James, if he didn't seem to enjoy that, a familiarity that only annoyed Compton. "Not so much," he said. "Remember that test? The estate failed. Up that dead-end at the mailbox, over the fence… It wasn't hard to take out the cameras, and it was even easier to take out your two guys. You don't have a thing here that can protect her. You need me."

"The offer," Compton said tightly, because he had to, "is still open." And even through the bitter bite of that, he felt the tang of waiting triumph.

James only nodded. "I'll let your guys loose." He pulled a knife from his pocket, tossing it once to snatch it from midair—a substantial folding Buck knife with a heavily swept blade. He thumbed the blade catch and it snicked open, locking into place. "Back in a moment."

Yes, James had certainly recovered.

Now Compton would have to start again. Break him down. Make him vulnerable…destroy what he thought he knew about himself, just as he'd once done with Leo James.

And then, finally, he'd move in for the kill.

Natalie Chambers wasn't much happy with Devin. Her stiff, straight shoulders told him as much; so did her overall silence as she showed him around—the various outbuildings, the exterior of her casita, and finally a walk around the perimeter of the grounds.

He didn't tell her he'd already seen these places—that he'd checked the estate in his own way, with the two erstwhile watchdogs tucked safely aside. He listened with half an ear, watching the brisk movement of her legs, the slender nature of her body beneath her coat, the deliberate, economical gestures with which she pointed out the estate's features: their sluice gates from the canal, the venerable old foundation in the corner from the original family settlement, the working chicken house and the kennel where the Schutzhund watchdog had been kept.

"Had?" Devin asked, watching her profile as the sun glinted off hair and lash and brow, bringing blue eyes into brightness.

She frowned. "He was a good dog. A German shepherd, the old blood lines. But he started reacting to Mr. Compton. His handler thought it might be a new scent—soap, aftershave, *something*—but we never had a chance to figure out it. The dog got so sick...he died very quickly." She glanced at him. "Mr. Compton paid the handler for the loss, but I guess the man couldn't deal with it. He never came back."

"So, no canine protection." Devin stopped himself from reaching out to touch her hair, and then quite suddenly grinned. "And no dogs to watch out for, either."

She glanced at him. "You're more or less incorrigible, aren't you?"

"More or less," he agreed, standing in edges of the lacy leafless shade—elms along the property edge, thick and tangled; cottonwoods closer to the canal, and all manner of low brush in between, encouraged to grow. Anyone in this area using the canal ditchrunner paths for horses or ATVs would barely be able to perceive the estate at all.

His response didn't impress her. Not nearly. He found

himself grinning—that damned silly grin, just at the heart of her.

That didn't impress her, either. She jammed her hands against her hips, snug doeskin on her hands and a soft scarf at her throat, and she glared at him. "What did you think you were doing, anyway?"

The grin made way for a shrug. "Like I said. A test. Nothing to lose. If they caught me, then maybe he didn't need someone extra on you after all. And if he didn't, then that was something he needed to know. About me, about his guys."

She made a small impatient noise. "I understood that the first time."

"Then—?" He walked a few steps onward, crunching small branches under his feet—so it was with elms, always shedding branches.

Her impatient noise came louder this time. "What did you think you were doing," she repeated, "to leave me hanging that way? I was worried about you!"

Devin returned to her—maybe more closely than she expected. She took a step back. "No need for that."

"I can see that *now,*" she said, and her mouth—so easy to watch, that mouth—had flattened.

After all, the last time she'd seen him, he'd been stitched and reeling and slipping onto the wild road without any notice at all. But if he'd paid the price for his unwilling partnership with the blade, he also reaped the benefits.

He'd snipped his stitches out that morning, twisting awkwardly in front of the bathroom mirror. He'd done rope work and weights and beat the hell out of a heavy bag. And if he still felt the wild road beside him, it at least ran parallel to his own path, and no longer tried to converge upon him.

For now.

But she knew none of that. She knew he'd been hurt; she knew he'd been sick. She knew he'd very nearly killed a man in cold blood—a man cowering stunned behind the wheel of his car, no longer a threat. She'd driven him home, stayed the night, and only reluctantly left him there—and if he hadn't called her...

Well. Maybe he'd needed to prove himself first. To him, to her.

A test.

"You don't even get it, do you?" she asked him, and he was startled to see her mouth softening to hurt. "Dammit, I was straight with you. There, on the street. Or did you think it was easy to say what I did?"

Devin stepped closer, snared by sunlight glinting off lash and barely tamed wavy hair and maybe by that genuine feeling coming up raw in her voice.

Except she pushed him away, a firm shove. "Don't crowd me. I've had days to think about this. Dammit, I gave you—"

"Truth," he said suddenly. He took those steps again, and more—backing her right up to the nearest elm trunk, where rough furrowed bark caught the wool of her coat. Her eyes widened, then narrowed—but there was no pushing him away. Not this time.

And she didn't really try.

"*Your* truth," he said, running the spread of his fingers over her hair—not quite touching, as if the sudden glint of it in slicing sunshine would burn as much as the blade's sharp reminders, and yet…wanting. It didn't help, the way she looked at him. Anger in the lift of her chin and awareness in eyes gone wide and dark, and just a little fear at the corners of her mouth, the faint flare of nostril.

No, that didn't help at *all*. "Your truth," he said again, and his breath stirred her hair where it had loosened from the twist at the back of her head. "That's why I'm here. Didn't you know?"

"I—" She might be pressed against a tree, but she'd stopped pushing at him. Her fingers rested lightly against his chest; she gave them a puzzled glance, and shook her head.

He leaned in, breathing of her—making it obvious. "That's *my* truth," he told her, barely a murmur. "Now see how long it takes you to get back to me."

Her eyes widened; after an instant of hesitation, she snorted gently. "You are so full of it!"

He laughed outright, pushing away from the tree. "Guess we'll see, huh?"

That's why I'm here. To see.

And because the blade would hardly let him do otherwise, even if he wanted to keep it out of her life.

Natalie hadn't been surprised to learn that he'd brought a duffel, or that his truck lurked half a mile away from the back approach to the estate. Not close enough to

give him away—or to draw attention to them. He broke
away from her little tour near the back access, left the
way he'd come in, and brought the truck in through the
front gates in less time than she'd thought possible. That
extra bounce in his stride…it added up.

Normal Devin James, as far as she could tell. It wasn't
as though she had anything to gauge him by. Just deadly
shadows and blurring speed, and then wholesale strange-
ness.

And yet when she closed her eyes, she didn't always
see *him,* fighting for her in a dark parking lot. She saw
the alley, those years ago. *A cry of surprise, a flash
of white-hot metal, suddenly extinguished; life extinguished.*

Her own life changed forever…

And now she showed him to the second floor—not
that he hadn't already spent some unknown amount of
time there, but he politely offered the pretense that he
hadn't—and to the small but complete guest suite—a sitting area, a small nook with modest appliances, a niche
for the bed and an attached bath. "It's not necessary,"
he'd told her. "I only brought gear in case I get caught
here sometime. My place isn't that far."

"Mr. Compton would prefer that you stay," Natalie said, and for the first time in the two years she'd
been here, she felt a faint wash of embarrassment at the
words—the ostentatious nature of them.

"We'll see how it goes," he said, and dropped his duffel on the immaculate bed.

"Thank you," she said, and meant it. "There are sev-

eral other rooms on this floor in which you'll be welcome—the library, for instance. Most of the rooms on
the first floor will be open to you. There's a workout
room, and the kitchen is always available." She stopped
in the doorway as she headed out into the short hallway
on this north wing of the house, turning back to catch
his attention. "I'm going to show you which refrigera-
tor is open to house use. Do not—oh, I mean this!—do
not get into the True." Of course he had no idea what
she meant; the face he made said as much. Eyes gone a
little squinty, mouth a little amused. She let slip a rueful grin. "The big double-door steel fridge. Hands off.
Unless you want to lose them."

"That would be the cook's fridge, then? Because I'm
betting Mr. Compton has a cook."

"Jimena, and she's wonderful." She glanced down to
the first floor, where she had the sense the man in question listened to every word. Cameras in the corners, not
to mention the natural acoustics of the place.

And he did. Listen, that was. He knew everything that
happened in this house, and she'd long ago learned to
take that into account in phone and email conversations.

Not that she'd rebuilt her life to include many connections outside this house. Not when she'd come here
so soon after hauling herself back on her feet.

She suddenly realized that Devin was grinning at
her—and when she gave him the slightest of double
takes, heading down the wide slate tiles, she was startled to realize he'd winked at her.

He knew it, too. That they weren't truly alone here.

Distracted, she waved at the other guest rooms—currently empty—and at the solarium sprawled across the end of the hallway, double doors leading to a second-story porch. She pointed to the sitting room, where Compton kept a display of art and fine things, and as they crossed the exposed area of the mezzanine, the viewing room—soundproofed, full of speakers and a huge-screen television, comfortable seating, and more remotes than Natalie had ever cared to figure out. She read his expression as a quiet willingness to absorb what she had to show him.

And then she realized she'd lost him. Heading down to indicate the library on the corner of the south wing with the door looking out over the mezzanine balcony and the entry below—and turning to indicate the area of private collections and the special guest suite that he should not approach—she lost him.

The bounce of his step faltered; he slowed. She found him with that faintly puzzled, faintly out-of-focus expression, the one she'd so quickly learned to read.

Or no…not quite the same. A little more self-aware this time. His head ever so slightly cocked, a faint frown of puzzlement on his brow…as if he listened to something that no one else could hear.

"Devin?" she asked.

"I—" he said. "There's—"

"Toes," she told him.

He closed his eyes; one hand went out to touch the heavily textured wall. Straight shoulders lifted, and if he kept his head tipped in that odd listening attitude, when he opened his eyes, they were nonetheless clear. "Never mind," he said distinctly. "I'm fine. Just the dregs of what happened."

She opened her mouth—she meant to push him on it—all of it. To find out what those vague looks were all about, to ask once and for all what she'd seen in the darkness.

But he caught and held her gaze, as steadily as he'd ever done. No sudden lighthearted grin, no breath-taking piercing connection. Just steady.

And then she realized. She all but clapped her hand over her mouth.

They weren't truly alone here.

And what she did now would tell him—would tell herself—exactly how much of a leash Sawyer Compton held on her. How tight, how strong. It would, she sensed, define not only what she was, but what she was to become.

Maybe what *they* would become.

"Well," she said briskly, as if continuing the conversation just barely left off. Not pushing him, not exposing him. *Dregs of what happened.* "That's to be expected, then, isn't it?"

Sudden relief flooded her—a sense of self she hadn't quite realized to be missing. All this time, thinking she'd been making her own choices, and it turned out she had been focusing on the small things, the obvious things. That deep down, she was as much of a follower as she'd ever been.

Not any damned longer.

"Toes," he told her, as if this was somehow a safe subject. But they did have to start the conversation again, and start it fast, she knew—and knew it suddenly and strong. Compton was no fool, and saying nothing was just as bad as saying the wrong thing.

Devin ducked his head slightly, tipping it—looking at her, a faint furrow in his brow, catching her struggle, if not understanding it, as he spoke again. "How'd you come to think of toes?"

She looked down at her own, ensconced as they were in the black Gucci loafers she'd been wearing the night she'd been attacked. It didn't matter what Compton heard; he'd hired her coming out of a difficult time, and he'd known it.

Though it did suddenly matter what she told Devin James.

She said, "They're *real*." And then at his lack of comprehension, she offered a little shrug. "A while ago, I… well, I was where I shouldn't have been, and I saw what I shouldn't have seen." *Hidden in the murk down a tight alley, a flickering light; a deep sudden flash.*

Strobing movement had revealed a man in silhouette, his broad stance full of strength—held back in hesitation, moving in sudden determination, and lost in the following darkness. A grunt of pain, a cry of surprise, and the alley lit like a fancy stage production.

A man, staggering out of the night, a dark stain spreading across his shirt, his face revealed only in the ephemeral, bewitching-hot light, stark contrast and harsh, twisted features.

Even now, closing her eyes, she could see him fall. Death coming over him, dulling him…turning him into nothing more than muscle and bone.

She could still feel Ajay's hand on her arm. And she felt the cold rush of understanding—that he had known what would happen here, that he had somehow been *part* of it, even if he hadn't gotten what he'd come for, somehow—flooded her mind with revulsion, and from that, panic.

Because what, then, was she?

This was a life she'd chosen. A man she'd chosen. And then, she'd let him do every bit of the choosing for her. As though she'd turned her brain off completely, pretending their wild moments amounted to nothing more than hocking a few stolen goodies, smoking campus bammies and letting the haze of the pot convince her that life was good.

She took responsibility for it—she took responsibility for it all. Learning to live with that had formed who she was now.

She found Devin still watching her—concerned, about to reach for her, his stance and his intensity sending a shiver of déjà vu down her spine. She cut his inquiry short with a shake of her head. "I saw something. I had a hard time after that, and I was…" Alone and struggling, school dropout and life dropout and living one step shy of homeless. "…trying to pull myself back together. I came to realize that thinking of here-and-now things did that…and the better the detail, the better it worked. I did some reading…you know. Very Oprah."

Now the concern had disappeared. Now he looked faintly startled.

She laughed, if without much humor. "Maybe you don't know."

"Me. Oprah. Like *this*," he said, holding up two fingers and twining one around the other.

"I suspected," she said, and felt humor take hold at the corners of her mouth, if only briefly. "Anyway, it works. And since it's good for focus, when I saw…" *You, so lost, trying to find yourself…* "Well, I just thought it might be useful."

He glanced at her hand—the one she held alongside her leg, and the one she now used, so automatically, to settle herself. Her past tense, he seemed to be saying, wasn't quite as *past* as all that.

But he didn't push the point. He had other things on his mind. He looked at her hand; he looked at his own. And he looked at her. "Show me," he said.

If he tried to make the words casual, he failed.

But nothing about this man said *casual*. And nothing about what had passed between them so far could be called remotely that.

Nothing, she suspected, ever would.

Chapter 8

He hadn't expected to be jogging with her; here, over the local hard-packing sandy clay. Holding casual conversation in breathless little puffs of speech.

"Event planning," Natalie said, answering his last question—the one about just what did a personal assistant do for a man like Compton, anyway? "Targeted shopping. Travel preparations. Message management. You want more, or—?"

"I get the idea." He moderated his pace, but only slightly. "So, what? There's a school for that? A degree?"

"No, I went to school for—" She stopped, and she might have just been catching her breath, but Devin knew better. She was catching her thoughts. When she spoke again, the words were simple and final. "I took some courses."

He left it at that for a while. Didn't have much choice, as they passed a property where three massive rottie-pit mixes paced them, barking thunderously. A marginal fence…the blade warmed to the potential of it.

Natalie glanced at him—her face flushed with cold and exercise, her hands gloved, clad in simple sweat-pants and a windbreaker shell over something thin and sporty. Her hair bounced on her back, a thick braid. "I don't do financial work or anything deeply involved with the business side of things. I just make things happen."

"Doesn't seem like there's any reason for someone to be after you, then." He fell back a few steps, check-ing over his shoulder at the racket as they left the prop-erty behind and the dogs made an extra effort to break through the fence. The blade gave a hopeful tingle. *Not today,* he told it.

She glanced back, and the look on her face showed suspicion that he hadn't yet caught up because he was too busy watching her ass.

She was right, of course.

She said, "Maybe they don't know what I do. You didn't."

True enough.

"Or maybe they just think they can reach him through me. In which case they don't know him very well."

He did catch up, then. "Maybe they knew better than you thought. Or did you think I was easy?"

She tossed him a dry look. "I'm sure you're worth every penny," she said, and ran in puffing silence an-other few moments. "Mr. Compton is a practical man.

Whoever's upset about that Alley of Life project, he doesn't intend to back down. This is one way to keep his business moving along pretty much as usual."

He said what she didn't. "Must be a pretty big deal, then."

But Natalie only laughed. "All of his deals are big ones." She led them over a rickety and informal metal-and-wood plank crossing, ten feet across a deep, seasonally dry canal.

He hadn't realized she'd be this fit. In his arms—*almost* in his arms—she'd struck him as slender, just the right amount of padding in just the right places.

Maybe they'd run some victory stairs next, maybe to some stirring theme music.

"What's so funny?" she asked.

Ah. Nothing to do but shrug. Few things were as inexplicable as his head, even in the best of times…and these were far from that. For years, had been far from that.

They passed another yard of dogs, all tiny little rat terrier types who poured out of a hole in the fence to swarm along at their heels. The knife gave a hopeful throb of warmth, and Devin directed inward scorn at it. *You must be kidding.*

Getting bored, that's what. Night after night, he walked the streets, following the knife to trouble…doing good in the name of bad, and trying so hard not to cross the line his brother had all but obliterated when he'd taken the wild road.

Not that Devin truly blamed him. That was the worst part. His brother hadn't been forewarned—hadn't seen it happen to anyone else. Had first come across the blade by chance—although Devin knew better than to believe any of it was by chance any longer—without seeing the de-evolution of the man who'd once held it.

Devin had seen.

Devin had watched.

His brother, changing. Gone dark and silent and obsessed. Gone heady with his power—the awareness that the blade would eventually put him back together after all but the most grievous wound, that his fighting skills came as inborn, that his strength and quickness required honing but not building.

The blade had whispered him onto the wild road, slowly but surely. Turning on him, wearing him away from the inside out. Until Devin hadn't even known him any longer, and saw only—

"Devin?"

He looked up at her. He looked down at his feet. "We're not running," he said, because that was the most intelligent thing he could come up with, the world not quite real around him. Just his feet quiet on the ground, and not pounding against it as they should be.

Not actually all that intelligent, really.

She moved closer, all bright flush and bright eyes, individual strands of hair glinting bright. "Look," she said. "Look at your hands."

He lifted them, turned them over—found hands that were used to work—the odd jobs between classes at Enrique's and the security gigs and of course the cash commandeered from the pockets of those he stopped on the streets. No guilt there. Had there once been guilt? Had he once thought twice? Or maybe these weren't his hands at all, square with long fingers and neatly clipped nails, healing knuckle scabs from who knows what. Maybe they weren't even attached to his—

She stepped into him. One hand slipped into his; the other touched the side of his face.

Quite suddenly, that was all he felt. Not his feet on the ground or the exhilaration of a heart pounding from good exercise while still wanting more.

Just the crystal clarity of her hand in his and the profound sensation of her fingers touching his face. Soft skin, a gentle touch. A polite touch, and yet…

The touch of a woman who claimed familiarity. One who had dragged his bleeding body into her car, into his house…who had walked the halls with him all night.

He sucked in a breath. He closed his fingers around her hand; leaned his face into her touch—and realized, suddenly, that he had done these things. His eyes snapped open—he hadn't known they were closed—and he stared at her in a mixture of confusion and regret.

"Feel it," she said. "Every nuance of it. Where are my fingers touching your hand? Where are your fingers closing across mine? Where on my face—*oh!*"

For he'd taken her face between his palms, threading his fingers into the base of her braid—soft, wavy texture anchoring him to this new clarity. He pulled her closer, watched her eyes widen—her mouth fall open.

She didn't resist. But *not resisting* was a far cry from wanting.

Devin *wanted*. He knew that much. Not just what she'd done to him—what her presence still did to him. Not just the slender beauty he found in her. But that which he'd seen in her this past week and more. The distinct lines she drew around herself while still utterly respecting his own. The resiliency of her. The empathy.

And there her mouth was, barely a whisper from his. "Up to you," he managed, if barely.

Your choice.

She understood that—understood further that he knew what it meant to her. It showed in her eyes, right before she closed them, and when she lifted her mouth, there was a hint of a smile at the corners.

God, yes, clarity. As if he could think of anything else other than the shape of her mouth beneath his, or the movement, or the warmth of her lips. The taste of her, the immediate tease of her tongue. *Gusty breathing, cold air chilling his neck, fiery warmth in his hands, fingers pulling at his hip, a hand pressing against his back—*

Every bit of him alive and aware and *present.* And when they separated—maybe she'd done it, maybe he had—and he gulped air, looking at her with a kind of awe, he found her flushed with more than just the running, her eyes widened again. He knew the exact moment she realized how low her hand had dropped, as it tightened slightly around the curve of his buttock.

"Oh," she said. And then he fell just a little bit in love, because instead of growing flustered, retreating to her proper executive assistant self and snatching her hand away, she let it linger. Just a moment, but so definite, before the touch turned to a trailing caress and she stepped away.

Not far, but…

Devin sucked in another breath.

"That help?" she asked him, watching him. Watching closely.

What the hell? "That's not what that was about. Don't—"

She held up a hand, then bent to scoop up the gloves she'd pulled off—there, back when he'd lost himself—and said, "Okay. *Okay.*" And then, glancing at him with a small smile, "Good."

He relaxed slightly. At least, until she sent him another small side glance. "But did it?"

He sighed, and didn't have it in him to lie about it. "Hell, *yes.*"

The small smile got just a little bigger. "Good." She tugged on the gloves and tucked away the hair he'd loosened from her braid. "So here's another thing to try. It's practicing thinking what you're doing, to anchor yourself." She took a slow step, every movement distinct. "It's like paying attention to the details of your toes. Or—" she shot him a look, and he swore it was a wicked one "—the details of kissing. Feel what your socks are like against your skin, where your shoes touch your feet, how your muscles flex—"

Right. There it was, right in front of him. That tightly shaped posterior. The one he'd just missed his chance to—

"If you don't mind," he said, abrupt at that, "I think I need to run."

Chapter 9

The blade warmed Devin's jacket pocket all the way to the estate. Smug and satisfied, as if it had somehow gained from those moments on the canal.

He faltered.

What if it had? What if the whole thing—the intensity of his reaction to her, his lingering impulse to return to her—hell, to sweep her right off to the nearest excuse for privacy—was truly only part of what he'd been running from all along?

Hell, no. He'd know. And those moments…they'd been so clear. So very real. None of the fog, none of the flickering pain and inner strobe.

And yet…

It made him cautious. By the time they returned to the estate, it made him mighty damned cautious indeed, here in this place where cameras watched every move and everyone pretended they didn't.

That Compton was one hell of a control freak.

"Don't tell me," she said, eyeing him…seeing it. She paused to stretch out in a way that purely made him ache. "You don't get involved with the people you protect. Some sort of professional code."

"Wouldn't know," he told her promptly. "I'm not a pro. Told Compton that from the start."

But his words rang a little hollow even to his own ears. He'd pulled back; he'd pulled in. And she knew it.

But she wasn't a woman to be played with, either.

And he knew it.

That kiss.

It had been the kind of kiss every woman should savor.

At least once.

Natalie didn't know what had come over him on the way back to the estate, but she knew enough. She knew what she saw.

A troubled man. A man full of darkness, if with contrary glimpses of sunlight in his humor, in the bounce of his step, in the unabashed grin he'd turned on her.

But still, full of darkness.

And now, with the mood on the estate wound tight and threat hanging over all, it was no time for exploring what was missing in her tidy little life.

So the moment had happened, and then it was over.

Or they pretended it was. Inside, she and Devin talked

about the weather, the latest kitchen delight and Natalie's schedule. Outside, they talked about her life here, or the estate, or sometimes nothing at all.

More rarely, they talked about him. But never what happened that night at the parking lot or at his home, because when she did bring it up, he simply looked at her—a little surprise, a little amusement. As if because she had asked him, again, that which he had made clear he wouldn't discuss.

She sometimes found him in the workout room, practicing thoughtful walking…going through Tai Chi forms with a slow intensity that told her he'd applied the concept to existing skills as well as those she'd suggested. If he noticed her, he only grinned, that startling glimpse of who he might have been if—

If whatever rode him, didn't.

And after a week, during which he took her on errands, walked her to appointments, scoped out the venues in which she'd be attending events and lurked on the grounds while she toiled in the office, he joined up with her for another walk around the estate, and his mood had changed. Troubled, now; reluctant.

He might well keep certain things to himself, but he'd not yet shown an ability to keep himself from her. Not the truth of him.

So when he bent to pick up one of the fallen elm branches, flinging it toward the canal with a practiced flick of his wrist, she caught the expression on his face and she said, "What's wrong?" before she could even stop herself.

Because it said too much about her, too.

He glanced sharply at her; of course he'd noticed. "Nothing," he said finally. "Other than the fact that I'm the worst kind of idiot for kissing you like that, and then not doing it again. But then, you knew that."

She couldn't help but laugh, as short as it was. "I hope you're not expecting an argument." She jammed her hands in her pockets, wishing for gloves on this deep winter day.

He, of course, wore nothing more than the hoodie under his vest. Devin James ran hot, no doubt about it. And he flashed her that grin, the one that made her hold her breath, if only for an instant. "I think I'd be disappointed if you offered one."

Frustration reared into place. Never mind the thoughtful logic of it all—her recognition of his conflicted nature, her impatience with the secrets left over from that night, her growing awareness that his life touched too many pieces of those things she'd fought so hard to leave behind. Thoughtful logic was crap compared to that grin.

Or compared to the way she could *still* feel his touch from those few moments on the canal.

So she said, frustration evident, "Then *why*—"

He cut her short with a shake of his head, an oddly panicked look. And while she was in the astonishment of that, he looked away, gathered himself, and said— evidently unable to look at her at all— "Because I can't do that to you."

"I—" she said. "What?" She turned a scowl on him,

drawing herself up. "Did I hear you right? You're making that decision for me?"

"No." He turned right back on her, and spat the words out low. "I'm making it for *me*." And then spun away, walking a few hard steps down the property line, leaving her stunned.

Only a few steps, though—there he stopped, tipping his head back—she'd think he was simply regarding the bare branches overhead if she couldn't see from this slight angle that his eyes were closed. After a moment, he reversed course, but only for a step. "There's nothing happening here," he said. "Whatever last week was about…there's been no sign of it since."

Stunned again, and blurting words without thinking them through. "How can you be so sure?"

His glance was wry. "I know," he said. "Let's leave it at that."

"Let's *not,*" she told him, so buffeted by the quick turns this conversation had taken, one after another, that she forgot to be smooth and polished.

But he only looked at her with regret, as if he understood entirely, and yet still…had no intention of explaining. And if his expression held a certain deep pain, she wasn't inclined to acknowledge it.

"Maybe you're right," she said. "You *are* all kinds of idiot. And *I* can't do that to me."

Compton listened to Natalie with an increasing ire— one he found difficult to hide.

But she could have no sense of it, not for this to work.

"It's not about the money," she said, and though she stood before him in his office with her usual composure, a stack of newspapers tucked into her elbow, she couldn't quite hide her flustered nature.

He wasn't sure which was the greater distress— her awareness of failing him, or the dissent that had so clearly risen between her and Devin James.

Bitter possessiveness curled deep inside at the knowledge that while he preferred it to be the latter, the former would best serve him right now.

She took a deep breath, held the papers a little tighter. She slowly flexed her other hand, and some of the strain drained out of her. "It's about the need. That's what he said." She shook her head. "As in, *other* people have need. He's willing to work with us for specific events, but staying here—" She seemed to run out of words. "I'm sorry. I tried to talk him out of it. I'm afraid it might be my fault."

Perfect. Compton laughed shortly, gratified at her startled expression. "Natalie," he said, "men like Devin James do the right thing." *For now.* "The honorable thing. Fighting him on this would only backfire."

She nodded, a slow gesture. "I'm glad you see it that way. How would you like me to handle it, then? He plans to leave in the morning."

"I'll talk to him before he goes," Compton said, waving a deliberately negligent hand. "In one thing, he's right. There's been no sign of further threat. Perhaps those who sought to discourage me have thought better of it, or perhaps they see that the project has gone beyond stopping." He shook his head. "I'll arrange for him to work with us per occasion. It should be sufficient to then hire on an extra man from my usual source."

She hesitated. "I'll call them in the morning, then."

Not that he was done. Not when he needed her believing, and trusting. He took a step away from the massive window that fronted his office, closing the distance between them. "Feel free to speak frankly, Natalie. Will you feel safe?"

He didn't miss the wistfulness that passed so briefly over her features, clouding blue eyes. It didn't show in her voice—it wouldn't. Not his Natalie. "I believe in his ability to assess the threat, sir. He has a…" She stopped, shook her head. "He seems to have a sense of such things."

"Indeed," Compton murmured. And therein had been his mistake. He'd brought the man under his roof; he'd trusted his interest in Natalie and his interest in the job to keep him here while Compton studied him…felt out his weaknesses. He hadn't given enough respect to James's very real ability—his blade-gifted ability—to assess threat.

He hadn't respected the way the blade thirsted for just that.

Compton, after all, should know.

And he also knew just what to do next.

Devin woke with the blade in his hand, rolling out of bed. Disoriented, lost in a fog of darkness and a pure zing of lust for action.

Toes.

The nubby texture of some expensive carpet beneath bare feet. The precise awareness of how much weight fell onto his heels and the balls of his feet; the swish of expensive high-count cotton falling away from bare legs.

The blade twitched, white-hot runnels of light flaring along the spine and front quillon, the belly of the blade gleaming an unnatural blue-white in the darkness, then subsiding. It was enough so he knew what he held, could feel the heft of it.

A knife eager to be deadly, with a double edge halfway down the spine, a finger ring at the butt...cool agate handle a contrast to the warmth it drew from within Devin. It had come to his hand in a reverse tactical grip; he flipped it, more appropriate to combat not yet engaged, the knife his primary weapon.

To think, once he hadn't known these things.

The blade had taught him. Hard and fast.

But the pull of it wasn't enough to get him outside in the cold without shoving his legs into jeans, his feet into shoes and his arms into sweatshirt. Not once he realized the threat wasn't literally upon him.

And then it hit him.

Outside. The casita. *Natalie.* Dammit!

He bolted out into the wide hall, noiseless on the tile, and down the center-tread carpet of the old wood-and-wrought-iron stairs. *Alarm code—!* He skidded to a stop on a silent snarl of impatience, stabbing the code into the control box. Couldn't risk alerting his quarry...or just as bad, risk alerting witnesses.

They weren't all as discreet as Natalie had been. *Damn,* he had owed her an explanation.

Just as he had owed her the kindness of keeping her out of it altogether.

Out the door, finally, the blade blasting eager heat through his body, centering there beneath his heart… the mark it had left on him there. Threatening to burst out even as the tendrils of it spread into a fog of clouding obsession.

Get back, you demonic son-of-a-bitch! He didn't have time to slow down, to think of toes or movement or glimmers of reality.

He thought of Natalie.

Where the blade now tried to cloud his mind, it still left him its subtle advantages—the black and grays of the night distinct to his eyes, the scents strong to his nose, the sounds crisp. The hoarfrost told him they'd reached early morning; the moonless sky told him the same. Not long before dawn, when so many people slept the most deeply.

Natalie, beware—you're not alone!

The blade told him as much, tugging him into a sprint toward the casita. The scent of old cigarette smoke on a leather jacket, unwashed hair…the crunch of a misstep on gravel.

Not one of Compton's security hires—no unkempt habits for Compton's men.

The casita's motion-sensitive entry light flicked on with sudden, excruciating brightness. Devin flung a hand before his eyes and twisted away, but it was too late. Even as the intruder shot out the light—the short, sharp sound of a silenced pistol giving away his weapon of choice—Devin saw the significant bulk of him silhouetted against the entry.

But with the light gone, he saw nothing—his night vision squandered, his eyes watering. The cold bit into him as the blade absorbed the shock of it.

It wasn't without its vulnerabilities.

He braced himself; it surged back with renewed fury—something personal in it this time.

"Hey, dumbass." That was his own voice, barely recognizable. His own words, unplanned—an instinctive attempt to get the man away from Natalie's door while stalling for his own vision to return. "She's *mine*."

The man was good. Too good to spar with words; too good to do anything more than pivot and turn the gun on Devin, the metal of it glinting dully in the sudden flare of the blade—no longer a tactical blade, but—spurt of flame and a shocking reverberation of pain up his arm and there it was, a throwing knife balanced and quiet in his hand, begging to fly.

He gave it that. A quick judgment of distance, a quick snap and release—the blade flew heavy and true, slamming home with a meaty thump. The intruder cried out, disbelief as much as pain, and the gun spat muzzle flash—aim wild, even if Devin hadn't been rolling aside, coming up against the house and ready to dive in from the side.

No need for that. The man looked down at his abdomen, where the knife pinned his coat to his shirt and then to his body. Clear enough to Devin's returning sight—liver hit to the hilt, blood gushing out to stain the shirt. One hand clawed at his belly; the gun grew limp in the grasp of the other. A few stumbled steps away from the house and down he went.

"Dumbass," Devin growled. "She's *mine*." And then froze, hearing himself. Hearing both truth and distortion, and stunned by it.

And then recovering enough for reality. "Nuh-uh. No dying until *after* I know who sent you and why." But when he crouched there, he found it already too late.

Ah, hell. Only one option, if he was to learn anything at all. Do it through the blade. Open himself to its invasive claws after the past week of desperately fighting it off.

Or keep himself safe, yank the blade and walk away.

No choice at all, really.

He wiped his hand against his thigh, reaching for the hilt—hesitating there, fingers spread wide, ready to wrap around cool lace agate—the tactical blade form again, taunting him. Strutting, the only way possessed metal imbued with blood and tears and sanity could do strut at all. "Bastard," he said under his breath, and closed his hand around it.

It swept into his mind with a moaning cry of victory, wind and groaning blood and brimstone stench, and it brought with it the taste of someone else.

Get her bring her, a flash of a dark vehicle waiting, an obscured license plate, money in a backpack, ammo spilled out across leather car seats. *Find out what she knows*. The blade shoved images into his mind—photos tossed carelessly on the center console, showing a younger woman with a less defined facial structure, unusual but not yet striking with somber blue eyes and unstyled ash and blond waves. His own blue-gray eyes, familiar and haunted and dangerous, watched some unknown quarry from a shaded doorway.

And then the scene faded away, while Devin snarled both for more and for his freedom, the tendrils of the blade wrapping through his mind and tightening down, a hiss of laughter snaking along a dozen insidious pathways into his soul.

The demon blade snared him—and then in its way, the demon blade saved him. From the casita came a thump and crash and cry, a thunderous cacophony to hearing gone blade-sharp, and he knew with startling certainty that he'd made the most unforgivable mistake of all. *More than one of them—*

He snatched the blade from the man's body, ignoring its unearthly wail of protest. A bounding kick and he'd smashed through the closed front door, into the open floor plan of the casita. Kitchen to the left, appliance clocks glowing. Flat screen dark in the corner, couch directly in his way. He skirted around it, just in time for Natalie to come careening out of the bedroom, running smack into him with a cry of surprise.

He wanted to grab her arms, pull her close—tuck her up tight and bury his face in her long, loose hair. He couldn't believe how much he wanted to—

"It's me," he said, voice low, and set her aside—

hesitating only long enough to be sure she was steady, breathing in the nighttime scent of her just enough to be sure there was nothing of fresh injury about her.

"Devin?" And then, as he went straight for the bedroom—all light scents and lavenders, linen curtains and pale sheets, "My *door!*"

Only once he'd made a circuit of the bedroom, detouring into the bathroom to slap the shower curtain aside, checking all the windows, checking the glass patio door, did he begin to realize that there wasn't anyone here. The bed—a double, on a wrought-iron frame with lazy curlicues at the head and foot—hid no one underneath. No one lurking behind doorways, escaping through broken glass—

He came back to the living room, struggling to put reality back together.

"My *door!*" she said again in disbelief, stabbing a hard finger at it.

"Where—?" He frowned, working at it…flexing his hands around the blade's agate hilt. "I heard someone—"

"You heard *me,*" she said. "You broke down my door to guard me from *me.*"

"You—" He looked back at the bedroom, where a single bedside lamp lay in pieces on the floor, a simple straight-backed wooden chair lay askew against the wall.

"I heard something outside—it startled me." She gave him a dry look she probably didn't realize he could read through the darkness. "I'm guessing that was you. Devin, my *door*—"

He got it, then. She had no idea. Not that a man had

come for her; not that he lay dead in the landscape gravel just off her porch.

"You heard *some*one," he said grimly, pulling his thoughts together—clamping his hand down around that cool agate, one finger sitting in the strong choil right before the blade went edged—letting it dig in a little. Keeping the blade at bay, and feeling the righteous hiss of its anger.

It was supposed to have been a trade-off, that vision it had provided him. It wanted its blood payment. And barring that, it wanted what it had always wanted…a lingering path on the wild road before the next hapless wielder put Devin out of his misery, leaving the blade in new hands.

Natalie's expression had gone wary—as if she could discern his struggle. As if she suddenly didn't quite trust him. She hugged herself, obscuring the curves beneath her flannel sleep shirt and girl-cut boxer shorts—and it wasn't clear whether she shivered from the cold rushing in through the open door or whether she suddenly wasn't entirely secure in his presence.

"I don't know," she said. "Something woke me and I knocked over the lamp—and then you came crashing in. Devin, there's no one else here, in *or* out." She crossed to the couch, grabbing a soft shoulder blanket, and pointed out with more calm than seemed reasonable, "If there were, you wouldn't be standing there talking to me."

He said, without quite thinking it through, "You've done this before—" What, that she'd been woken in the middle of the night by crashing doors and gunshots?

That she'd learned to assess, so quickly, what mattered and what didn't?

Except this time she was wrong.

Her head lifted; the look might have been called imperious, if he'd thought she could truly see him at all. "You keep your details, I'll keep mine."

He closed his eyes; he pressed the heel of his hand to his brow—pressed hard, as if he didn't already hold the blade in that hand. Hunting reality. He grappled for it, found an opening…just barely found himself.

"You heard someone," he said, finding words again, even if his voice came out low and strained. "He's dead, but he's out there. And we don't know for certain that he's alone. So shove your feet in some shoes and let's go."

"He's—you *killed* someone?" Her hands clenched on the shoulder blanket. "Just now?"

He couldn't help it that the blade licked at his voice. "Did you think I wouldn't? If they came for you?" And when she just looked at him, he took the few steps between them, grabbed her arm and escorted her to the side of the door where the shoe tray held a neat line-up. "Boots, whatever. We need to get to the big house." Then he'd take care of the body. He'd feed the blade, and he'd decide whether to hunt the grounds or stick close to Natalie.

She had her boots on—and from the little secretary by the door, she grabbed a small flashlight. "Let's go," she said, and took a step toward the exposed doorway—

and then, before he could stop her, held back. Let him go first.

Just like moments earlier.

Just like that first night. Hit by the crazy, the unexpected…still thinking her way through it.

He stepped onto the porch, lifted his head to the night. Listening with the blade's ears…scenting the night. Waiting for the rush of warmth that bespoke the blade's anticipation.

Nothing. Silence. Not even the satisfied bass thrum from moments earlier.

"Devin," she whispered, a plea; her teeth chattered. She shadowed him, just enough to the side so she could see beyond him, crowding him for warmth and safety and one hand resting lightly on his hip.

He gave himself a moment to absorb the feel of that touch—a deep breath, eyes half closing—and then moved out.

Her little light swept the path before them, hindering more than helping. He reached back and gently placed a hand over hers, steadying the light—aiming it slightly off the path as a compromise. Aiming it, as it happened, at the body.

No. Aiming it at where the body had *been*.

"What the fu—?" He cut himself off in his own disbelief. "It was—I left—*right here*. It was right here!"

"What was right here?" she asked, remarkable patience for someone who shivered up against him so.

"The man I—" He stopped, let it hang there. He'd felt the blade's triumph; he'd known the man's death.

She pushed right up against his back; her flashlight sweeping the ground.

"Right here."

"Or the whole thing was a dream, and you broke my porch light when you broke down the door!" she snapped. "God, Devin, can we just get inside? Are you insane, keeping me out here like this—?"

This time she was the one to cut herself off, as he stiffened from her words—as the impact of what she'd said bounced back to her. *Are you insane?*

Maybe just so.

Chapter 10

Trust. A fragile thing.

Belief, even more so.

Stretched thin, now, both of them—no matter how Natalie rued it.

The man had saved her. He had nearly died for it; he had endured a night of pure torture in the wake of it. He had touched her with his strength, with his grit…with his self-honesty and with the glimpses of his startling capacity to embrace random moments of humor.

Staring out her office window at her little casita with its newly installed front door, Natalie ached at the conflict of him. At the memory of blue-gray eyes, light-footed stride along the canal path and then his sudden presence and strength, hard intensity beneath her hands. Eyes darkening…body *wanting*.

His hadn't been the only one.

But he'd sidestepped her direct questions about what she'd seen that night. And though she thought she'd helped him with his frightening distractions...

She found herself thinking of the lapses. The moments in the main house, outside the private wing—more than one of those, now. And the night before, when he'd burst into her house...

If he'd killed a man and let the blade have the body as had happened in the parking lot, he'd had such a lapse that he didn't even remember the whole thing.

The other option wasn't any better—that he'd made up the entire incident.

Her own memory echoes didn't help. Those moments Natalie had tried so hard to leave behind—flickering alley light, a man silhouetted in the midst of it, another staggering out of the darkness to die before her, features hauntingly familiar and yet unrecognizable, too broken into light and shadow by the strobing night.

"Natalie?" Compton's voice held a hint of censure. "You're ready for this afternoon's meeting?"

As she'd certainly better be, if she'd been caught staring mindlessly out this window.

But she couldn't quite bring herself to turn away from it. Not when Devin James came into view, walking careful steps between the big house and her casita. Searching the sparse dried winter grass—crouching here, touching the ground there...touching the slash side pocket of his vest. Shaking his head.

Now, Natalie glanced at Compton. "Yes, sir. The presentation folders are ready." Thumb drives tucked into leather portfolios, preselected business cards tucked into slots meant for just that. Complementary built-in calculators, of course, as well as slim solar-powered digital clocks. A sleek Fiberstone paper notepad and matching pen, as well as a series of diagrams and plot drawings that no doubt complemented the flash drive contents. The Alley of Life restaurant development…time to woo the movers and shakers whose support would make all the difference to this project.

"And your bodyguard?"

One last glimpse of Devin—standing, now, and gazing off over the estate—and she finally turned to him. "Sir, I…"

"Natalie, relax. It's only natural that you might feel some response to him. He saved your life, and you continue to entrust yourself to him." He looked no less dapper than ever—ready for the presentation in a tailored charcoal suit that set off his silvered hair to perfection.

The steely businessman, still full of the vigor that had led him to his success, honed by maturity into a formidable opponent—wise and experienced and used to the taste of victory.

So why that bitter edge to his tone?

It meant she was careful when she said, "That's not it, sir. I just… I do think something's troubling him. I'm not sure it's not interfering with his judgment."

Her words startled him, which she hadn't expected, either. He came up beside her, looking out across the yard between the two homes, large and small. "I understand there was some confusion last night," he said. "But I have to admit, I'd rather mend a door broken in overprotective zeal than depend on a man who does too little, too late."

Natalie took a breath, holding it as she searched for the right words. Words to say, "It was more than zeal" and "He has secrets you wouldn't believe" and "I think maybe he's losing his mind."

To know that he thought he might be losing his mind, too.

But she couldn't say those words. None of them. So instead she said, "Of course you're right, sir."

"Not to mention," Compton said, "a man who seems to have a certain extra motivation to keep you safe. Don't you think?"

She looked straight at Compton, meeting those cool eyes. "I wouldn't know, sir."

There was a flicker in his expression, something else she couldn't read. "We had a nice little talk this morning. He'll be staying on here until we're completely satisfied the threat is resolved."

Natalie swallowed hard. Outside the window, Devin James touched his pocket and glanced up at the window. The intense version…a little brooding, a lot dark. She felt as though he was looking directly at her—and asking something inexplicable of her.

She wanted to reach out to the window…. She wanted to run. She wanted everything and nothing, all at the same time.

She said only, "That's excellent, sir."

* * *

Not far from the deliberately charming streets of Old Town Albuquerque, the architectural firm held its corner in just the right bold complement to the buildings around it. Not too tall, perfectly Southwest and sleekly modern. The parking lot was newly paved and striped, and the doorway greeted Natalie with a gentle blast of warmth.

She juggled the presentation materials, striding in one step behind Compton. Devin James—dressed for the occasion in unexpected black suit pants under a deep gray wool overcoat, grim efficiency in his movement—ranged slightly behind the both of them, and then stood off to the side as Natalie unloaded the materials into the hands of the admin assistants who met them.

At a word from Compton, Devin hung back in the lobby—not relaxing, but lurking. Assigning himself an obvious station in the corner.

The receptionist gave him an unsettled look, shifted as though she might say something, and then subsided.

Natalie didn't blame her.

She entered the presentation room with brisk efficiency, laying out the folders and preparing Compton's work space—not with the primary presentation materials, which Compton himself had created with a consultant, and then absorbed through hours of study, but with things of a practical nature—his own coffee, brewed fresh in his own kitchen and transported in a sleek little executive thermos. His small digital recorder, set just so off to the side; pen and paper just so. A discreet wireless web camera, tiny surveillance gear of the highest quality for Compton's convenience when it came to reviewing the meeting.

But Natalie's presence became redundant as soon as she had his work area set up, and she quickly withdrew, the press of hearty greetings already ringing falsely in her ears.

She was just as grateful to escape. It unsettled her, the way Compton's business persona settled around him so easily—so effectively. She left his empty briefcase by the door and slung her own slim leather bag over her shoulder, already reaching for her notebook.

Just because she wasn't in the meeting didn't mean she wouldn't be working. Each of these highly placed men and women would receive a courtesy basket of goodies, and Natalie wanted those baskets waiting at their respective homes.

Still on the move, she glanced up from her notebook to find Devin James watching her from the lobby, his gaze a hooded, single-minded intensity that made her brisk steps falter, her thoughts skip a beat and the flush at the base of her throat spread both up and down.

You don't know him at all.

Or so she told herself. A distinct part of her seemed to think otherwise.

Or maybe it just didn't care.

The receptionist sat stiffly, glancing Natalie's way with both accusation and relief—an expression that said *Good, you're back. Now* take *him.*

Too raw for this ultrapolished world of surfaces and shiny things. Too *real.*

For the first time Natalie realized that she, too, fit neatly in this world of excessive polish and little depth— that she'd learned to slip it on like a glove.

She looked at Devin, found that he hadn't moved— but that he still waited.

She fit in his world, too.

"Walk with me outside," she suggested, heading straight on for the door, not looking back. Knowing he'd be there.

And he was. Not behind her, but beside her. "Hey," he said, as if it meant something. As if it was all he needed to say.

Maybe it was.

She dug into the bag, pulled out her phone and tipped it away from the sun. "You look nice," she said.

"Mmm." It was a noncommittal response, so neutral that as they moved around the shaped juniper landscaping, she lowered the phone to glance over at him—found his grin.

She found herself grinning back, but pointedly lifted the phone again.

"I think I scared the receptionist," Devin said. "What do you think? Do you think I scared her?"

Natalie lowered the phone, gave him a look. *See me being patient?*

If he got it, his expression didn't reflect the fact. Not with that smile at the corners of his eyes, the grin lingering.

She sighed, stuffing the phone away. And really, she'd made these calls. She'd just intended to double-check them all. "Let's walk," she said, and held out an inviting elbow.

"You don't think I scared her," Devin said, and briefly, visibly, considered disappointment before shrugging.

"Maybe if you hadn't shaved," she said kindly, but when he slanted a sideways glance at her, she burst out laughing again. Just because. Because the night before suddenly seemed long ago and far away, a nearly forgotten incident between two people who, in that moment, had been different people altogether.

This man, she had jogged with along the canal, walked with on the estate, partnered with for slow-motion games in the workout room. This man had rhythms she had come to know.

His grin faded away; he seemed at once taller and more solidly grounded, and infinitely less approachable. Not the dazed look that sometimes still overtook him, but a complete clarity of focus.

Quite suddenly, hunting.

And here we are, out in the open as if there hasn't been any threat at all. Her fault.

Devin scanned ahead to a small cluster of tough young men taking up the whole sidewalk, not enough in the way of jackets, wife beaters and flannel shirts and posturing every step.

Doesn't matter. Whoever wants me isn't working with such blunt instruments.

She glanced quickly behind, orienting—finding them alone in this clean parking lot except for an older man coming up behind them—someone's grandfather—

That's when she realized that Devin might have been looking ahead, but his true attention was inward—alarmed, the faintest of frowns…a searching.

And as the older man came quickly up behind them, Devin turned on him. At the last moment, turning away from the young men and their tattoos and their gang signs and turning on the old gentleman with equal intensity—eyes gone dark, hand emerging from his coat pocket with gleaming brass knuckles and the glint of a short, sharp blade. A new weapon altogether.

Natalie froze in horror. In the old man's face she saw flashes of vulnerability and fear, the awareness that he had no defense against violence blooming to dark eminence. "Devin!" she cried, even as the old man shied away—nearly lost his footing, one hand sticking in his pocket—and then gave them wide berth, one aghast glance back at them as he made good his retreat.

And it was over. Only a moment of time. Short, sweet and fading.

An inexplicable moment in which the previous night suddenly loomed big and the laughter died away entirely.

The gang members jeered, offering exaggerated gestures of how impressed they were. Devin didn't appear to notice. He pulled the brass knuckles from his hand, gave them a puzzled glance and snicked the curved blade closed. For a long moment he held it there, his fingers wrapping down around it…his eyes, in losing their intensity, also losing their focus.

"Devin," she said again, her voice low; she stepped

up to him and touched his face, barely cupping his jaw. Not tentative. Not guessing. *Knowing.*

He sucked in a sudden breath; his hand snapped closed over her wrist. "Would you—" he said, and it was a request—quiet pleading. *"Would you—"*

But he closed his eyes, and released her wrist, and lifted his face from her touch, all without quite stepping away. "Yeah," he said harshly. "She was right to be scared."

Natalie only shook her head, if ever so infinitesimally. *Smart woman.*

Much smarter than Natalie herself, it seemed.

Sawyer Compton glanced at the one-word text message displayed on his phone screen.

The man had lived, it seemed. Good.

Not that Compton had cared particularly about his fate. But he was a good resource, even at his age—able to approach without raising alarm, presented to create assumptions, yet still spry and capable.

And he'd been instructed to kill.

Not that Compton had ever expected him to succeed. He'd expected one of two things—that the blade would warn James and the old man would die, or that the blade would warn James and circumstances would allow the man to retreat, switching to frightened grandfather mode to make good his escape.

Either way, James wouldn't realize that the blade hadn't gone rogue, sending him at an innocent man. Either way, he'd carry the stain of guilt and uncertainty.

And this way, Compton didn't have anything to clean up.

He smiled, and continued with the business pitch— the one that in spite of all the implications he'd made, had nothing to do with the attacks on Natalie and nothing to do with the heightened security around the estate.

It was a shame Natalie had trusted him so thoroughly. A flaw, really.

One he was perfectly willing to use.

Chapter 11

What were you even thinking?

But Devin knew the answer to that.

Nothing.

There on the street in broad daylight, the blade in his hand, its warning heat singeing his mind…an old man frightened out of his wits.

Devin counted himself lucky the old guy hadn't had a heart attack on the spot, slain by intent if not by blade.

And now the pull of it still worked on him—inexorable, unyielding. The blade woken and still hungry. The wild road beckoning. His concentration shattered.

He wasn't any good to Natalie like this. And now—?

What?

What was he doing out here on the estate mezzanine, staring blankly down the private hallway?

He scrubbed his hands over his face, suddenly weary. Wanting nothing more than a night sprawled on his couch, a half-eaten bowl of popcorn waiting for random attention, an old Western murmuring in the background, the privacy of the little house snug around him.

Not this. Not standing at the echoing juncture of a hallway that meant nothing to him, swaying slightly...

Lost to himself.

Only for a moment. That's what he told himself.

A moment too long.

He'd been on his way to the workout room, full of burning and drive and needing to do something with it— thinking himself tied to this estate, to Natalie's safety.

He knew better now. Compton would have to hire another.

Devin had other mysteries to solve.

Had he killed a man the night before? Had he imagined it all? Or had he only imagined parts of it?

There were no good answers. Not even if his memory was right in every detail. That only meant that someone had indeed come for her...had died for it...and had then disappeared.

Not been alone?

He'd have known. He'd have felt it. The blade would have told him.

Would it have?

No assumptions. Not anymore.

And Devin found he'd somehow gone a third of the way down that private hallway, the big window at the end of the hall sending a sharp glare of late afternoon light across his body.

He heard her footsteps, and yet somehow didn't register the significance of them, of being where he was, until they suddenly stopped, so close. He jerked around to face her, both startled and defiant and something, somewhere deep within him, ready for a fight.

She took a step back, and at her side, her hand flexed, closed…relaxed. When she spoke, her voice didn't quite strike *normal*—but it wasn't far off. "You shouldn't be here."

"I know," he said. "It's the secret hallway. Abandon hope, all ye who—"

"That's not funny," she said.

He didn't respond at first. Not quite floundering, just…

What did one say, anyway? *Sorry about the completely random acts of insanity and violence.*

Or almost-violence. Or imagined violence.

"No," he admitted. "Probably not funny at all."

She let out a breath. "Devin…" she said, and reached out, probably not even realizing it—one hand barely raised.

His reality, that's what she was. Glinting golden blond-in-brown, an open blue gaze framed by sharp cheekbones and that strong, narrow jaw…the mouth he could watch forever. All fired up about protecting her own path, her own choices and full of a strength she didn't even seem to recognize.

Devin saw it. He saw it all. Every piece of him warmed to it.

She watched him with...what was that? Confusion or regret? But whatever it was, she tucked it away, and drew herself up. "Dinner's almost ready. I'm afraid it's not optional tonight. Mr. Compton is celebrating."

No, he thought. Longing. Longing and sorrow.

Sawyer Compton reigned charming over the meal. Visibly pleased with his day's work, confident about the outcome...not inclined to notice that neither his personal assistant nor her bodyguard were good company.

The meal itself proved a multicultural tasting opportunity—not too much of any one thing, but all of a theme. From South American pastes and Philippine fish to India's southern dishes to Thailand's hottest offerings...definitely a night of spice.

Devin hardly noticed when he washed it all down with a laced espresso.

He hardly noticed any of it, truth be told. Too caught up in the inescapable conclusion that the wild road was putting his feet on its path.

"Devin?"

How long had he been staring at his plate of tiny desserts? The clear sugar gelatin from China, the miniature Thai fried bananas, the Filipino budbud pilipit with rich coconut cream and—

Well. At least it wasn't *spicy.*

Devin couldn't pretend he hadn't been completely distracted, or that he hadn't lost track of the conversation entirely, or that Sawyer Compton hadn't just caught him at it. Natalie watched him in dismay, the several other guests maintaining a polite preoccupation.

"I should head to the kitchen," Devin said, "and let Jimena know that was the best several meals I ever had in one sitting." He stood, scooping up his plate. The meal had been mandatory. Natalie had made that much clear. But it was over.

By the time Devin walked away, the conversation had already turned to other things—the most recent charity fundraiser, the most recent society gaffes. Dessert discussion.

Devin took the plate to the kitchen, thanked Jimena and turned around to find Natalie in the arching doorway behind him, looking both bemused and concerned.

"You're going for a walk," she said, barely even guessing.

"It's what I do." Walking the cold night grounds, hunting trouble—one hand on the blade, listening, while the rest of him tried not to hear at all.

"Are you all right?"

He moved on out of the kitchen, heading for the small room off the entry that served as a walk-in coat closet and keeping his voice low. "It helps," he said. "The things you've taught me."

"But *what*—" She stopped herself just barely short of asking it, as if she sensed she'd never get an answer. And then she did it anyway. "It's got to do with that knife of yours, doesn't it? With what I saw. That's what."

He found his coat, retrieved his very favorite alpaca

wool scarf from the sleeve where he'd stuffed it and pulled leather gloves from the pockets. "Does it matter?"

She yanked her own coat from the coat rack beside the row of hung outerwear. "Oh, *please*. Did you think I would stop asking?"

He zipped the coat. "I'd hoped," he admitted. He reached out to straighten her coat collar, not asking the obvious—if she was coming with him. Walking with him. Too battened up for the simple walk to her casita, which could be done with a quick dash and an unfastened coat. So he smoothed the collar down; he tucked a wayward strand behind her ear. At his lingering touch, at the gentleness there, her eyes widened. He couldn't help but smile—something small and wry. "What?" he asked. "Did you think I would stop trying?"

"I—" she said, and swallowed, all her courage there on her face. "I *hoped*—"

And Devin grinned, because he saw what that meant. Knew it in his bones. Just the opposite of what she'd said, given those words left unspoken.

Natalie suddenly looked as though she wanted to kick his shins—she suddenly looked as though she'd do it. She glanced behind them out into the entry, although no one was near and no one could hear the conversation in this tucked-away little room either way. She said, low and fierce, "You drive me nuts. One moment you're a hero, the next you're full of crazy—*mad* crazy, the kind that nearly kills innocent old men. You scare me—you scare *everyone*. And never, *never* do you tell me the whole truth. You don't even pretend!"

"It would be stupid to pretend," he observed, even then pretending his pulse hadn't kicked up into overdrive—the nearness of her, the fervency of her emotion, the high flush on high cheeks...

"All of that," she said, as if he hadn't spoken, "and every time I get anywhere *near* you, it's all I can do to—*not* to—"

He grinned. Slow and unrepentant.

Natalie swore under her breath. She took a step back, spreading her arms in a sharp gesture. *Here I am, then, you fool. What are you waiting for?*

Nothing, that's what.

Nothing at all.

Not so long ago, Devin had kissed this woman by the canal; not so long ago, he'd been so responsive to her touch that he wondered if it was his own response at all or pulled from the knife, all heat and clarity and trembling detail. He'd wondered if what he took from it wasn't his to take.

Days of wanting, days of watching himself—examining every step, every reaction—looking for impulses that weren't his own. Not ever finding them. Not when it came to Natalie.

Looks like I make my choices, too.

Damn, *yes,* he kissed her. From hesitation to, oh, sweetness, just the briefest hesitation, a soft exploration—but that wondrous mouth of hers was as mobile as he remembered, as responsive—as wonderfully clever against his. And her hands—oh, hell yes, they went straight to his butt again. More of that any day.

The coat room shifted around him, its pleasant warmth suddenly stifling and not nearly private enough; Devin pulled away from her. She would have protested; he put a light hand over her mouth, listening. She raised her brows and, oh, yeah. She bit his hand.

Not *ow*. Not in the least. Clever lips on his fingers, a soft tongue. He closed his eyes tightly, awash in the battle for self-control and not the least bit above laughing at his own predicament. She tugged him a little closer, and that's when he suddenly realized it—how very far in over his head he was.

How very good that was.

He opened his eyes to find her, yes, laughing, bright blue gaze, lashes tipping up at the outside corners. He indicated the dining room with a nod, and then gave the door an obvious glance. Snagging her hand, he tugged her toward the door. They emerged from the house at a tumbling run, laughter bursting out to fog the night air.

Halfway to her place, he had her hair out of its upswept style and his fingers lacing through it. Two thirds of the way there, she'd unzipped her coat and started on his shirt. By the time the repaired entry light flicked on with their arrival, she'd pulled him in close and tight.

Only when the light flicked off did either of them think to fumble for the doorknob. And by then, who needed lights or indoor heating or any such thing at all?

* * *

Natalie managed to get the door open and then closed; she let Devin drag them to the couch, where he pulled her over the end. He bounced off the couch and she bounced off him, and in another moment there they were laughing on the floor, tugging on coats and clothing and tugging on each other.

She dove for his earlobe; she tickled her breath down his neck. She pushed his hands up her shirt and twined her legs around his, rueing the material between them as she moved against him.

He grunted, a ragged sound—his hands, searching to release bra, lost coordination. When she did it again, his strangled noise became a curse as he pushed her away, instantly rolling on top of her—pinning her hands by her head, his weight settling over her hips. But holding her there—holding himself slightly apart. "You," he said, through clenched teeth, "have *no idea*."

Deliciously buffeted, blood singing, she only gave him a slow smile. *Maybe I do.*

Maybe this wasn't her at all, this uninhibited creature who'd made her decision and now gave herself to it completely.

Or maybe it had been her all along...waiting.

He leaned over, fitting them together for a kiss of deep and lengthy entanglement, until she tugged her hands free from his token grip to wander and play and touch, bringing him back to that gasping place.

Until he suddenly pulled away, resting his forehead on her shoulder.

His body had lost some of its tension; his ragged breathing seemed less invigorated and more simply breathless.

"Devin?" Her hands, heading for his snap and zipper, came back up to his shoulders, then either side of his face. "Are you—?"

"It's not that," he said, quickly enough, and nuzzled her an apology. She scraped her fingers lightly through the hair behind his ear; he groaned in appreciation.

But in another moment he'd made the slow transition to the floor beside her, his leg still thrown over her body and one arm pulling her in tight. "Just…give me a moment."

She reached over him to pull the shoulder blanket down from the couch, covering them both. "It's not—?"

"It's…I don't know. Not familiar."

In that, at least, she heard utter, nonevasive truth.

"Leo never—" he started to say, but cut himself short. "Tell me how you got here. Tell me where it is you learned to think on your feet, and why sometimes I see Compton's perfect little assistant and sometimes I see a fierce little hell cat."

She rose up to one elbow, letting cool air under the blanket. *"Perfect little—"*

He tugged her in closer again. "Am I wrong?"

She wanted to stare at him in horror—and at the same time found herself completely gratified to be in darkness. She knew what he meant, all right. How polished she was, how well she knew the routine. How perfectly she functioned within it.

Oh, she wanted so badly to go back to pounding hearts and moving bodies....

"In college," she found herself saying, "I was in it for the party. We grew pot, we inhaled, and we thought we were pretty tough."

His grunt of response sounded a little too amused for her liking. "Tough," he repeated.

"I know, I know." She wanted to run from this, no matter how his warmth beckoned her and his body had come so close to being *hers*—and yet somehow, there was her hand, tracing over his chest, tucking in between the unfastened buttons of a well-worn casual shirt. "Really, we were just slackers, always at the edge of trouble—until suddenly it got to be more than that. My fiancé—"

She stopped. Just how foolish had she been, back then? Not to see how Ajay had pushed and nudged and taunted them all until suddenly one day they *were* rough... They were in over their heads. No longer pretending to be college students at all, most of them dispersing back home to their various flavors of failure.

Not Natalie. She had Ajay. And she'd always had an edge to her—slapped around at home, driven to escape the dictatorial hand of accidental parents. Driven to control her own fate, in ways good *or* bad.

He shifted beside her, a restless motion; it reminded her of that first night. The moments in which he'd finally been able to pause but couldn't quite be still. Beneath her hand, his breath caught.

She flattened her fingers over the dusting of hair on

his chest, deepening the contact. "Ajay," she said finally, telling the story, "*was* tough. And he ran with some guys who were tougher— I never really met them, though he always thought I went behind his back with one of them. But this one night—" She shook her head. "He'd set something up. A meet or something, though I didn't realize it until later. And it went wrong, and I still—" She hesitated. Were there even words? *Blinding lights, the silhouette of conflict, a man staggering out to die at her feet, more blood—*

"More blood than I even thought a body could hold," she murmured.

"What?" Vague, that voice…not quite there. She stroked down his ribs—using the touch for herself as much as him, to keep her here, now. Not then, in the alley.

"He died," she said. "Right there at my feet. And Ajay, I still don't know why, but Ajay went into that alley—not once, but twice. I thought he was going to die, too."

But it wasn't Ajay's face she saw in her mind's eye, it was the dead man—his features obscured by blood, marred by a broken nose and a split lip. She'd seen only enough to know he'd been slightly older than she…features once handsome.

And then he'd died.

"Ajay?" There, now he was back with her.

She spread her fingers over his side, kneading gently at faintly quivering muscle there. "Mad as hell over something. I don't know. Didn't get his way."

"This is the guy you were with then?"

"Hey," she said, digging her fingers in just a little. "Did I mention I was stoned a lot?"

"Speed," Devin said. "My crowd liked speed. But I had—" He stopped. More truth evaded. Or maybe not, for she felt his chest expand, the deepest of breaths. "My brother had—"

But no.

He wasn't going to go there.

He said, "So a man died at your feet, and it was your personal epiphany." He laughed, a low sound, and she didn't understand why except that it was dark and bitter and not aimed at her at all.

"Something like that ought to be, don't you think?" She hesitated as his arm tightened around her, and ran her hand down to the hard line of his hip. His sharp exhalation came in acknowledgment of her touch; he nuzzled her temple...kissed the skin just beneath her brow. Not demanding, not needy, just...

Sweet.

Damned sweet. One of those sudden grins, gone straight to her heart. Oh damn.

"Yes," he murmured, and threw a leg over hers again. Okay, that was needy. But it was fine by her. Even finer that he moved from her brow to her neck, still nuzzling... singing warmth back into her blood. "Something like that...*is*."

She wasn't even thinking when she said, "Kind of ironic that place turned out to be one of the first Alley

of Life projects. All that beauty, in that place of death…
no one even knew."

The gentle breath stopped—held, for a long moment.
"It—*what?*" And then, not to her—not to her *at all*—a
sudden tension, a recoil, and the desperate sound of protest. *"No—"*

Chapter 12

"Not now," she told him fiercely. As if she didn't know the signs by now. As if she didn't know that they came upon him when he pulled away from her. Responding to her story...to her life. Pulling away, and then losing himself.

And oh, he did more than pull away from her—he jerked himself free of the shoulder blanket and rolled up onto his knees, his movement laced with an emotional panic new and ragged.

Except she'd had enough. She wrapped her arms around his shoulders and said, "*No.* You *don't* get to do this to me again. Do you hear me? You don't get to rip me open and turn away!"

"I don't—" he said, just as dazed as ever. "It can't—" Upright didn't quite suit; he lurched down to his hands.

"I'm not kidding!" she told him, tears suddenly stinging at her eyes, unfulfilled in both heart and body. Bereft in both. "Not again! You make your choices, too!"

But when he fumbled forward, it was away from her. Not enough to break her contact, only loosen it—at least not before he suddenly stiffened, and became, again, someone else altogether.

Some *thing* else altogether.

The disjointed fumbling snapped into focused tension. Her hands, slipped to his upper back, felt a vibration…a body-wide growl. *"Where?"* he snarled, and his voice didn't sound like his, either—the knife, suddenly in his hand, couldn't possibly have been with him all along. Not that full-length hunting knife with a sweet killing sweep to the streamlined belly of the blade, handle shaped perfectly to Devin's grip and metal gleaming blue-white where the room was too dim for it to gleam at all…

Strobing alley light, blinding her, dazing her—

He lunged to his feet—lunged at her door, all swift deadly movement, but so very focused on whatever lay *beyond* that he literally flung himself at the door.

Only to cry out in sharp surprise. And this time, when he went down, he stayed down.

For a long moment, she just stared at him. Too hurt—the taste of rejection a bitter thing along her lips—to rush over to check on him. Too wary to get near that blade.

And yet too compassionate to leave him alone.

Slowly, she reached for the blanket he'd rejected; she pulled another from the back of the couch—soft and decorative. She tugged her clothes back into place, and eased over to him...not finding the knife at all.

She covered him, sitting behind him...resting her head on his back. Holding her heart as safely as she could while giving him the only thing that had ever seemed to help.

But the contact did nothing. Not this time. This time, he twitched and trembled and grunted and sometimes cried out—and if she'd never seen him fight his strange fugue, she'd have said he was simply caught in a terrible nightmare. A bad trip. A big mistake.

Sometime before morning, she fell asleep.

Sometime before morning, he left.

He left her home, he left the estate...

And he left the sad, deep part of her that had so stupidly come to love him.

Forgetting would have been a blessing. Going hazy... losing himself to the clawing edges of the wild road... any of those things.

Instead, Devin remembered the night with a crystalline clarity. Not just the coat room and the wild abandon, the deep and mutual fervor that had taken them from one house to the other, shedding clothes and sense along the way.

Every strand of her hair brushing his face, he still felt. Every curve and flex of her body beneath his hands.

That, he could happily remember forever.

Here at Enrique's in the early morning hours, the heavy bag reverberated beneath his fists, a solid pounding rain of inner conflict beating its pattern on canvas. *Jab, cross, left low kick...*

Because he could also remember the way he'd pulled back from her, even as she poured her heart out to him. He remembered her hurt—he remembered turning from her.

And just because his body had turned into some sort of badly jointed puppet didn't mean he hadn't seen her shock—*oh, please don't do this*—and then the hard acceptance.

You did it.

And especially, he remembered the part where her expression had said it loud and clear—*And now it's done.*

Because truthfully, there was only so much a man could ask. And he'd already gone above and beyond on the very first night they'd met.

Bag chains rattled; dust sifted. *Jab, cross, hook, right low kick...*

And then there had been the blade. Waking for no reason, prodding him into an oddly mindless and animalistic state he could only describe as territorial defiance. *Mine.* Raking him with its claims, trails of fire that had no business being in his brain or body. Leaving him so defensive and wary that even now—

High blitz kick series, slam, slam, SLAM... Sweat dripping, now, his breath coming in fast little explosive puffs.

Yeah, forgetting would have been a blessing.

"You gonna buy me another one of these again?" Enrique's voice startled him, too close behind, too sudden.

Devin whirled on him—saw that glimmering challenge in Enrique's eyes, and pivoted back around to slam a final punch into the bag that lifted it on its chains.

Not a macho challenge from Enrique—not "See if you can hit me." But "See if you can NOT."

Control. Enrique knew it as much as Devin. Enrique had been the one to hold him the night Leo had died. Enrique had cried with him.

And then he'd told Devin that he'd done the right thing.

"You scared off my morning kids," Enrique pointed out, coming around opposite to where Devin now simply leaned against the bag.

"Good," Devin grunted, panting. "That one kid—what's his name, Greg? He's got that look in his eye."

"Gregorio." Enrique nodded. "It won't be long now. Try not to break his nose."

Devin gave a short laugh, blowing sweat off his upper lip. "The nose is a given."

Enrique frowned. "His family cannot fix a nose. We should assign you both to a spar with helmets."

"Fine," Devin said. "Whatever. Whenever. Maybe you'd better make it soon."

"Not for the boy," Enrique said, understanding behind his narrowed eyes. "For you."

Devin looked away. "It got Leo."

"*Leo* didn't know it was coming." Enrique gave the heavy bag a push, just enough to make Devin take a balancing step back.

Devin shook his head, snagging the Velcro on his

hand wrap and ripping it free with a vicious twist. "Might not be enough, Rick."

Enrique pushed away from the bag, coming around to look Devin up and down. "What happened?"

Devin laughed. "What *hasn't* happened?" But this was Enrique, so he rerolled the first wrap and started on the second, shaking his head—but he answered.

He offered the details Enrique hadn't yet heard about the night Devin had been hurt, about the nights since then. What it was like, how hard it was to fight…how sometimes he didn't even know it had him. How Natalie's exercises helped, but…

There'd been the old man. The way he'd lost himself in the private hallway. The way he'd killed but could find no evidence of the body. And then night before—

All of it.

Enrique snorted. "That part sounds more like a mean high. Peyote, maybe."

Devin scowled, finishing up on the second wrap; he tossed them both on the phone table to grab his sports bottle and squirt a stream of water down his throat. After he'd swallowed and before he bothered to wipe off his chin, he said, "It's no secret what that stuff tastes like. I think I would have noticed—"

But he hesitated. He couldn't bring himself to voice it; he couldn't even bring himself to fully think it. *Would* he have noticed it, during the previous night of spices and indulgence?

"What happened at the end," he said finally. "That was…it wasn't the same."

Enrique shrugged, unwrapping the towel from his neck to throw at Devin. "You want all answers to be the same. Maybe there's more than one thing happening here." Now, finally, he hesitated, dark eyes careful. "You felt the wild road, yes? Now you think every failure comes from the call of that road."

"I—" Devin scrubbed the towel over his face, frowning fiercely. Thinking it through. "Yes," he said. "We've been waiting for it, and now it's here." And they still knew nothing about it. Nothing about the knife. Only what they'd learned by hard experience, he and Leo. And Leo had told them things with an assurance Devin hadn't understood until the blade had filled his own hand with claiming warmth. Terms, concepts...things he had once been told, but now he *knew*.

And far too much that he didn't.

"It's here," Enrique agreed. "But is it the start of *all* these things? Or is it just part of these things?"

These things. Natalie. A bad injury; a gruesome night. Compton and his estate, and a job he wasn't suited for under the best of circumstances.

The knife wanted motion. It wanted activity and prowling. If it couldn't feed off blood, it fed off fear. And if it led Devin to innocents in peril, it did so in order to leach both blood and fear from those who had been the threat.

For Natalie, he'd stayed at the estate. For Natalie... how could he have said no?

She hadn't learned it yet—she might never learn it. But he didn't think he'd ever be able to say *no* to her.

Not that astute blue gaze; not that mouth. Not the way she moved beneath him.

"You're thinking about her," Enrique said.

"Huh?" Devin said. "What?" And he glanced at himself.

Enrique laughed. "It was in your eyes, *hijo*. Your face." He shook his head. "Devin. You thought of the *woman*. Not the wild road. Don't make this all about the wild road. Not *all* about the wild road." He pulled the damp towel away from Devin's unresisting grip, tossing it unerringly into the laundry service bin along the wall. "Listen to your heart, too. Your instinct."

Devin had plenty of instinct. He'd just been too afraid to reach for it. Too afraid of where it would lead him.

"Huh," he said. "Wisdom with age, is that it, Rick?" And ducked, just barely evading a swift towel flick. He grinned and headed for the shower, shedding intensity for action. "Hey, what about this Sawyer Compton guy? You hear anything about him on that street radar of yours, or is he as clean as he seems?"

For with Enrique's perspective on board, he suddenly thought bigger. Wider. He thought of Leo's death spot, turned to the very first Alley of Life; he thought of Natalie, beset by thugs near an Alley of Life who wanted Compton's plans.

Compton's plans.

Compton's Alley of Life gardens.

Because that was where it had *started*. The first step. The common factor from which every other tangled experience of these past weeks—these past years—had flowed.

Not Natalie. Not the blade or the wild road. But Sawyer Compton.

Chapter 13

Natalie licked away the last gluey blob of hastily prepared instant oatmeal and rinsed the bowl, leaving it in the sink out of deference to Jimena's need to load the dishwasher *just so*.

"I'm so sorry," the woman said, fumbling to line up fresh chives on the chopping board. "I don't know what came over me last night. To have left this kitchen in such a state!"

"It's not your job to make my breakfast, Jimena," Natalie said, giving the woman's wan appearance a frank assessment. "I'm spoiled, that's all. And if you aren't well, you should take the day. You have plenty of personal days built up, I happen to know—and plenty of nutritious, absolutely delicious preprepared meals in that freezer. Mr. Compton would want you to take care of yourself, you know that. And you deserve a break, after the meal you pulled off last night."

Last night. Devin and his hands all over her and her body arching in responses completely out of her control—

Devin and his startling rejection of who she was because of who she'd been.

Devin and his wild eyes and his inexplicable pain and his need...

Devin, gone.

Jimena frowned at the chopping board, creating the neat, chunky garnishes for Compton's late omelet. She opened her mouth, her brows drawn tightly together, and then shrugged ever so slightly, reaching for a single, perfect red chili.

"What?" Natalie asked her.

Jimena shook her head. She said, "It was a puzzling meal. I did my best with the request, but...for company..."

"They loved it," Natalie said. "It was unusual. And he took all the credit for the theme of it."

"Letting me off the hook, you mean?" Jimena shot her a dry glance, but looked quickly away. "I shouldn't have said that. Whatever comes out of this kitchen is my responsibility. And..." She briskly gathered up the diced condiments, green and red and sharply enticing. "I have concern that the dishes might not have digested well together. But you heard of no one else who wasn't well?"

"No one else?" For a moment Natalie floundered— and then she realized, "You?"

Jimena smiled, a little wryly. "Your young man left some pieces untouched. The others, too, if less so. I made myself dinner from them."

Your young man. Natalie hesitated—struck by how deeply those words hit, how absurd it was that it should matter. She said, "You think it was the—" and then saw the embarrassment on Jimena's face and quickly shook her head. "No," she said. "I haven't heard anything." Because with Devin there was no telling, was there? She added a quick, distracted smile as Jimena broke eggs into a bowl and reached for the whisk. "Take it easy today, okay? I'll let you know if I hear anything."

She left Jimena looking more relaxed as she headed upstairs, ducking only briefly into the guest hall bath to brush her teeth and check her appearance.

The mirror offered no reassurance at all. There she stood, a grim young woman, impeccably dressed and presented—and as wan as Jimena, if in spirit instead of body.

As if in teaching herself to make her own choices, she'd forgotten to allow herself to just *be.*

Devin James…that grin of his, it knew how to grab the moment. His hands, his mouth…those knew how to grab the moment, too. They'd known how to grab *her.* From the inside out.

She turned out the light and headed briskly for the office. Damned briskly.

Compton had been working already—he would see this quiet day as a chance to work unimpeded, his workout accomplished early and his late breakfast break now imminent.

Natalie pulled out her notes from the day before, entered the pertinent items into his online scheduler and printed out crisp, updated copies.

Focus on the job at hand. It kept away the creeping memories from those days of what she'd once been; it kept away her endless, nagging guilt that if she'd just *done* something, *said* something, even *screamed* something at just the right time, then the man in the alley would not have died at her feet.

She took a breath, shook out her hands and brought herself back to this day, this now. And on this day, she had thank-you calls to make and bills to pay and the next event to arrange, not to mention a skip tracer with whom to touch base.

She took the schedule pages into Compton's private office, where she routinely handed them off directly. But the office stood empty, the windows still lightly veiled against the morning light. Caught off guard—she couldn't remember a time she'd been in here alone— Natalie hesitated briefly and opted for efficiency, the few quick steps to lay the printouts neatly beside his keyboard.

The monitor flickered to life; she stepped back, averting her gaze—but not quickly enough to avoid absorbing the screen image, a security camera feed frozen on an inexplicable frame of smudged shadow and patchy gray. *A room.* At night. Here on the estate? *But why?* And so she glanced again, confirmed that impression, found tiny blurs of light here—and there—just pinpricks. But there was nothing recognizable—no face, no human form. So why? And where?

Not her business, that's what. Just because she'd nudged the mouse didn't give her license to pry. She stepped away from the desk and took her mind to her next task. Phone calls.

"Natalie."

It wasn't a voice filled with warm approval.

She hadn't heard him coming—hadn't seen him. For a moment, startled, she saw the same predatory gleam in his eye that so often overtook Devin. "I'm sorry, sir," she said. "I left your schedule." And realized, with dread that took her by surprise, that he would see that she'd knocked the computer out of sleep mode.

"In the future, Natalie, you may leave the schedule on the desk in our shared space," he told her, no forgiveness in cold eyes.

"I understand," she said, because it was the only thing to say. And then, because she didn't dare look at the monitor but she knew it needed more time to sleep, she added, "Are you well, sir?"

He arched a brow. Silver hair styled crisply, features mature but not aging, every aspect of his appearance tended. "Completely well," he said. "Did I give you occasion to ask?"

She felt the immediate impulse to defer…pushed back against it, but no less respectful. "Not at all. But I do know that Devin wasn't feeling well yesterday after dinner, so I've been concerned."

"Ah." Compton relaxed, ever so slightly. "Perhaps he was unaccustomed to something in the meal. I don't expect it was his usual quality of fare."

"No," Natalie murmured, wondering at that little dig. "I don't expect that it was."

"I have queries out for his replacement," Compton said, because of course they'd discussed Devin's departure first thing.

"I was still hoping—" But she stopped herself, because there was nothing to hope. Even if Devin wanted back, he had walked out on the job. Compton wouldn't have him.

And she knew better than to think Devin would want it.

She didn't dare glance over at the monitor, but surely it had been long enough for the screen saver to kick in. Surely it was safe, now, to go back to her own space.

Not that it should have mattered. Or that she should be second-guessing his lack of concern for the welfare of a guest at his table, given that guest's sudden departure from employment.

But something inside her did. Something inside her took note.

And it was that part of her that Devin James had brought back to life.

Devin stared down the quiet Alley of Life—garden patches put to bed, litter neatly patrolled, graffiti painted away. He stared and took note, breathing deeply—

grounding himself in its details. The wild road started in on him the moment he'd left her.

Devin twisted aside from it, clawed away from it, held every determined moment of himself from it.

Without Natalie, it came hard on him.

But she'd given him ideas; she'd given him tools. She'd given him things that Leo had never had.

So he centered himself in thoughts of Natalie—the high cut of her cheekbones, the slant of them; the unusual shape of her mouth, and the way the very corners curved upward, humor coming out even when she had no intention of smiling at all.

Soft hair in his fingers, soft flesh beneath his hands, soft noises in his ears.

That, he found, was a sweet, fierce pain that never failed to bring him back from the edge of the road.

And now he had something to do.

For now he had a beginning. He had, in the past several days since leaving the estate, discovered an architect who didn't exist—for the man who'd ostensibly given Natalie his new office address not only no longer had the old office, he no longer worked in Albuquerque at all—and hadn't done so for a number of months now. Still listed online, still in the phone book…but otherwise, no sign of him.

And Devin had put out word on the men he'd killed, looking to identify them in absentia…looking for a trail. Too generic, most of the men, but the one with the tattoos? He thought he'd get a ping on that one.

And Enrique. "Be careful," he'd told the old man.

"If you're right that I was drugged the other night, that means Compton is definitely dirty—even if I can't figure out how."

But Enrique had only smiled, a mean expression. "This is my neighborhood," he said. "You—you're my people. This man should have stayed to being dirty among his own kind, if he didn't want to be noticed."

And so Enrique, too, did his looking.

But for all Devin's questions and all his thinking and all his effort to separate what was happening within him from what he still had of himself, here was where he found himself time after time. Early morning, sharp afternoon, fading day…deep midnight. *One of the first Alley of Life spots,* Natalie had said, and for as garbled as he'd been, he'd understood her well enough—absorbed her well enough. The horror of her experience here— here where he stood, his mind's eye even now seeing a man stagger out of the alley.

My brother.

Easy to imagine what it would have looked like, two men silhouetted in battle, the one wrenching free from a grievous wound to rise up high above the other, the blade suddenly in hand…the blade turned traitor to them both.

And so Leo had died, and Devin had lived, and now he stared down this alley buttressed by dried winter plume grasses, stakes marking the summer vegetable rows and honeysuckle vines winter-sere along the fence, neat patches of earth already prepared for the following spring. A thing of beauty…a thing of nurture. Here, in this place of death.

Ironic.

But what Devin felt most, amid the turmoil of what Natalie's words had wrought in him—aware that once she *knew,* he could never expect her to look at him with that smile or take him with that mouth or make demands of him with those hands—had nothing to do with Natalie, or with Leo, or with Devin himself.

It had to do with what he'd been too wounded, too grieving and too new to the blade to notice, when he'd been here with Leo years earlier. It had to do with the angry thrum in the air, a spark of metal hackles—still resonating in the blade, these years later, if not with the intensity of what it had felt that night. *Intruder, other, warning*, hiss and spit—

And it had to do with what he'd felt in this blade only a few nights earlier. That same fury, that same territorial gnashing—that same insane fever of reaction, overlaid on a mean peyote haze that had left him with no defenses. Not against the blade, not against Natalie's touch in his heart.

And maybe that was the beginning, after all. That reaction…that fury.

Years earlier, his brother had died for that insanity, that fury. Just over a week earlier, Devin had survived it—in the arms of the woman who had been there for both events.

The common threads. The alleys.

And Natalie.

So maybe Sawyer Compton had some questions to

answer—but first, Devin thought, he'd have to talk to Natalie. First, he thought, she deserved the truth.

No matter what came of it.

Sawyer Compton found himself displeased.

Truly, the game was only worth playing so long as it was pleasing. Failing that, it was time to bring things to a close.

Options, options.

He stood before the vast window of the shared office—beside the drafting desk, there where he cut a striking figure in black slacks and black turtleneck—a working day, with his hair not quite as crisply styled as usual and the suggestion of a smudge on his hand.

Plans for the restaurant spread before him on the desk; the estate spread before him out the window. His future spread before him in his mind.

Nothing spontaneous about any of it. And he wanted Natalie off guard today, her mind deeply involved in work. Unprepared.

"Have you decided?" he asked, just as abruptly as he'd meant to—startling Natalie from her careful research. A new caterer, he believed. As if it truly mattered.

She lifted her head, tucking that wavy strand of sun-brushed hair into the darker mass of it. "About the bodyguard, you mean?"

She'd been avoiding the subject for days. She might not still hold hopes that Devin James would return, but she wasn't ready to cede that position to anyone else, either. Compton had no difficulty reading it in the flush that came up across those exquisite cheekbones anytime the subject came up.

She might have had some questionable moments on the streets, but she'd never been cut out to lie.

Not from that first moment he'd first—and finally—met her, at the first Alley of Life dedication—lurking on the edges, a young woman too thin, too anxious, too jumpy. Dressed in thrift-store chic, everything worn but everything neat.

There hadn't been much to see at that dedication. A short, grumpy alley, still resonating with the flavor of death—not that anyone else could taste it. The ground broken, what there was of it; the seeds planted. A perfectly placed arrangement of potted plants brought in to start things off right.

But it hadn't been a coincidence that the dedication had been planned on Natalie's morning off—from both school and work. Not coincidence that she was there at all. For if at first he'd kept track of her because of what she'd witnessed, he quickly grew to recognize her as a potential resource—and he'd known just how to guide her along.

The right words, at the right time…and she found herself back in school. Taking business classes, basic office software classes…and excelling at it. A nudge from a helpful friend here; a kind word at the right time, there; a stroke of good luck just when needed.

Until there she was, in the right time at the right place to strike up a startled conversation with the man who'd started the Alleys of Life project. One step closer to becoming his assistant.

No coincidence at all.

Of course, he'd hoped to learn more from her, along with his intentions to use her however he could—knowing her background, knowing her weaknesses. And he'd expected, from what Ajay had first told him, that she'd spent more time with Leo James. He'd expected that she'd spent at least *some* time with Devin James.

Ajay had thought it of her…accused it. But Ajay was often a fool.

How fortunate that she'd turned out to be such a good assistant. No trouble at all to keep around until the time came when he could make better use of her.

Now.

Because that look on her face said it all. She hadn't known Devin James then.

But she did now.

And now she carefully closed her notebook and put her pen aside. "I've been thinking," she said. "There's been no sign of trouble. And the restaurant is moving ahead. I think whoever wanted the project stopped has seen the inevitability of it. Do you really suppose…?"

Wise, she was, to let the words linger unspoken rather than directly contradict his intent. But as it happened… her careful suggestion suited him, too.

She took a breath, hesitated on it and came as close to blurting words as she ever did. "May I ask you—"

"Of course, Natalie," he said, truly curious.

She pushed her notebook aside. "You've done so

many good things…so many projects that could tie in with this one, and help build the goodwill factor. The wells project in Brazil…the latrine system in that little African region. The clinics in the Balkans—"

Death in the favela…memorialized. Death in the dusty brush, memorialized. Death in the mountains, memorialized.

He said, "I don't recall mentioning those projects to you."

"I'm sure you didn't." Good for her, facing it right on like that. She stretched her hand open in that odd gesture of hers, relaxed it again. "I stumbled on to them while I was looking into the first alleys. I guess the restaurant got me to thinking about them again."

"Your life has changed significantly since the days you lived in that area." As if he didn't know just what she'd seen there. "What do you gain by dwelling on them?"

Paternal concern. The perfect touch.

She frowned, looking at her notebook. "It somehow all seems to tie together, is all. That we met there…that you started the gardens, and now you're starting the restaurant. And I just had no idea that you'd been doing this all around the world."

"I enjoyed traveling when I was younger." Keep it simple. No need to mention what he'd brought home from those travels.

That which he also intended to acquire from Devin.

"About your new bodyguard," he said.

"I'd really rather not." She hesitated after those bold

words, then shook her head. "Please…maybe I can talk to Devin's friend Rick. If I could only understand—" But she stopped herself, smiling a little wryly. "I guess that's personal, though."

Compton allowed himself a small snort. "Natalie, it's perfectly human. You shared an intense near-death experience together. Of course you're invested in his presence. But he is not a man without troubles. I would hate to see you hurt."

In fact, I would find it perfectly convenient.

Her phone rang; she glanced at him for tacit permission, and picked it up when he nodded. That the following conversation surprised her, he could tell; other than the mention of a tattoo, the details of it were quickly lost to him as his own line rang through.

Ajay. Calling here, where Natalie could have overheard his voice, or possibly even picked up the phone. "There will be consequences," he said, not bothering with a greeting.

Ajay didn't bother with a greeting, either—or with apologies. The man had some sense, after all. "Enrique Perez," he said. "James's old man buddy. He's been calling in favors. He's asking about you and the gardens. About *that* garden."

"He is nothing," Compton said, and shifted to hang up with no further ado.

"He's been in that neighborhood for a long time," Ajay said—as usual, coming just short of calling Compton *boss* as if he was in some gangster movie. "He's got a lot of favors to call." He hesitated. "If someone puts us together—"

Compton held his words for a moment. A long, tense moment, his mouth tightly pressed together. A glance at Natalie showed her deep in her own surprise, and paying no attention to him.

Just as well.

It looked like he had someone else to hurt.

Chapter 14

Devin sat on Natalie's tiny covered entryway. Waiting. The manila envelope had frayed slightly under the constant attention of his fingers—worrying the edges, turning it over in his grip.

If Compton's men knew he was here, they didn't approach him. Wise. Not that he'd advertised his presence—his truck was out on the street, his footprints light in the soil along the property line. But here on the porch, he was hardly inconspicuous.

All the same, Natalie was deep enough in thought as she approached, late in the afternoon—head down, legs striding in graceful movement, coat open to the failing sunshine—that she stopped short only at the last moment, one foot about to land on the entry flagstone. "Devin," she breathed.

"Hey," he said, and shrugged. A rueful thing, that shrug. "Listen," he said. "About—" And realized suddenly that he didn't have any idea how to go there. He shook his head. Maybe there was too much to it, anyway—too much to fix.

But there were still things to make *right,* and that was a different thing.

"Are you okay?" she asked, taking her foot back off the slightly raised stone on which he sat. Her words struck him as wary.

Couldn't blame her, really.

But maybe there was something else, too—something of concern, something of anxiety—something that very nearly wanted to blurt its way out, except she, too, shook her head and kept it to herself. "Devin? You're okay?"

"Missing you," he said, which wasn't what he'd meant to say, either. He laughed at himself and looked away. "Helluva thing. I didn't think I'd known you long enough."

Out of the corner of his eye, he saw her mouth tighten, her head lift. He wasn't sure what it meant, but it didn't seem likely that there was any good interpretation. "Sorry," he said, and scrubbed a hand over his face. "I've decided that you deserve some truth. But I wasn't expecting that particular truth to come out."

"Truth would be good," she said, without relaxing. And still, something lingered in her expression. A decision, being made.

He handed her the envelope. Not sealed, not official—

an old scratched-out address on the front. Just enough to hold the photos.

He didn't watch her hands as she opened it. He watched her face. Watched her eyes widen at the first photo, the very first Alley of Life—potted flowers in full bloom, container vegetables thriving, the pampas grasses arcing gracefully in midsummer growth. *The* Alley. She met his gaze, mouth open—and he shook his head. Nodded at the pictures. And watched.

She slipped the next picture to the top, and inhaled sharply. "This—" She looked at him, looked at the photo…gestured at him with it. "This is—"

"My brother," Devin said.

"Oh, my God," she said. "It was in the alley. In *this* alley. It was your brother! I saw him die!"

And then, finally, the words didn't seem hard to find at all. "Yes," he told her. "And you saw me kill him."

Natalie's fingers tightened around the photos—wrinkling them in a rustle of paper protest. "No," she said, taking a step back from him, because of course it was true. He'd never say such a thing if it wasn't true. And still she shook her head and repeated, "Devin, *no.*"

He couldn't quite look at her—sitting on the small rise of her entry, his knees drawn up and his body tight with tension. Not fuzzy, not distant, not faded. Totally here. Totally real.

Totally telling the truth.

He said, "Leo had the blade then. I think he got set off by something similar to what happened here the other night. Peyote, Enrique thinks. Not a lot, but…you know how it is with me right now. Probably wouldn't take much."

"Jimena," Natalie found herself saying, a mere breath of a word.

He threw her a sharp look; the setting sun glimmered over the horizon one last moment to glint off the gray of his eyes, the line of his jaw. Fatigue and resignation settled in deep, but…determination, too.

"She had some of your leftovers." Natalie's voice went on without her; her body stood locked in place, enthralled by the horror of what she'd heard.

"Leo was further gone than I am," Devin said. "With the blade, I mean." He pulled a face at himself, waved that off. "Thing is, he didn't know what was happening. He was fighting for his life, but he'd been doing it a lot longer—and he didn't have you to help him."

"I don't—" She shook her head. Behind her, the porch light flickered on, having decided the dusk was shadowed enough. "I don't understand."

He made a sound of frustration, pushing off to his feet in a single, powerful thrust—a few hard steps away from the porch, a few steps back. "I know," he said. "I *know*. So look at it this way. Think about last night. Pretend that whatever's been going on with me has been going on for a lot longer, and I'm in a lot worse shape—I'm barely sticking with reality half the time, my reasoning is skewed, my motivations are driven by darkness. *How do you think it would have turned out?*"

Natalie closed her eyes on that particular truth.

"Something threatened you," she said. "You tried to strike at it. And I was there—"

She couldn't go any further.

He didn't fill in the silence.

And finally she looked at him and whispered, "Leo… tried to kill you."

He pushed his palm against his brow—looked like he was pushing back pain. "He very nearly did."

Natalie looked down at the photos—at the man who shared Devin's eyes and the set of his mouth, but whose chin wasn't as strong and whose facial structure wasn't as defined. *Brother.*

And then she looked again at the alley. There, where she'd been with Ajay. There, where crystalline memory showed her a man silhouetted against wildly flickering light, braced and strong, the wide set of his shoulders suddenly familiar, the lean lines of a strong body, those she had since come close to claiming for her own.

Her throat ached with the enormity of it; she shoved an impatient hand along her wet cheek. "I don't understand," she said. "How does it all…I mean, Ajay must have known your brother. He must have gone there for… but I know he wasn't expecting…" She shook her head, impatient with the jumble of pieces. "And now? All of this? How can this be coincidence?"

He looked as grim as she felt—as shaken. "I don't think it is. There's something going on—something bigger than you and me and a chance meeting in a dark parking lot. I'll find it. I just wanted you to know…." He gestured at the photos; his expression tight with grief.

"I didn't want to believe it at first, but…you were there. You, and me…and Leo. It was the worst night of my life…and you saw it."

"You killed your brother," she whispered. She traced a finger over the thriving plants in the alley photo. "And now it's a place of life. The very first one. How can *that* be coincidence?"

"It's not just that one," he said; his voice had that distracted sound, and when she gave him a hard glance she discovered what she suspected—that he'd lost himself for a moment—in the grief, in the memories, in whatever thing it was that had had a hold on his brother and now had a hold on him. And that he probably hadn't quite meant to say those words out loud. Reluctance clear, he added, "They all have the same taste."

"The alleys," she said, somewhat flatly.

"Death," he told her. "Fear. Anger. It's sharp and hot and hard to breath… It's the blade, reacting to them all. Just like the other night."

"The blade," she said, just as flatly, thinking about steel gleaming first one shape, then another. Thinking about a man, crumbling to the asphalt before her eyes.

Thinking about Devin James—fever-hot one moment, shivering the next. Gushing arterial blood…and cutting out his own stitches three days later. Deep and brooding and torn, just as quickly turned to that startlingly honest grin—or equally honest, irresistible desire.

Questions and inconsistencies. And she'd been holding on to them for far too long. Far too long for what hung unresolved between them.

And yet he closed his eyes; the look on his face was nothing but pain. Her chest tightened, stealing her breath—for she knew his answer. And she knew her own.

His words came as though torn from him. "I can't—not yet. I just…can't."

She thrust the photos back at him, already reaching for the door handle. "Then you're on your own. I hope you figure it out."

You're on your own.

As it should be.

But telling about the blade meant telling her *all* of it. The men he'd killed since, the inexplicable street hunt that had become his life, the not-so-inanimate object that drove him.

The inevitable and pending loss of self, the wild road already tugging at him.

Tugging hard.

She might not want to be with a man who wouldn't give up his secrets, but she was no more likely to be with one who was about to lose his soul.

With some care, he slipped the photos back into their envelope, pressing the clasp securely closed, and walked away into the darkening night.

Natalie put her back to the closed door—eyes closed, head tipped back.

Even just standing there, she'd felt the pull of him.

But she wouldn't let herself follow anyone blindly, not any longer.

What about Sawyer Compton?

"That's not the same," she said, words loud in the empty room. "That's a *job*."

The words didn't sound as reassuring as they would have even a few days earlier.

Standing there, with the cool of the door against her back, she suddenly couldn't see her life clearly any longer. With the memory of the pain in his face…the memory of her body responding to his…the memory of his instant honesty in every moment in which it truly counted…

Her reasons were good ones. It didn't mean she wasn't doing the wrong thing.

The sigh built from deep within her. She lifted her head from the door, opened her eyes to the dark room.

Blinked in sudden déjà vu confusion.

Light patches, dark shadows, vague assertions of form…the familiar glow of the kitchen clock, just barely visible from this angle.

Déjà vu.

What if she took a single step to the right?

Dreading it, Natalie did just that.

And found herself looking at the security web cam image from Sawyer Compton's computer.

Chapter 15

Devin hadn't truly expected any other reaction. Not from a woman so clear about her boundaries. Not when he would give her truth and trust but not *all* of it.

Didn't mean he hadn't let himself hope. Deep down, where he didn't truly have any control. And he'd learned a lot about control these past weeks.

He'd see Natalie again. He didn't have any doubt. Fate had brought them together not once but twice, and now they were too entwined to avoid another encounter.

He just wasn't sure if he wanted it. Because *damn,* he couldn't help but put his heart right out there when he saw her—when he wanted to draw her close and breathe in the scent of her hair and feel her hands dig gently into the muscle along his spine.

Watching her reject that…wasn't going to be so good

for that heart. Twice he'd walked away from her; lacking courage; now she'd drawn the line a final time.

He pulled the truck up alongside the curb outside Enrique's. If he went into the gym like this—closed now, but Enrique would be in the back cursing over bills and paperwork and laundry—Enrique would take one look at him and kick him out on his ass, tell him to get right back over to Natalie and straighten this out.

Enrique had a matter-of-fact philosophy when it came to affairs of the heart. *Don't screw around, hijo. Don't waste it.*

Devin trailed his fingers over the battered envelope sitting on the passenger side of the bench seat. *The alleys, the deaths...the territorial response of the blade.* The gardens, the new restaurant...Sawyer Compton. Way too many pieces, far too little understanding of what tied them altogether. Just the bone-deep awareness that something *did.*

Maybe Enrique had found a thing or two.

He flipped the truck's door handle, gave the door itself the extra kick it needed on a cold night like this, and slid out to pavement, high-top martial arts sneaks silent by both habit and nature, the hoodie and vest no longer nearly enough to keep out the night.

The blade snarled a warning.

Not the eager thrill of anticipated blood, but the same edgy feel from the evening at Natalie's. The same lingering territorial anger as the alleys. Faint but distinct.

Devin knew it this time. Not just pending violence, not just the chance to bite flesh. But a threat perceived.

He ran for the door, hit the entry bar in frustration—locked, as it should be. Fumbling for the keys merely filled his hand with the knife; he flipped it to his other hand and went back to his watch pocket, digging out the key he always kept tucked away there.

He wasn't surprised at the hot burn flooding his arm; he knew the knife had flung itself into the tactical blade, sweet in his grip and ready to bite. He found the key; the key found the lock.

He left it there as he ran into the dark gym, orienting…listening. Heeding the deep inner burn of his own personal directionals, bypassing the still-lit office and slamming through the swinging double doors to the back hallway—permanent odor of bleach, cleansers, sweat and wet shower tile.

A grunt echoed hollowly down the dim hallway. An old man's pain. *The showers—*

He knew better than to run for it—to give up the advantage of those habitually silent feet in their dance-light shoes. But he moved fast enough, threading through a row of lockers and up against the wall outside the showers—hesitating just long enough to hear the sound of someone spitting defiance.

Ah, Enrique. Don't you know you're an old man?

Still snapping back in the face of defeat, as he had in the ring. Never giving up. Just that thing he instilled in his students now.

This time, it might just get him killed. The blade knew as much, burning hot up Devin's arm.

"Who did you tell, old man?" The growl echoed in

that shower room, coming with a loud rustle of movement. Devin had no trouble interpreting the actions that
made them—a second man had Enrique, had jerked him
to his feet—

Threat, the blade murmured.

Devin stepped into the communal shower. Hard tile
floor, dripping shower head in the corner, someone's
forgotten shampoo tipped over on its side and filling
the room with a manly fragrance.

That, and the raw smell of blood.

There were two of them, all right—both of them
macho tough in black leather jackets that would have
fit better with a little more shoulder and slightly less gut;
both with snug black gloves; both with faces exposed.

If they thought they'd scare Enrique past identify-
ing them—

No. Of course they didn't. This was about gathering
information and leaving a body behind.

Or it *had* been. Now, they would discover, it was
about staying alive.

"Gently," Devin said, his voice cold and tight; he gave
Enrique a quick once-over. Nothing too serious, not yet.
Maybe a broken cheekbone; stitches for sure. And the
way the older man hunched over, could be a rib or two
gone. "You'll put him down gently. And then, if you can
get past me, you might get out of here tonight."

Want. The blade pulsed with it, thirsting for their
blood, thirsting for their fear. Enticing Devin to play
with them, to kill them slowly…one cut, one blow at
a time.

Didn't matter that there were two of them, or that the man not holding Enrique up would go for a gun at the very first opportunity. These men wouldn't get past him. Not tonight, not ever.

Enrique lifted his head, squinted at Devin with the one eye that wasn't already swollen closed. "Keep it in here," he said, his expression hard and bright. "Easy to clean up the blood that way." He spat again, hitting the shoes of the man in front of him. "Even fool's blood washes off tile."

Not that the blade would leave a trace.

"Don't kill him yet," the senior of the two ordered of the man who held Enrique. Curly hair cropped close to his head, big beefy hands beneath the gloves, coarse features. "We don't yet have what we were sent to get."

Enrique looked at Devin. "They want to know about the alleys. They want to know who cares that people have died there. They want to know who cares about a big man named Sawyer Compton." He lifted his lip in a snarl of blood-smeared teeth. "I want to know who cares that someone cares."

Abruptly, the man who held Enrique tossed him aside—from defiance to a heap of brittle bones in the corner, just like that.

They'd thought Devin would snarl fury; they'd thought he would hesitate, or make some aborted attempt to reach the old man.

Part of him did. Some inner part, the part not blade-honed and street-trained and battle-scarred.

The rest of him knew better.

He stepped in—a duck, a whirl, blade slicing air and whispering through leather and skin; his foot landed in the gut of the leader, trapping his hand as it reached for his gun. Breaking a bone, maybe two.

When he came to rest, one man had only just begun to realize how deeply he'd been cut and the other had dropped his gun—and Devin was no longer within reach of either.

From the corner, Enrique grunted something that could have been a laugh.

And the rush of the blade swept through Devin, gripping his soul. He shuddered, fighting it—losing to it. *Kill them. Kill them now. Drink of them.* He set his jaw, staring at the innocuous floor, tile smeared with more than just Enrique's blood now. Staring hard. "*I* want to know," he said, right through clenched teeth, "who *cares.*" *Kill them. Drink of them.* He lifted his head; he let the blade's darkness show. "And does *Compton* care if you come back alive?"

"Shit," breathed the man who had already tasted the blade's edge, taking a step back. "Oh, shit. Ajay, let's go. Let's just—"

Ajay—*Ajay?*—turned suddenly sly and crafty; he dove for the gun.

The blade surged up within him, and Devin knew, he *knew,* if he rode the full strength of it, it would win this time. He wouldn't be able to stay his hand. Never mind that he needed answers from these men, never mind that they could tell him what he needed to know. *Natalie. Leo. Death alleys, masquerading as life.*

Ajay saw Devin coming and fumbled the gun, his short, harsh cry of fear echoing off the tile. The beta guy's eyes widened—

Threat! Fiery resentment flared down Devin's arm, throwing him off balance; metal sparked and flowed, strobing light reflected off dull yellow ceramic. The feel of it shifted dramatically in his hand and he knew better than to question. He pivoted, the blade a sturdy, shaped quarterstaff of metal, perfectly placed, perfectly balanced—deflecting the blow that had been aimed for his head from behind.

Just a blur, that's all he saw. Another black leather jacket, darker skin this time, rough-stubbled jaw and a meanly triumphant sneer turning to surprise. Metal crowbar clanged against mutable steel, a blow that reverberated down his arm.

But he wasn't done moving by far. His other hand swept up, took the staff at the end; he whirled into the motion, soaking up the lightning glee of the blade set free, the metal reforming, the saber flowing into its graceful curve—

An extra whip of motion as he completed the pivot and the blade took what it had been looking for.

Life.

Control.

Sanity.

The crowbar clattered to the floor, chipping tile.

The body followed, eyes already dead, form already crumbling to the blade's hunger. Devin stood braced against it, his body still fighting what his mind had

already lost, the darkness swirling in around him—
vaguely aware of Enrique's shout, a harsh and liquid
sound, and of a second body falling—the beta, succumbing to blood loss.

An explosion rocked the shower—gunfire, contained
and echoed and magnified. Devin jerked; he hardly felt
it. His leg went numb. A second shot; his entire torso
rocked with it.

Ajay.

But when he turned, the blade a knife and ready to
throw—no matter that his legs slowly gave way beneath
him—Ajay scrambled to his feet, cast one last look at
the blade—at Devin's expression—and shook his head.
"As crazy as your fucking brother," he said, and fled.

Chapter 16

For a long time, Natalie sat in her car. Shivering inside and out…but no cameras.

Her home, under surveillance. Her life, unraveling, so many pieces proving to be only layers of truth.

And as she'd stood frozen in shock beneath the camera in her home, her very first thought had been of Devin. Not a logical thought, not strategic or practical.

Just that she wanted him.

Secrets and all.

For in the aftermath of this stark, undeniable betrayal by Compton, it was still his emotionally honest grin flashing through her mind.

She'd drawn her lines and she'd made her decisions and she'd been *wrong*.

What if there was more to it than just cameras?

Of course there's more to it. Once she started questioning her place here, none of it could be taken for granted. Especially not lately.

Starting with that architect and his incorrect address. She hadn't pulled that address from thin air; she'd gone where told. And it had put her in the position to be attacked.

To meet Devin.

And then Compton had insisted…

She closed her eyes. Compton's insistence on hiring Devin…his insistence that Devin stay here. Devin's continuing struggles in spite of the focus work he was doing, the quick progress Natalie had seen.

Had there been a battle fought outside her door, a man killed and then removed? And what about the intent look on that distinctly mature gentleman's face as he approached them? And that night, at dinner…two people sick on Devin's meal. Peyote? She'd seen how sensitive he was…how he eschewed even caffeine. It wouldn't have taken much.

Too many pieces, none of them quite coming together.

The practical ring tone of her phone startled her; she jerked, huffing steamy breath into the darkness, car windows already fogging.

The caller ID gave her an unfamiliar number; she answered the phone with caution, relaxing only when she heard the voice of the skip tracer looking into the details and identity of the tattooed dead man from the parking lot.

But not relaxing for long, as she realized who had

provided her with this phone—as she heard the tension in this man's voice.

"Wait," she said, as he would have started the conversation. "I'm not sure…that is…this phone—"

There was a long silence. And then he said, so carefully, "Then you probably already know what I have to tell you. I'm tearing up your check, Miss Chambers. Please don't call me again."

The click of his disconnect startled her just as much as the ring tone. The abrupt nature of it, the finality of his voice. The fear of it.

She'd asked him to find out who the man was working for, among other things.

And she understood his message, loud and clear.

The man in the parking lot, the man in the dark, the man with the gun and the brutality, had been hired by Sawyer Compton.

Natalie rolled down her window and threw the phone out of the car.

She stared at it for a long moment, as cold air rushed in through the open window and the fogged air cleared out, and then she decided, yes. Leave it there. It looked as though she'd dropped it on the way to the car, and if it left her without a phone…it also left her without a device that was GPS-enabled.

She'd pick up a prepaid phone. Unless…

She worked here. She lived here. He'd been watching her. Did he have access to her credit accounts? Her bank accounts? Every little private piece of her life? Had he watched, the other night, as she and Devin very nearly made love directly in view of that camera? Or the times she'd so casually walked naked through the house, blinds closed and privacy ensured as she pulled on clothes while heading for coffee?

She had only one place to go. One place she *wanted* to go.

She stopped at a pay phone and called Devin, but he didn't answer. Not on his cell, which he so freely ignored, and not on his home phone.

A glance at her watch showed the hour growing late… she'd try Enrique's anyway. If Devin wasn't there—if she couldn't find either of them—she'd just go camp in his driveway.

But she wasn't expecting Enrique's gym door to be ajar. She pushed through, listening…. Her hand went to her pocket, pulling out the pepper spray…thumbing the safety to the side.

Inside was all darkness…she heard nothing but her pulse pounding in her ears. She peered into the office, found it empty…found the dim light smeared beneath the swinging door at the back corner. Men's territory.

She pushed it open, just enough to poke her head through. "Hello?"

A faint grunt, a cry of sorts—wordless, but pleading.

And then she glanced down—and gasped, and froze, staring stupidly.

A blood trail out the door, and she stood right on top of it.

She stepped over the blood, moving more swiftly now. Whatever had happened, her answers lay within—

through a door left ajar, through a few modest rows of bent-up lockers.

It wasn't hard to follow the trail.

Or, once she reached the showers, to find Enrique.

She stiffened, wasting a moment to clap her hand over her mouth.

A dirty alley, flickering light, battered features, blood everywhere—

But this wasn't that night. This was an old man, beaten half to death in his own gym. She ran to him, skipping over the pools of evidence—and already thinking like her old petty crime self. *Leave no fingerprints. No trace. Got to get out of here.*

"Enrique," she breathed, crouching by him—daring to touch him. When they'd met, he'd been boundless bright energy in an aging body. Now he lay crumpled and brittle and broken. "What—"

"Damned phone," he said, his words muffled—lower lip grotesquely swollen right down to his chin, one side of his face puffed out shiny and tight. "How to use such a thing?"

She followed his twitch of movement, and found a cell phone cradled loosely in his hand.

Devin's phone.

"Devin was here," she said, quite suddenly unable to breathe. Of course Devin had been here.

Except…the only blood Devin appeared incapable of cleaning up was…

His own.

"Help me," Enrique said. "Take me to the front door. Show me to call help. And then you *go*. Go to him."

"Take you to the—" Natalie frowned, involuntarily glancing in the direction of the front door. "Enrique, I shouldn't move you."

He grunted. "Then I move myself." And made as if to prove that point.

"No!" She panicked with it, imagining him dying right here before her.

If she helped him, he might die, too. But at least she would be *helping*.

"Tell me," she said. "Tell me first."

This made sense enough to him—it showed on that distorted face. Tell her, in case he passed out. In case his aging heart gave out or internal injuries worsened with the movement. "We ask about the alleys. We ask about Sawyer Compton. Three of them…I couldn't warn my boy…took him from behind." He gestured at the blood. "Two of them, dead and gone. The third, hurt and running. Devin—"

"This is his blood," she whispered.

He nodded, and his eyes, black in the shadows, nonetheless briefly turned sharp. "Take me to front door. Over his blood. Obscure it. Make it mine. If I live, they maybe won't test. An old man beaten in a bad neighborhood. Nothing to investigate. Take my cash box, too."

"My God," she said. "That's what you've been doing, lying here alone. Figuring out how to cover for him."

He didn't bother to respond to that. "Then you go to

him," he said. "*You go to him*. He is alone, and the wild road will take him—"

She didn't understand the words. But she understood the meaning. She understood all this blood. And she remembered with piercing clarity what had happened the last time Devin had been hurt.

She helped Enrique to the door. She showed him the easy sequence for dialing nine-one-one on the cell phone, she took the cash box, and she rifled the first-aid supplies.

And then she ran back out into the night.

It took forever to reach Devin's home. Forever, with her hands clenching and releasing the steering wheel, her mind slipping back into every little trick she'd taught herself. Focusing on the details of where she was.

It was the only way to keep that tentative, slippery grasp on control until she pulled into his driveway.

There she found the truck parked askew, the driver's door still open. She slammed it closed on the way by and ran to the front door—also open, with heat and faint light spilling out into the darkness.

She closed that, too. She flipped on the light, dumped her bag and the first-aid supplies on the couch, and shrugged off her coat, letting it lie on the floor where it fell. "Devin?"

The shower was silent. The house, silent.

She flipped lights as she moved more deeply into the house. Peeking into the kitchen, heading down the short hall, double-checking the bathroom…knowing, then, he'd simply gone for the bedroom.

The blood trail confirmed it. New hand prints on the walls. Splotches and smears across the carpet.

She hesitated inside the door, and for an instant, couldn't quite bring herself to turn on the light.

Until she heard his breathing—ragged and uneven and full of pain. Then suddenly she stopped thinking so hard at all, and the light was on and she'd found him, crumpled on his way to the patio doors.

"Hey," she said, coming up behind him—not daring to touch, simply because she didn't know where she could. Blood soaked everything; she couldn't see the wounds. Not through his vest and hoodie and flannel shirt and jeans.

He watched her—dazed, unthinking—not raging as she'd seen that first night. Beyond it. Blood trailed from his mouth, bright and frothy, staining the carpet by his face. She looked for the knife, didn't see it….

It was here somewhere. The inexplicable, the mutable, the gleaming wail of anger and steel—

She had no doubt.

Well, she didn't need it. She could cut his clothes away with Enrique's bandage scissors. And she didn't let herself think about the possibility that his amazing healing prowess wasn't up to fixing…*this*.

Compton. Compton had done this. Going after Enrique. Of *course* Devin had tried to stop his men—whatever the cost.

He choked, and blood pooled beneath his mouth.

"Devin," she said, still afraid to touch. "Tell me what I can do." No assumptions, about this man who had raged through the night, healing after what should have been a fatal stab wound—and now lay clenched in pain, his fingers working against the carpet, his faint movements purposeless and vague. *"Tell me."*

His body curled against a new pain—there, she saw it in him, the building heat. The same as that night, but weaker. *Not enough.*

"Tell me," she demanded.

His jaw clenched until she thought she heard it crack; a tear leaked from the corner of a closed eye.

She understood, then. Or thought she did. It wouldn't let him die…but it couldn't heal him. Not as it had the other night.

And she only knew one thing to do.

She touched him.

Kneeling beside him, her hand so gentle, still uncertain of his wounds, she hovered splayed fingers over his side, let them slide down across his ribs and over to his stomach.

He gasped like a drowning man finding air, arching into her touch. His chest labored beneath her hand; he cried something agonized—his hand found hers. She, too, gasped as his fingers tightened down—but she didn't draw back.

His eyes opened, dark shadows of a man who believed himself lost. His voice was little more than a wheeze carried on stolen air. "What—"

"I came to see you," she said, much more firmly than

she'd expected. She added, just as matter-of-factly, "Because I was wrong."

"But—"

"Hey." Her voice sharpened slightly, self-aware asperity. "It was a choice, okay?"

She didn't expect him to laugh—and it didn't last long, as he rolled over on a groan, his hand clamping down on hers again.

"Can't—" he said.

"No kidding," Natalie muttered. "Devin, I have no idea what's going on here. I have no idea what's going on with *you*. Let me help. Can't you tell me—?"

"Get them *out*," he managed. "Can't—the knife—" He opened his other hand, curled in so close to his body, and the knife spilled out. No more than an ordinary little pen knife.

Right. She didn't believe that for a moment.

"Take it," he said. Or she thought that's what he said, anyway, for just as soon as he spoke, the heat flared again—she felt it, this time, an amazing wash of dark impotent fury as it took him in its grip and shook him out and left him trembling. "It can't… It won't stop trying…it's going to…"

He couldn't finish, gasping for that shallow breath. But he didn't have to. She could see it. It was going to kill him. Whatever this thing was, trying to heal him as it had done so brutally the night they'd met, it was hitting a wall. But it wouldn't stop trying.

"Get them *out*," he said, eyes no longer opening, but words as distinct as he could make them.

Get *what?*

He glanced—toward his back. Down to his leg.

And then, suddenly, the blood made sense.

He'd been shot. Not once, but twice.

"Devin—" she said, aghast, at a complete loss for words. She *couldn't*. Never mind her nerve, which might or might not be good enough. She had no skill. She'd kill him, as surely as the bullets themselves.

"The blade will," he said, barely audible. Another seizure of that brutal healing—*not*-healing—took him, and left him limp. "Just...try."

Because if she didn't, she was going to lose him. Right here and right now. The forces battling within him would tear him apart. She didn't have to understand them to see it—this man, so full of life, so startling honest with that grin and that sudden light in his eyes, faded before her.

And the knife, suddenly in her hand, was no innocuous pen knife. It was stiletto, deadly and narrow, and she had no idea how that had happened, or even when her fingers had closed around the grip in the first place.

The blade will.

Fine. None of it made sense. Not from the first moment she'd met him. Crumbling men, healing wounds, a crazed hero battling some inner demon—

Demon.

It resonated through her mind, a hiss of triumph and threat. She almost flung the blade away—

Except she thought she would save this man's life, and make sense of it later.

"Devin," she murmured, and bent over him, touching her forehead to his upper biceps. "I'll try."

The blade will.

She found the neat bullet hole in his jeans. *Behind. They shot him from behind.*

Of course they had. What other chance had they had?

Not a huge caliber. *Carrying concealed and cheap.* Those days with Ajay had taught her something after all. But still the blood pulsed steadily outward, soaking denim, and still the flesh tore raw beneath. And what was she supposed to do with a stiletto? Even if the bullet was close to the surface, a knife could hardly pluck it out.

The blade will.

As if he'd done it before.

Her hand shook, poised. "I hope this is what you mean," she murmured, more for herself than in expectation of a response, for he had gone beyond it.

Or she thought he had, until she probed the stiletto into that wound.

"Son of a *bitch!*" He stiffened, a series of pointed curses spitting out through gritted teeth and his hand latching unerringly on to her elbow, tears damping the side of his face and his body clenched and trembling and just as honest as the open grin and the open desire. *"Son of a—"*

"I'm sorry!" Her elbow ached and her throat had tightened down so hard she didn't know if she would ever breathe again. *Oh, this is so wrong!* She should have called for help, she should have pushed Enrique for answers, she should have slapped Devin awake and insisted on them before doing *this*....

Oh, so very wrong!

Except there, in the instant of silence between his cursing and his harsh, bloody and damaged breath, she heard the faintest of *clinks*.

And when, startled, she looked at the stiletto—withdrew it from the several inches it had claimed of that wound—on the end, she found a misshapen slug of metal.

Devin made a noise that could have been a sob, and passed out.

Nothing kept still in Devin's world. The floor shifted; the ceiling rotated. Fiery coals burned his back, his lung, his leg, and flushed on through his entire body.

But he wasn't alone.

And he wasn't wearing any clothes, either.

At least, not many.

Cool air brushed over one leg where jeans had been; his shoes were long gone, and blood-soaked socks removed. Vest, jacket and shirt, gone. The furnace turned up to offset the chill of it all—set high enough so sweat dampened the nape of his neck and along his temple. "I'm naked," he started to say, except it didn't turn out that way. Just a groan of unintelligible words, forced from an aching chest. Aching back. Aching self.

But not dead.

"Hey," he said, with more success. "Not dead."

"Hey," Natalie said, a cool hand resting on his side.

"Not dead." A warm damp cloth brushed along his leg, catching briefly on the crusted blood there. "But don't expect me to sew you up like Enrique did."

Alarm surged up—so did he, but no more successfully than he'd first tried to speak.

"I found him," Natalie said, guessing his concern. "He sent me after you." She hesitated. "I came looking for you in the first place because…"

"Compton," he muttered.

"I don't understand." Her voice caught; her hand stopped moving. But then she took the cloth away, dipped it in water somewhere, and wrung it out, coming back for more. "There's so very much I don't understand. But none of this is coincidence. I know that much. Not what happened in the alley years ago…not what happened the other night."

"No," he said, voicing it on a sigh. And then, "Cut up my clothes, didn't you?" He managed to twist his head just enough to see her—the overhead light bringing out the glimmer in her hair, the warmth of the room bringing out the flush on her cheeks.

Unless, of course, that was just the sight of his barely clothed ass, having its way with her.

Ha. Self-sarcasm. Must still be alive after all.

Flame licked through his body, reminding him. His breath caught; Natalie's hand stilled, just for a moment— touched a little more firmly, just for a moment. Reassurance in silent understanding. She said, "Your clothes were wrecked. You really did it to yourself this time."

No kidding. *Stupid.* He hoped the blade was paying

attention, such as it could. That it knew, as he did, that he never would have been taken that way had he not been struggling with the wild road while he fought Enrique free of those thugs....

She didn't seem to need an answer. Her hands—hurting, soothing—kept their steady work. Gently buffing away the gore of the night. She said, "Handy thing, your knife. Or sword, which I'm probably supposed to pretend I haven't seen. Or the stiletto I held earlier tonight, the one that pulled bullets like it had a mind of its own. The folding knife that cut off your clothes—" She stopped. She put a hand on his shoulder. "Devin. Please."

Yes.

Because it was time. It was fair. And it was too late for anything else.

"C'mere," he said.

She didn't ask what that meant. She moved aside whatever she'd used as a washbasin, stood. A moment later, the lightweight comforter from his bed settled over his shoulders. "The slugs are out," she told him, moving around with a pillow—lifting his head with a firm confidence, sliding the pillow beneath. He closed his eyes and let her, and some part of him, in the middle of all this, thrilled to it. To more than just the touch, but to her assumption of the right to touch him in that way.

"I cleaned the wounds as best I can—I used some of Enrique's stuff on them. And they're not bleeding any longer. As far as I can tell, once I got the slugs out, whatever it is that you do..."

"Right," he murmured. He'd learned that one early

on. As long as a bullet sat in his flesh, the blade could do nothing to heal him—just reflexive, battering attempts at it.

"C'mere," he said again, in case she'd missed that part.

But she hadn't. She was already settling down on the floor with him, tucking in under the comforter, tugging out a corner of the pillow for her own use. A hand resting on the side of his face; fingers scraping lightly back through the damp hair at his temples. He closed his eyes, thrilling to that, too.

"My brother had the knife," he told her. "That was chance, we thought, but now I'm not sure…now I think it chooses who it wants. Someone it thinks it can ride for a long time, turning us to its purposes. But there's so much I don't really *know.*"

Her thumb stroked the tight skin at the corner of his eye where those so very human tears of pain and distress beyond endurance had recently traced a path. "You realize that makes no sense."

He laughed—no strength behind it, and even that much made his lung ache, brought a hot flush of pain through his body—caught up his breath and held him there, while Natalie fiercely kissed his forehead and his eyes and picked up his hand and kissed that, too. Finally he was able to say, "If it actually made *sense,* I would have figured it out a long time ago. *We* would have figured it out, and Leo wouldn't be dead."

"Okay," she said. "It doesn't make sense. Tell me again."

He sighed, a shallow breath. Careful. And he let himself pull her in just a little closer. "It's leaving me alone," he said. "I think it knows…it's not done with me just yet. It's hedging its bets."

"Mmm," she said. "More sense than that, though, please."

"Demon blade," Devin said. "That's how it thinks of itself."

She stiffened slightly against him…but said nothing. Waited.

"You don't choose it. It chooses you. I didn't want it, that night Leo died. Didn't have any choice." He made a wry face. "Once it has you…nothing is the same. It… *drives* you. It wants blood. It sends you out into the night, hunting an excuse to find it."

"Vigilante," she murmured.

"I always give them a chance," he said, but his raw voice betrayed him. Too much blood on his hands, because the blade had pushed him into places where the men he faced couldn't and wouldn't back down. Bad men, murderers and rapists and the worst of both at that. "They *could* walk away."

"But most of them don't." She understood that right away. "And then the blade takes what's left of them."

Relief. "You believe…"

She laughed. "With what I've seen? How could I *not?*" And then she added, "All of it. I want all of it."

"Aside from the way the thing is so careful to heal me up once it shoves me out in front of knives and guns and the like?" He didn't laugh again, no matter how darkly—

he'd learned that lesson. "When I fight…it helps. It gives me an edge. Not much, but—"

"Enough," she said softly, a contemplative tone. Thinking about what she'd seen, no doubt. She ran her fingers along his jaw, and he shivered with it. "And then there's the wild road."

"Enrique," he said.

"You mentioned it, too," she said. "I'm not sure you meant to."

"Probably not," he muttered, just enough strength in him to put a little edge to it. He pulled her in a little closer, fully reveling in the curves, everything toned and still smooth beneath his touch—at first resistant, and then softening against him. Even her breath, soft against the base of his throat. He let the rest of the room fade away, clinging only to the sensation of her. "The blade…*takes* you. Where it is, what it is…who the hell knows. We never found out. I only know what it does. What it *did*." The hot fingers of it, slicing through his soul…setting its hooks into his being. "I know there's no escape."

"Shh," she said, which seemed a strange thing, when she'd been the one to ask. To insist.

"Only you," he told her, his hand tightening on the swell of her hip; she pressed against him in response. She'd shown him how to keep hold of himself, if only for a little while longer.

"Shh," she said again. "I'll be here." Her lips landed on his neck; her lashes came to rest against his collarbone as she tucked her head up against him.

And Devin ached, and Devin fought the blade within, and Devin knew that death likely waited from without…but he still fell asleep with a faint smile lingering at his mouth.

I'll be here.

That's what she'd told him.

So Natalie didn't tear away, and she didn't throw herself into a corner in a fetal ball of denial.

She faced it.

After all, she'd asked.

And who was she to deny the existence of a thing called *demon blade* when she'd seen it at work? When she'd been waiting, these past weeks, for him to finally speak out loud of it? To tell her this, which explained so much.

But it didn't explain all.

Either he'd fought a man on her porch, or he'd hallucinated it.

Either that old man—*old man*—had been a threat, or Devin had, in that moment, lost all perspective.

Either he could still be trusted, or it was already too late. No matter the work they'd done together.

"Shh," she'd told him, when she'd come to realize he had no idea the weary pain on his features, the despair that drew his brow together or the faint clench of his jaw between words.

Just as she doubted he'd realized his own faint smile, lingering on his mouth even as he fell asleep in her arms—hurting and wounded and yes, already healing.

Pulling her closer, a reverence in his touch. Needing her—gently rousing to her even in his battered state. And so she'd be here.

Chapter 17

Devin's mouth tasted like death and old blood.

He opened his eyes to deep night, the lights on and Natalie fast asleep beside him, rolling slightly away as she'd relaxed. Not so hard to disengage, to climb to his feet—pulling himself up on the bed and then moving from the bed to the wall and down the hall to the bathroom.

The hall was, of course, a mess. No little wonder this place always had a new carpet smell to it.

The bathroom yielded his toothbrush—oh, small mercies—and the harsh vanity lights. No mercies there. They showed the smudged fatigue under his eyes, the tight stress…the pain, with his lung a burning ember and his leg a smug, fiery throb that had little intention of truly supporting his weight.

But he'd been right. The blade was all about survival…about keeping its puppet useful for as long as possible. It had tortured him when that seemed the best strategy; now, when he had been so close to death that another such night would have killed him, it merely healed him. As in the old days, the first days. The accelerated healing had its own price, but tonight that didn't include his sanity.

He looked in the mirror, gave himself a hard grin of a challenge. A lifted lip, a growling voice—seeing the blade in his eyes, where the darkness lingered. He told it, "Or maybe she's just got you on the run."

Sullen, shooting pain pushed back at him; he gasped a laugh, doubling briefly over the sink. "You," he said to the blade, *"really suck."*

It had no particular opinion about that.

For all he knew, the notion pleased it. There, where it lay tucked up against his leg in quiescent pen knife form, having gotten back into his pocket who knew how or when.

He straightened again, eyed his jeans—one pants leg entirely missing, though she'd left him his boxer briefs. Who knew where his shirt was, and an uneven film of blood still washed over his side like a grisly real-life watercolor.

But the hole in his back had a distinctly healing look about it. Not a man raw and wounded, but a man who could take a deep breath if he wanted.

He tried it. Hell, yes, it hurt, but for a man who'd been spitting up blood mere hours earlier…

The leg told a similar story. Not happy about bearing weight, not ready to run any marathons…but healing. Healing fast.

And that told him exactly how much the blade had put him through for that simple arterial slice he'd taken the night he'd met Natalie. "Bastard," he muttered at it.

A smug tickle of awareness was as much warning as confirmation.

The blade used him, all right. It wanted him out there stalking the bad guys like prey. Chasing them down, taking them down.

He knew it wouldn't end there, either—the innocents would come next.

But he also knew something else. He knew that Leo hadn't simply snapped that night in that alley those years earlier.

He'd been driven.

He'd been manipulated.

He'd been known and he'd been used—not by the blade, but by some outside force.

And maybe it was now no different for Devin.

Except that it was. He *knew.*

And he had Natalie.

He rinsed out his mouth another time, took a deep slug of water.

He had Natalie.

Didn't he?

With careful, unsteady steps, he returned to the bedroom. She'd moved into the spot where he'd been, as if seeking his missing warmth—curled up around herself, limbs long and slender, hair a mass of wavy brown and blond. Her hand rested quietly over the carpet where he'd so recently lain.

With nothing of stealth or power or grace, he lowered himself beside her and gently pulled her hair back from her face, revealing the amazing angle of cheekbone beneath.

That, he bent to kiss.

And the corner of her eye, and the corner of her mouth. And he felt every minute variation in the softness of her skin, the flicker of her lash, the twitch of her cheek. When she opened her eyes.

"What are you doing?" she murmured.

He didn't answer right away—not until she turned to look at him, there from a hairsbreadth away. "I want you to know," he said then, deadpan, "how very hard it is not to say the obvious thing here." As in, *what do you* think *I'm doing?*

She rolled over to face him, and gave him a somber look—but not one that could hide the deep humor behind her eyes. "That must be very hard indeed." Damned if her gaze didn't flick down below his waist.

He didn't hide his amusement—or his intent. "I'm finishing what we started, that's what." *While we still have the chance.*

Her expression lost the humor, turned direct—still so close, as she reached up to touch the side of his face. "You could have done that a long time ago, if you hadn't walked away at the canal. You must know that."

"I know it wouldn't have been right for you," Devin

said bluntly. "I know it wouldn't have been a true *choice* for you, with so many things unsaid. You wouldn't have been happy when you realized that."

"No," she admitted. "But I wasn't happy the way things were, either." She touched his face, his shoulder...she stroked his side. "There's something about you that makes me feel free. I see you in the middle of all *this,* and you give me that *look*.... You make me see that avoiding life...that's no choice at all. So you know what?"

He didn't answer. He didn't dare. Not to mention that her hand had found its way to the inside of his thigh and he'd forgotten how to speak.

"I choose you," she said.

"Thank God," Devin muttered, and lowered his forehead to hers, the relief on his face bringing a sweet pain to Natalie's throat.

Come here, she wanted to say, but that throat wouldn't let her, so she did the first thing that came to mind, brushing nails across the inner thigh she'd already claimed. There, up very high, bare tender skin. Sensitive skin.

Then she welcomed him when he abruptly settled over her; she ran her hands down his sides, feeling the play and flex of muscle along his back and spine, the tight clench in his buttocks. She shifted to fit them together more precisely. Her sound of utter satisfaction didn't entirely smother a little laugh. "I guess you didn't lose as much blood as I thought."

"Saved some," he said, his voice thick, the words distracted and all the more charming for it, one hand working on the buttons of her blouse. "Special occasion."

"I approve." But then the breath hissed through her teeth and she arched up against him, pushing into his hand as it overcame the obstacle of her bra and found her breast—reverence and demand wrapped up in clever fingers, followed by his own groan.

She wasn't sure what her own hands did then. Or her body. She was suddenly aware that he'd stiffened, his breath gusting out across her now-bare shoulder, a strangled noise in his throat. It brought her back to the floor and the winter night and the oddity of legs wrapped around half a pair of jeans. Concern flooded her. "Dev—"

"Nnng," he said, or something like it. "Don't—no— it's okay—*gah*—"

She laughed, breathless, he nibbled along her exposed neck, and when she reached for him again, he trapped her hand and said, "Uh-uh," before bending to her ear to whisper, "Think about *this*. Feel *this*." Her own words of these past weeks, driven right back at her.

The carpet disappeared. The night became irrelevant. There were only his hands—the one at the side of her head, angling her mouth just the way he wanted it, strong and gentle fingers, inexorable grip. The other hand roaming her body, touching…skimming and undressing. Pausing to lavish attention, stroking and warming and finding all possible sensitivities. He came down on her mouth, nipped her lower lip and turned it into a deep kiss. "Feel that," he told her again. "Feel *this*."

And so she lost her mind as his hand found her, all clever and gentle and then *plunging,* so she pushed up against him, desperate to open to him and tighten around him at the same time, no longer able to do even as much as kiss him, only crying out into his mouth. Clever, clever fingers, striking sparks everywhere in her body at once, winding her tighter…letting her back down again.

She took advantage to reach for him—he wasn't hard to find. He twitched in her hand, a throb of response that came with a gust of breath on her neck. She stroked him gently, learning him—smiling against his kiss when he thrust against her and growing bolder with her touch.

He made his strangled noise again, clamping his hand on her hip and quite suddenly holding her still, but this time she understood, and this time she wasn't willing to wait. She found her hands clenching into his back— demanding. And reaching into his back pocket for his slim wallet, tapping him on the ass with it.

"Nnng," he said again, reaching for it—fumbling it between them. She released him to join the effort, applying herself to the task of covering him with eager and inventive fingers. And where moments before he'd had her right at the edge of sanity, now he quivered beside and above her, and now his fingers clawed into the carpet, and now his breath gusted hard onto her skin, his head bowed and his forehead resting against her shoulder. "I," he managed, a mere grunt of a word, "am…

so…going to—" was that a whimper, between clenched teeth? "—*take* you…for this."

"I *choose you*," she reminded him, a whisper of a laugh and invitation, reveling in the quiver and tremble and restraint of him, but ready for the fulfillment of promise—that which he'd offered her from the beginning: glimpses of honesty and passion and completeness.

Oh, *there.*

Like *that.*

"Oh," she breathed, the wonder of it. And *"Oh!"*

And what he said, she wasn't sure. But it sounded like honesty. It felt like passion.

And it left her complete.

Whoa.

Gahhh.

It was as sentient as Devin got, right in that moment, his muscles collapsing and only half successful in rolling his weight off Natalie.

All the aches suddenly shrieked; all the wounds suddenly throbbed. The fire of it wrapped around him, darting through his inattentiveness to take control. He had nothing left to hold back a heartfelt groan.

"Devin?" she said, twisting up to her elbow, her legs still wrapped around his hips and showing no sign of releasing him anytime soon. "Oh, I'm so sorry! What was I even thinking?"

He laughed, low and true, startling her into silence. "Oh, God," he said. "That was *so* worth it." Even if it took another moment of struggle to get control of it, another grunt of pain, a hiss, a restless shifting as a swell of it washed through him. "Not kidding," he panted, feeling her worried gaze on him, her touch at the side of his face. And then, finally, as the piqued blade eased its grip on him, he tucked her in closer. "Be with me," he asked her, and she relaxed again. She reached behind him to tuck the ultra light comforter back into place over them both.

For a moment, he thought of nothing else but the touching—the places they touched, the ways they touched. The warmth of her skin, the scent of her hair and her body. His own scent, just a little bit sharp—stressed—and the raw hint of blood lingering in the background.

Natalie whispered, "What are we going to do?"

"Make love," he muttered, not truly thinking about it. "Repeatedly. Until I pass out."

"I think," she told him gently, "you might be just about to do that."

He grunted a denial, and she held him a little tighter for just that moment, affection filtering through the worry in her voice. "I mean what're we going to do about what's happening. I think…" She took a breath. "I don't think this has anything to do with the restaurant—that's just a ruse. I think it's been Compton all along. He's had cameras in my home. The guys who came for me that night…they were on his payroll. That's what I came to tell you."

He considered that, and frowned against her shoulder. "Thought you came because you were wrong. About us."

"Well, *obviously,*" she said, in a tone that made it clear he was lucky she hadn't tacked the word *doofus* on to that response. "But I came *now* because of what I learned. I can't make it make sense, but I know…somehow, Compton is tied up in this."

"I know," he said, and even if it still came out in no more than a mutter, there was heat behind it. "The alleys…they're part of this, too, somehow. My brother. And I think…your ex-fiancé." *Ajay.* Too much coincidence, to hear that name from her lips and then from the man at Enrique's.

Her voice sounded subdued. Miserable. "Yes," she said. "I don't know exactly how, but…"

"We'll sort it out." He said it with utter confidence, and tucked her a little closer. Or at least he made the effort. They were already pretty much as entwined as they could get.

"But—"

"Tomorrow," he said simply. "Tomorrow, we go to him."

Silence, as she absorbed that. But her body remained relaxed against him. Her hand, comforting on his arm; her lips, just barely resting against his temple. Then she said, "Tomorrow."

"Love first," he said, so low she might not even hear it, except her body tightening around him told him that she had. "Repeatedly."

"Okay," she whispered. "But I think you're going to pass out first."

And he did.

* * *

Devin woke toward morning, and found she'd been busy. She'd cleaned up; she'd brushed her hair into gleaming brown and blond. She'd acquired one of his button-up shirts, old and soft and a red that looked so good on her that he instantly vowed to put it aside in his closet as a shrine.

She'd turned most of the lights off, leaving more intimate illumination.

And right. She sat on him, straddling him, rocking her hips ever so slightly. Just enough to bring a rushing swell of pleasure streaking through his body and up behind his eyes, a gasp in his throat and his head tipping back to ride it out…to absorb it. To revel in it. "How—?" he rasped, when he could.

She smiled, lips still kiss-plumped, a flush of pleasure spreading along her cheeks and neck and collarbones, tightening her breasts through that shirt. "Not *all* of you went to sleep." As if to illustrate this point, she reached behind herself to lightly stroke and tickle.

He jerked—a gasp, a curse, his body arching. "Oh, yeah," he said, when he could. "You—*you*—"

"Repeatedly," she said, her voice a low and husky warning of intent. And though a faint worry fluttered in her gaze, reflecting words unspoken—*while we can*— she didn't voice them. She ran her hands over his chest, tracing the dusting of hair, and followed the narrow line of it down his stomach and beyond.

His skin fluttered beneath her touch; he swelled within her. And though he waited for the habitual interference from the blade—demands and nudges and licking, fiery forays at his soul—it couldn't reach him. Not now—not through the clarity of her touch.

"Repeatedly," she warned him again.

"Okay," he managed, all too aware that she'd turned the earlier conversation around on him. "How about—*nng*—*uh*—right—"

"Now," she agreed.

Chapter 18

Morning found Natalie alone. On the bed, now and in her own pool of warmth beneath the blankets. For the moment, she heard nothing. No shower running, no kitchen noises.

Tomorrow we'll go to him.

Surely he hadn't gone on his own—

No. There. Something in the kitchen. A muted sound; water running. She relaxed. She let herself take in the sensations of being—here, now. All the intimate parts of her, tender and sore and even startled at so much attention after the dry spell since…

That was enough. Since before.

She touched her lips; found them sensitive—found them smiling beneath her fingers. A pleasant whisker burn brushed her cheeks; the rest of her more or less melted right down into the bed, not inclined to move this day or possibly the next; the very scent of him permeated the sheets around her, enveloping her in the reassurance of reality.

Yes. I slept here. I made love here. Repeatedly.

So many things she'd learned during the night—how Leo had wrested the blade from the wild man who'd attacked two youths at the La Luz trail head. How it had instantly changed him…and how those changes had shifted over time.

Until Devin had killed him in self-defense, and eventually found himself in exactly the same situation.

No wonder he'd latched on to her little exercises with such dedication.

I can find more.

She'd been a young woman in a difficult situation, battling to regain her life. But she'd been healthy; she'd had determination. She'd had plenty of incentive. That hadn't made it easy—not any of it—but when she'd found things that helped—things that gave her confidence and eased anxiety and kept her focused on her goals—she'd been able to stop looking.

I can find more.

What was she, if not a woman who had trained herself to do just that? Find what was needed, when it was needed? Make it happen?

The thoughts got her out of bed. Feet on the floor, she discovered that she still wore his soft old red shirt… marginally. She buttoned it, headed to the bathroom to tidy up and padded through the house to find him in the kitchen, just as half-dressed as she.

No welcoming smell of coffee here; he glanced up from a small blender as she hesitated by the end of the breakfast bar, and though he grinned at her—his mouth looking every bit as kissed-all-night as hers—there was something somber lurking in his eyes.

He lifted the blender. "Want some protein?"

No coffee. Okay, she could deal. But she eyed the blender most dubiously.

Some of the spark returned to his eye. "It's chocolate."

"Oh, *well,* then."

He pushed a button and for thirty seconds made a whole lot of noise, pulling two glasses out onto the counter while he waited. "Meal replacement stuff," he said, thumbing the blender off. "Lots of calories, but after the blade pushes up a healing like that—"

"You've got a lot to replace," she noted.

He nodded, pushed a glass in her direction, lifted his in a small salute and drank the thick liquid down.

Natalie sniffed hers; gave it a tentative taste. Not *food,* but…not bad. She waited for him to finish. "How are you?"

He rinsed the glass in the sink, turned it upside down in the half-sized drainer there and turned his back to her, tugging his old T-shirt up from the fresh boxer briefs beneath.

Oh.

"My *back,*" he reminded her after a moment.

"Oh," she said, raising her gaze. "Right." Maybe she

should blush, but then again…after the previous night, maybe she was just taking in what was hers to take in.

So she smiled, and damned if he didn't flush. She reached for his shirt, brushing skin, and bit her lip when his butt cheek clenched in response. But now…now was the time to face what lay ahead. She lifted the shirt just another inch, and found the healing wound. *Healing* being the operative word.

"Wow," she said.

"It doesn't fool around when it wants to make sure I'm available for its purposes," Devin said dryly. "At the moment, it feels threatened. But putting me back together like that…" He shook his head. "It doesn't leave me much to work with. I can slug back protein shakes and meal replacements all day—it'll still take time to come back."

Still raw, still angry; still clearly injured. But his voice sounded normal; his breathing was light and casual.

"Your leg?" she asked, suddenly a little numb.

"I can get around." But a glance told her it hadn't made half the progress, and he turned to share a wry look. "Call it triage healing."

Natalie ran a worrying thumb over her lower lip— realized what she'd done, and stopped herself. Not one of her good signs. "Do you really think we should go back today?"

His gaze went hooded and dark. There in the kitchen, half-dressed and walking-wounded, he suddenly became the dangerous man she'd first seen in that dark parking lot. That his face was paler, his hair scruffed up in guy bed-head…didn't make a bit of difference. "No, I don't think we should. Except I don't think we have any choice."

"Uh," Natalie found herself saying, and leaving it at that.

He shook his head. "You didn't say anything to Compton when you left, did you?"

She shook her head, shifting her feet on the cold tile of the kitchen floor.

"So we have a window. He knows you're gone, but he doesn't know why."

"Once I realized there was a camera…" she said slowly, going over those moments in her mind, "I didn't say anything at all. I never even turned on the light." She met his gaze, gray gone to dark. "It wouldn't be hard to convince him that I found myself emotional over our situation and left. He knows my past. He knows how I had to pull myself back together."

Right. Pretend to be as weak as she'd been when Compton had first found her. The very last thing she wanted to do.

"Might not come to that," he said, gently enough so she knew he understood all her unspokens. "All we really need is for you to be able to get into the main house unchallenged. But the longer we wait, the less likely that is."

"And then what? Confront—"

He shook his head, sharply. "I want a look around. That hallway…the blade almost took me there a number of times. You saw it."

"I didn't understand it," she admitted. "But I saw it."

"I *still* don't understand it. But we need to know." But still the dark look, the borderline glower. Not at Natalie. At…*himself?*

"Those are all reasons to go back," she said. "But why *not* go? You said—"

He turned away from her. "Because I've got a week before I'm what I should be, for starters. I've got no business heading into enemy territory like this, and no damned business at all asking you to do it beside me."

"Enemy territory," she said, and shook her head. "I can't believe—"

The man who had given her a job to grow into. Goals, when she so badly needed them. A stranger, meeting her in a newly dedicated alley and offering a helping hand.

Except he'd apparently never truly been a stranger. He knew Ajay…somehow. Probably Ajay's doing, one of his schemes. And he'd known *her*—what she needed. How to reach her.

Why?

She looked at Devin—his weight shifted off his bad leg, his shoulder stiff to guard his back.

This was why.

She'd been there. She'd talked freely of it to him— but she'd been unable to answer questions about the two men in the alley, whom he'd somehow thought she'd known. *Because Ajay had always believed it—that she was stepping out on him.* Eventually he'd stopped asking…and then evidently decided to use her another way.

Attacked in the parking lot, drawn together under Compton's roof…watched. Manipulated.

It didn't matter how hard she tried to return to that nice clean world view where her boss was an intelligent, driven and wealthy man who did good things with his life….

Recent facts told her otherwise. Her instinct, stirring back to life, told her otherwise.

"Yeah," Devin said, watching her—the whole story of it that must have been playing out across her face. "I know. It's hard. But once we figure out what it's all about…it'll get easier, then."

"I hope you're right." She threaded fingers through her hair, combing it away from her face. "And we can't wait. So, we go."

A day or so earlier, she might have missed the faint wince at the corner of his eye, or the way his gaze went subtly distant. This day, she knew better. She left the protein shake on the counter and closed the distance between them, bare feet and red shirt and concern. "What?"

She thought, from the faint desperation in his eye, that he would have given everything to have been across the room again. To have been in a different house altogether. Or even to find whatever it would take to break the gaze between them.

Instead he let her see the desperation, and the darkness. "Because the blade wants me there," he told her. "It wants to go. And that might be the biggest single reason not to."

She shook her head. "But I thought you listened to it. I thought that's how you found me."

"Like *that,* yes. But this…" He rubbed fingers across his brow. "Leo felt it, the last days. The blade, curious about things. Nosy. Demanding. More than just the usual—the hunting. And, Natalie—" Here came that *desperate* again. "I'm trying, but…it's already coming back at me. Fog, there around the edges of what makes me…*me.* I'm *trying*—but I don't know if I can stop it."

She saw that fear—felt it strike deep within her, a cold slice of weakness up her spine. She swallowed it back. "*We* can stop it," she said. She lay her hand on his arm—a lover's touch in the territorial familiarity of it, but not a sensual touch. Distinct fingers, a distinct hold. A grasp on reality.

But even as the clarity of it surged up through his expression, so did a ferocity she hadn't expected. "That's not why I'm with you! Not why I wanted you—God, why I want you again, right here, right *now*—"

And for a moment she thought he'd follow up his words, the tension between them crackling and his expression so nakedly possessive—she thought he just might toss her up on this counter and take her.

For a moment, she thought she'd let him.

But somehow the moment passed, even if it left them only inches apart, his breath stirring her hair and his body tight, forgetting it had ever been hurt at all. He bit his lip in what looked like regret; he turned his head away.

"Devin," she said, refusing to release when he would

have pulled away, "if I'd ever thought that, I wouldn't be here, and you know it. You *know* that."

Right. That might have been a nod. It might have some subtle shift of air around them. Her fingers weren't kind, now, clamping down as she gave that arm a little shake. "Don't you dare stop me from doing what little I can do to help, Devin James."

Something in him gave way. He ducked his head, looked up at her from lowered brow. "When you put it that way, it makes me sound kind of stupid."

"Then don't be." But she softened her hold on him, gave that arm a gentle rub.

"As long as we're clear." His head didn't come up, but his eye held a gleam she'd come to recognize. "I still want you. Right here. Right now."

Her hand slipped lower, confirming the truth of his words—evoking a surprised and startled noise from him. "And so you should," she told him, and glanced behind him, a pointed look. "Maybe you should just keep that counter clear in the future."

Natalie drove.

Cleaned up, tucked away in her tidy slacks and his red shirt, purse-borne makeup only pretending to obscure the whisker burn, the love nip on her neck, the bright glow of her cheeks…

Natalie drove, and Devin watched her. Without even pretending not to.

They'd had his protein shakes, they'd stopped for do-nuts—*healing hangover,* he'd explained, at her askance expression. Right, street fighting vengeance kickboxing dude with demon blade, chomping down on the sugary carbs. But hey, a craving was a craving.

With the blade in his life, he should know.

With the memory of Natalie in his arms, he should *damned* well know.

Not that he couldn't multi-task, flipping closed the cheapo prepaid phone she'd picked up. "Finally. Enrique's at UNM. They won't say crap over the phone, but they didn't tell me to rush in and see him just in case, either."

"You can call one of his other guys?" Natalie suggested.

Pure irritation set his jaw. "Not until I have my own phone back," he said. "We've got a calling tree, but that's where I keep it."

"Then we need to see him soon," she said simply. She might not know the details, but she clearly understood enough.

He shifted, easing his leg—stretching it as he could. That it burned with a deep, hot and abiding fury was a given—the extra kiss of the blade's healing. As did his back, and deep within his chest.

Distractions. Moments of endurance. He was, after all, breathing.

"You're sure—" he started, and Natalie didn't let him finish—a little amused, a little exasperated.

"If I say it again, will you believe me this time? I set up the man's schedule. He's at a meeting this morning. Security will be light. The lower house is being cleaned;

Jimena has the morning off." She shrugged. "After what happened last night, did he cancel everything? Is he waiting for us? I don't know. He's a brilliant man, Devin. He gets what he wants."

Devin grumbled, deep in his throat. "That would be why we have to figure out what he *does* want."

"Yes," she said, and the look she gave him held an affection he hadn't expected. Desire, they had in plenty. A raw and naked attraction. But that look...

That look said she *knew* him. She understood him.

Maybe that they could—

Leo. Blade. Doomed. And don't forget it. What she could do for him was temporary. And even if neither of them was inclined to deny the moments they could have, that's what they were. Moments.

Don't forget it.

"Give me twenty minutes to freshen up at home and make it to the main house alarm, and you can come in through the kitchen. I'll meet you there—we'll use the back stairs and head straight to the private wing. In and out, everything's quiet, and we can decide where to go from there." She gave him a wry smile, glancing away from the road to do it. "If something's there to find, I have the feeling we won't be left wondering."

He laughed shortly—a dark sound, little humor. "Yeah," he said, and when she looked back at him again, a little startled, he found himself looking away. *You have no idea.*

Chapter 19

Just as planned.

Natalie breathed a sigh of relief when she found her phone in front of her little home; she breathed a further sigh of relief at the completely undisturbed nature of the door and the living space beyond.

And she never forgot she was on camera.

Didn't matter that he might not be watching this moment—he clearly had the capacity to store the recordings…as well as the inclination.

Although perhaps that night had been a special one. If he'd truly drugged Devin…if he'd wanted to keep track of the results, whatever his purpose behind it…

Oh, God, we nearly made love right there on the floor.

But they hadn't. They'd had that particular moment in privacy, and now she'd come back to reclaim her life.

Devin's life.

So she for sure didn't look up at the spot she knew the camera occupied—probably in the smoke alarm. She made a show of examining the recovered phone, and then of plugging it into its charger, and then she did as she might normally do—she shrugged out of her coat, dropped her purse on the couch and unsnapped her slacks, shedding them on the way to the bedroom. *Eat your heart out.*

From there, she made quick work of it—pulling on fresh underwear and jeans, taking a few moments to gather up her hair, clipping it into a casual twist at the back of her head, the back length of it still tumbling free.

It was, she realized, instinctively calculated. As if she'd suddenly allowed herself to see that Compton had always treated her as more than just a personal assistant. Something controlled, something desired…something *owned.*

Something *wanted.*

But if he wanted her, then that gave her power in return. So if she ran into him, and if she could throw him off balance—even just a little—she'd take that power.

She didn't need much makeup; her skin still shone burnished by kisses. She gave her eyes some drama, made the blue of them *pop*—and then tucked Devin's shirt into the jeans.

Compton would know. Let him think about *that,* instead of whatever plans he'd made and inflicted upon her. Upon Devin.

Supposing he was here at all.

Please don't be here.

It's not what this day was about. Even Devin didn't want it that way.

Not yet.

She pulled her coat back on and headed out the door at a brisk walk. Natalie, making it to work late after a night out. No precedent for it, but she didn't owe this estate her life…much as she'd somehow ceded it that very thing.

The security, as usual, was invisible. Whoever watched her did it unseen. She slipped in the front door, quickly disarming the security system—and, through force of long habit, snagged her coat over one of the hooks just inside the coat room.

Normal is as normal does.

Except she didn't quite make it to the kitchen door in time.

A woman's cry of alarm, a harsh sound, a slamming door and then metal clattering across tile—for an instant, Natalie froze. *Jimena?* But this was her morning off—

A high, thin cry, Spanish words cut off in midvoice, and Natalie found her feet again—started running, reckless through the kitchen door and breathless not at the short sprint but at what awaited her there.

Devin, jammed up against the closed back door, his expression hardly *Devin's* at all. Calphalon pans scattered across the floor, a saucepan canted at the edge of the counter—and a pan tipping out of Jimena's fingers where it had quite obviously been clutched as a weapon.

Jimena's gaze, dark and frightened, darted between Natalie and the eight-inch Wusthof chef's knife just out of her reach. *Help me.*

Oh, Jimena...

"Devin," she said, deliberately releasing a deep breath—one he would hear. One she hoped he would key in on. *Relax.* Because what she saw in his eye—

No. Not Devin at all. And nothing like the man she had left only moments earlier.

His hand closed around Jimena's throat from behind. And that throat suddenly looked so very fragile...that hand, so very strong. Long fingers, scarred over the knuckles...knew how to take a beating, knew how to give one.

Bloody fingers.

Finally, she saw the sleeve of his coat—the rent material, the blood staining the edges. Nothing like what he'd lost the night before, but so violent—

"The dog," she breathed. "I heard a dog—"

His expression went glowering dark. Jimena, faltering as she began to understand that Natalie wasn't going to help save her from this version of Devin gone mad, whispered desperately, "Mr. Compton brought it in last night."

Now? It had been two years since the last one. Longer. Almost since Natalie had first arrived. *Now?*

No coincidence.

She looked at Devin, and suddenly understood. "It came for you," she said. "You killed it."

He held out his other hand, palm open, the agate-handled knife displayed...traces of gore over bright blade. Jimena stiffened, her thoughts writ clear on her face. She couldn't reach the knife on the counter, but this one—

"No, Jimena," Natalie said softly, and she stepped closer. She took the pan from the woman's hand and set it aside, never removing her gaze from Devin's—hunting some hint of the saner man within.

He hadn't been prepared for violence. He hadn't been strong enough for it. Oh, strong enough to survive it—but not to keep the blade out. "Come back to me, Devin. Jimena won't be a problem."

Jimena's mouth opened; Natalie saw the words in her expression. The protest that they had come like this; the awareness that they were, somehow, working against Compton's interest.

Devin's hand gave a reflexive twitch at Jimena's throat; she stifled a cry.

It was the rebellious nature of his own hand that seemed to do it. He took a sudden, sharp breath, jaw working and nostrils flared, and quite suddenly pushed Jimena away from him—a hard shove at that.

Jimena stumbled, but it didn't stop her from making a snatch at the blade in his open hand. Something dark ruffled through the air—it might have been a silent laugh, as Devin closed his grip around the knife and moved it aside, an unhurried motion, skating just aside from her grasp.

"No!" Natalie put herself between them, taking Jimena's arm—leading her a few more crucial steps down the counter and, while she was at it, making sure there were no more potential weapons to hand. "You need to leave us to this, Jimena. It's important." She glanced back at Devin, found him shaking it all off…the knife, out of sight.

The look he gave her then was rueful and matter-of-fact. "She met me at the door with that fry pan. Nearly got me, too. But I—" he stopped, hesitated. "I wasn't in the mood for it."

No kidding.

Jimena straightened with some pride. "This is my kitchen," she said. "You shouldn't be here." But she, too, hesitated. "I didn't realize it was you when—" She glanced at the pan on the floor.

Natalie picked it up, set it firmly on the counter. "What *are* you doing here? If I'd had any idea, I would have told him to knock."

Jimena scowled, shaking back wavy black hair normally captured in a hairnet. "I said. This is *my* kitchen." She looked directly at Devin. "You became ill. So was I."

Natalie suddenly saw the signs—supplies in the sink, a few remaining items of food at the end of the counter. "You were cleaning."

"Trying to find—" Jimena stopped, lips pressed together. "At least cleaning to be sure."

Natalie exchanged a glance with Devin, who

shrugged, rubbing his arm…fisting his hand and then shaking it out again. He said in a low voice, "I'm sorry about the dog. That wasn't right."

"You need to go," Jimena said firmly. "I don't know what's going on, but it's not right for him to be here."

"You're right," Devin said. "It's not. But Sawyer Compton drugged me. He's been using me. He's been using Natalie. For years, both of us. Maybe we've been a little slow to catch on, but…" He grinned. Nothing of the exuberance, the honest humor—all teeth and darkness. "We're catching up now."

Jimena turned a troubled face away from them— only a swift glance to check Devin's reaction as she reached for her errant knife and placed it into its block with the set.

Finally, the words lingering behind that troubled look came out. "I found a powder spilled in the back of the True, where I chilled the finished servings. Very bitter." She looked at Devin. "*Lo siento,* but still, you stay out of my kitchen!"

Devin grinned at her, and it was back—just for a fleeting moment. Honest and right through to the heart of him. "*Lo siento,* Jimena."

She pressed her lips together again—glanced out into the main house…lowered her voice. "That man of his was here this morning. He stayed the night, I think. He left a mess! I heard him arguing with one of the others. About a shooting…a beating. I don't like that man; I don't understand why Mr. Compton keeps him around."

Scorn crossed her oval features, filled her voice. "Ajay Dudek."

Ajay.

Here. Now.

A glance at Devin told her everything. The recognition, the rising anger. Apology, and, dammit, compassion. She couldn't keep the accusation from her voice. "You *knew*."

He lifted one shoulder. "I've been putting it together." But then he hesitated. "Last night, he almost killed Enrique. He—" He glanced at Jimena. "He had the gun."

He'd shot Devin.

"Natalie." He took a step into the kitchen; the wild ferocity of the blade had deserted him. Now he looked every bit of what he'd been through the night before. Now she could see how he favored his leg, held his body to protect his back. "Now we know," he told her. "We know it goes deep, and we know it goes long."

Right. Had she just been coincidence back then? Tangled up with a man she'd never truly known, and then turned into a pawn over the years?

Maybe it didn't matter. She knew enough. She knew she'd been used—then, and ever since. None of her careful choices had truly been *choices* at all.

"Okay," she said, and forced the words through a tight throat. "Now we get to find out *why*."

Something sparked in his eyes—a deep smile…a deep pride. He didn't have to say the words that came next, and neither did she.

And then we stop him.

* * *

Compton turned away from the table at which sat his hopefuls—restaurant manager, hostess, chef—earnest people, ready to fire his Alley of Life project into reality. The project was now heavily supported by the city, various charities and a plethora of high-society leeches, in spite of considerable opposition from those who felt the whole project would create an unfair advantage for this particular restaurant over others.

For Compton, there was no downside. None. Not even if the project took years to turn a profit. The goodwill attached to his name was already priceless, and the project had already created allies among the valley social services—the food shelves, the shelters, the unwed mothers and battered women. To Sawyer Compton, all resources of the sort his grateful new cohorts never even imagined.

Vulnerable. Easy. Seldom missed.

His body flushed with the remembered warmth of the hunt, and how he had already taken advantage of that, too. The thought of his sycophantic wannabe counterparts, feting him and worshiping him with no idea what blood he'd washed off his hands only hours earlier...

Amusing.

But he was not amused now.

"I understand," he said into the phone, upon hearing of the newly discovered dead dog.

He'd underestimated Natalie—he'd thought her fled from it all. But that she'd not only gone to Devin James, but somehow become involved in the events of the previous evening and now had the nerve to return...

Oh, yes, he'd underestimated her.

"Find them," he said to the man on the phone, striding away from the conference table. He spoke with sharp precision and no hesitation. "Detain them. Do not engage. Do you understand?"

"How—?" the man said.

His voice, razor sharp and pitched low, cut the other man short. "They're heading for the private wing." He'd seen Devin James's awareness of the blade room—seen him falter in the grip of it.

That was nothing compared to what awaited him now.

"Let them pass unmolested, and keep them there. If they aren't, encourage them. And there, speak the phrases you were taught upon entering my employ. *Do you understand?*"

"But—" the man said, no doubt thinking of comrades dead and Ajay Dudek disgraced.

Compton took his voice lower yet, as if that could hide its cold menace. "Fail to heed me, and you will undoubtedly die. Fail *me,* and you will wish you had." Ah, it felt good to let the teeth come out every once in a while. "I'll be there shortly."

It was then that the amusement trickled back in. Never mind that Natalie and James had been unpredictable—that they'd broken the pattern of his hunt by coming back to check Compton's own trail. That to some extent, they must already be aware of Compton's efforts—and that surely, Devin James must understand, even if not consciously, the forces in play.

Because no matter the healing the blade had done for

him, it wouldn't be enough. And now they would both be trapped. Under Compton's control.

Awaiting his pleasure.

And then we stop him. Words unspoken, clearly understood.

A response floated through Devin's thoughts unbidden, and he recognized it in only a bemused way as his own. *The sooner the better.*

"Devin," Natalie whispered. "Are you—"

"Yes, dammit!" he snapped, keeping his voice just as low—even if they did believe themselves to be alone here in the house. "I'm fine!"

Because of course he wasn't, was he?

But he'd told her he could do this.

He hadn't been expecting the dog. More than just an arm turned to temporary sausage beneath his coat sleeve...it had been an opening for the blade. Wanting, pushing, demanding.

It was, Devin thought, as confused as he was. In its way, as battered. What did it take from the blade, to do a major healing? How much of the rising threat did it really feel?

How much of Natalie could it feel?

Nothing, he thought fiercely at it. *She's not for you.* Not any part of her.

The back stairs, tight and enclosed, spit them out at the end of the guest wing. The blade hummed in his hand, warm and anticipating. *Hunting.*

Well, let it. There wasn't anyone up here, and maybe it would keep busy. Keep out of his head.

"Devin—"

She'd turned to him again. He grabbed her arm, pushed her up against the textured paint of the wall, footsteps echoing like whispers in this soaring, open hallway and spilling out to fall silent in the high, vaulted ceiling. "Look," he said. "Maybe I am, maybe I'm not. Let me *deal* with it. You deal with *you*."

She jerked her arm away, rubbing it—hurt and offended and not hiding it. "That's not how this goes," she told him. "That's not what we're about any longer. Don't you dare pretend otherwise!"

He growled. Nothing else, just growled, jerking away from her. Not failing to see in her eye that she recognized it for the frustrated capitulation that it was.

The blade hummed. He got the distinct impression that the discord pleased it. "Bastard," he muttered at it.

"Wait here," Natalie said, pressing him against the wall before they emerged on the mezzanine. "I'll cut the video feed."

Compton would figure out that they'd been there. If nothing else, the dead dog…also a dead giveaway. But that didn't mean they had to leave him a road map.

She slipped off to the office end of the mezzanine… returned within moments. "Now let's see what's down here. I'm going to be really disappointed if it's a red velvet porn room." Past the workout room, there to where the wide-tiled hall led to the bright solarium.

And the blade snarled to life. Fiery resentment, territorial ferocity…

Fear.

All those things it had fed him from the alleys, multiplied and echoing and slicing sharply through his mind. Raw surprise tore from his throat; he staggered into her.

This time, she didn't ask. She took him—not supporting, just *touching.* Slender but strong, the shape of her a familiar thing. Just *being.*

And the reality that was Natalie sliced right back through the blade's effects, so Devin sucked in a deep breath. "Took me by surprise," he said, easing himself straight—testing soreness and even function.

"Pretty much answers the question," she murmured, looking back over her shoulder—nervous, here where she could no longer explain away their presence.

"Oh, yeah," he said. "There's something to find, all right. And you aren't gonna like it, but *this?*" He lifted the knife, ever so slightly. "This thing's afraid."

Eloquent expression left no doubt, but she didn't falter. "Then let it choose which," she told him, nodding at the doors before them. "We won't have much time. Even if they don't find the dog…"

Point taken. Devin gave himself to the blade, if only for an instant. His instinct, his gut reaction. The blade rewarded him, pinging off the farthest door with particular sting. *Threat. Snarl. Resentment and anger.*

He nodded at the door in question, knotty alder with a rustic finish, black wrought-iron hardware. "There," he said, shaking off the taste of it, a quick shudder of his shoulders that he hadn't meant to give way to.

She took note, as she seemed to notice everything. Quick, sharp...absorbing it without getting stuck on it. With another glance down the hall, she stepped up to it and grasped the handle as if *believing* would be enough to do the trick. "It's locked," she said, unable to hide her disappointment. "I've got keys in my desk, but I think it's a safe bet none of them fit this particular lock."

"Safe enough," he murmured, regarding the knife most thoughtfully...hefting it slightly. *Nothing.* "Don't be a baby," he told it.

Beside him, Natalie laughed under her breath—but nonetheless crowded him slightly, her worry hand pressed against her thigh. "If it's not cooperating, I can pick—"

He raised an eyebrow.

"Yes," she said. "I can."

Ah. The demon blade wasn't about to be shown up by—

Well. By anyone or anything. And so Devin felt the shift of balance in his hand, and knew this particular lock pick needed no skill to guide it. He grinned. "You embarrassed it," he told her, a stage whisper as he applied the thing, turning it only enough to let the blade find its way.

The lock went *snick;* the knob turned in his hand.

And they were in.

A room from another time, another place—the taste of old wood paneling everywhere, built-in shelves gleaming, the carpet thick beneath their feet and layered not with a Southwest weaving, but a Persian rug of exquisite design and execution.

Other than the books and the black iron fittings and light fixtures, the room was unadorned and lightly furnished. No wall hangings—only a few closed cabinets. No draperies...in fact— "No windows," Devin murmured. Only a single solar tube skylight, spreading bright light throughout the room, illuminating especially the wing-backed leather chair and the small table beside it.

"No window," Natalie said. "Ugh." She stopped herself, shook her head, glanced at the blade. "Still afraid?"

It was the tactical knife again, sullen...withdrawn. He looked at it in surprise. "Sulking."

She shivered a little. "Somehow I like it better when it's hungry."

He gave her a wry look. "Somehow, so do I."

Chapter 20

Natalie wasted no time. She walked along the book-shelves, assessing the books—reading the spines as possible, but discovering them old, worn...various first editions, leather bound...cracked and aging. One whole bright section she instantly thought of as the travel section, with colorful trade paperbacks and stout local guides. Familiar country names jumped out at her—the Balkans, Brazil, western Africa...

Places Compton had been. Places in which he'd started his humanitarian projects. It only made sense.

What didn't make sense was to hide them away.

She glanced at the door, suddenly wary. It was as they'd left it—just barely ajar. But if someone found them here—

"Relax," Devin said, but his own voice sounded tight.

"If Compton finds us—if *anyone* finds us, then maybe it means we just get our answers sooner."

She would have been more convinced had he not looked so strained—had he not suddenly so obviously shifted to ease his pain.

If he hadn't shaken his head, frowning, his attention nowhere in this room at all.

"Toes," she whispered to him, her fingers still trailing over the book spines simply because she hadn't yet turned away.

"It's not—" He looked at her, shook his head. "It's not that. Or…it's not the same. I don't know—" He looked down at the blade. Still in hunting mode—she'd learned to recognize that much—but otherwise quiescent. Not showing off, no special effects…lying in his relaxed grip.

She found her fingers lingering at a worn book spine—a spine cracked with use, and not sitting on the shelf as evenly as it might have been.

On anyone else's shelf, it wouldn't have meant a thing. On this shelf, in this house…

Natalie knew Sawyer Compton. And here, in this place that was so very private, Compton wouldn't idly leave so much as a twitch out of place.

The book meant something.

"Hey," she said, and tugged it from the shelf.

A thin volume, without heft or size. Old and worn, edges rubbed pale. It smelled of more than just leather and conditioner…it smelled of astringent ash, faintly stinging her nose.

For a long moment, he stood just as he'd been—

puzzled, his head tipped slightly, his body braced against its pain.

Too much. They'd asked too much of him, too soon.

But he shook it off and came to her as she opened the book—supporting the spine, and letting it open to whatever page it would.

The pages settled to reveal a language that Natalie didn't recognize—not even an alphabet she recognized. Hebrew? Arabic? Someone's secret code?

A whispery susurrus crawled through her ears and down along her spine. She stiffened.

Devin raised his brow. "You heard that?"

"Did *you*?"

"I hear things all the time," he said dryly.

"I heard it," she admitted. "Just…for a moment. I'm not even sure what it was. Or what *this* is."

"You know Compton," he said reasonably. "Does he decode this thing in his head, or does he have notes somewhere?"

"Notes," she said. "He probably does do it in his head, but he likes to see his work written down. He likes to—"

"Admire it," Devin said, and grinned—only half a grin, here in Compton's house and in his most private of rooms, faltering from the night and surrounded by mysteries they hadn't begun to resolve. But that half a grin—pure Devin. Direct gray gaze so clearly that of the man who had held her the night before.

"I don't think he looks at it that way," she said, not bothering to stifle amusement. She set the book on the reading table. "Notes, and within decent reach."

But a quick look around offered no enlightenment—
nor a second, more careful look. "Wait," Natalie said,
and crossed the room to the chair, gingerly settling herself into it.

It felt slightly creepy. Definitely trespassing.

But Natalie smiled, and she reached to the side of
the chair, beneath—and she found it. A discreet shelf—
not meant to be secret so much as convenient and un-
obtrusive.

And ohh, were there notes. Taken in Compton's
neat, thoughtful hand, precise and tiny letters march-
ing across the page. Natalie swept her hand across the
top page, unable to contain a certain reverence—if only
because Compton's reverence for his subject matter came
through.

Devin knelt beside the chair to look over her arm.
"What the hell?"

"I haven't the faintest idea." And she didn't. For of all
the languages here on this first page, none were English.

He reached over her arm, barely touching the page...
his fingers whispering over it. "All the same," he murmured.

"What?" Startled, she looked from the page to his
face, found him frowning. And though she could see
the pain at the corners of his eyes, otherwise she found
only concentration. "How can you read—?"

"What?" he said, just as startled as she, looking away
from the text. "I can't. But look—all the same length,
more or less. One language after another." He stretched
over her, the clean scent of him briefly enveloping her;

when he settled, it was with the book in hand, opened to the same page as before. There, set in a section of doubly indented text, was a bold block of—

"Is this even printed on a press?" Natalie asked, startled all over again. "Or is this just…completely impossibly neat calligraphy of some sort?" She bent to the book without thinking, sniffing it—and regretting it. "It smells—"

"Hot metal," Devin murmured, as if the words had come unbidden. "Forged steel."

Natalie put her hand over the open book. "This makes no sense. None of it."

"Less sense than *this*?" Devin held up the blade.

"No," she said, a little alto growl. "Not *less* sense. But that still doesn't leave it making any sense at all." She pushed the book aside, returning to Compton's neat notes—a whole sheaf of them. Devin flipped over the first page, then the second…and stopped.

She instantly saw why. *English*. The paragraph, finally done in English. "He with the blade is cursed," she read out loud—and her voice strangled to a stop.

For suddenly her life made sense.

Compton knew about the demon blade.

He knew now…and he'd known then. Working through Ajay and his schemes even then, and Natalie so unwittingly tangled up in it all. Leo's death, part of the scheme—for Ajay had gone there that night expecting to come away with the blade.

What a surprise it must have been when Devin intervened—and then prevailed. They wouldn't have expected it of any man playing fair, not over the blade.

And then he'd created his sardonic little memorial—there, and the other alleys. He'd manipulated Natalie, taken her in…had it even been her idea, to direct her class load toward those things that would fill out a personal assistant's skill set? Or had it been—

She remembered now. Just a casual conversation at school one ordinary day. Someone who'd seemed kind and interested and impressed by her. And she'd never thought twice about ulterior motive or manipulation.

"Compton wanted me," she said, her voice sounding so very far away to her own ears, "because of my connection to that night. I must have been a huge disappointment, as little as I knew. But Ajay…Ajay always thought I knew more about his crew. Ajay always thought I was stepping out on him."

"The blade," Devin said, sounding just as strained. "He's been waiting for this."

For Devin to feel the touch of the wild road, as his brother had.

For the time to make another try at the blade.

Devin flipped the book closed. "See what else you can find like this."

Her eyes went wide, clear blue in the natural light overhead. "You want to *take*—"

"Hell, yes," Devin said, taking her arm—holding her tightly enough so a flicker of uncertainty crossed her features. "Do you realize what this is? What it *means*?"

"Yes, of course—we just said—"

He cut her off with an impatient shake of his head. "More than that. *Everything* more than that. Natalie, these are *answers.*"

"He'll know!" she said. "Don't you get it, Devin? You don't take what Sawyer Compton *owns.* I may have been blind these past few years, but I saw that much!"

"He already thinks he owns *you,*" Devin said softly, honest words slipping past to widen her eyes even further—first with hurt, then, as she turned away, brows tightening with regret—with acknowledgment.

And that's when the door slammed closed.

Not much of a slam, not when it was barely unlatched to begin with. But definite. Distinct. Natalie jumped to her feet; Devin was already there, his hand closing around the blade in disbelief.

From the other side of the door, a man's voice shouted an awkward and unconvincing phrase, harsh nonsensical syllables. And then, more intelligibly—full of relief, as if some particularly difficult duty had just been discharged, he added, "Get comfortable. Mr. Compton wants to talk to you."

The door locked, metal snicking against metal—and a second latch sliding into place at the very top of the door. Discreet. And Devin hadn't even noticed it. Hadn't realized they could be locked in here.

Harsh whispers crawled around the room, barely audible—brushing against his skin, stirring his hair.

Natalie dropped the sheaf of notes onto the chair and turned to him, pale. "Compton—"

"Is a man," Devin said, his hand twitching as the blade shot out sudden alarm, hot tingles of anger tracing along nerves. "And, as it happens, he is not the boss of me."

Her smile flickered in response, a wan expression, and he saw it, suddenly—the realization that her carefully hoarded choices hadn't been choices at all; the understanding that now, she had none left.

"Natalie," he said, and simply that—until she met his gaze, held it. Until they'd shared, suddenly, a smile. Small and determined on her part, and something more grim, a little more deadly, on his. *Whispers edged with barbed wire, scraping nerves...*

And then she frowned, her gaze flickering down to the blade—there where his arm now trembled slightly in thrall to it, the heat building. "It didn't warn us," she said, looking back to him with bafflement. "I thought you said—"

He gave the blade a soft snarl, a lifted lip. Defiance, as tendrils of influence crept across his chest, scraping whisper and hot pain combined. "Did you hear the sound of his voice?" he asked, and heard the change in his own voice—the effort of it. "That man was never a threat— the blade never saw him that way. He barely had the nerve to lock that door and make his little chant...whatever the hell—" He strangled down on those words, that thought, losing them for a moment as the traces of fire flared hot across his torso—cursed to feel his eyes roll back and his knees give way at the chair. Cursed again, spitting the word, and climbed to his feet—the knife, still in his grip, left a slashing trail across fine material.

Her hands on his arm, on his back—a gasp of cool reality.

"What?" she asked him. *"What?"*

He shook his head, eyes closed—pulling himself back together. "I wasn't ready for that. Son-of-a-*bitch,* I wasn't ready for that." He leaned, for a moment, into her slender strength. Every line of her body touching his, every separate press of each finger. "I don't know what it—I don't—" One leg twitched and faltered; he snarled back the blade. Guttural mutters crawled down his neck, along his spine. "Those words. They did something…" He lifted his head, found worried eyes, sharp chin trembling on fear. "He's coming. But we're here with his books. With his notes. We can still learn—"

She snatched up the notes, held them unsteadily so he could also see. "He with the blade is cursed. But he with the three, and the three being of two minors and a major, may wield the balance." She frowned. "What does that mean? Minors and major? The strength of the blades?"

He shook his head, fingers digging into the back of the chair, knife resting along the top. "The other languages. You know any of them? If we could get perspective…"

"Not enough Spanish for something like this," she said. "You?"

"Darlin'," he said, laughing shortly, "I can barely think in English."

She made a sound of dismay. "What is it *doing?*"

"The words," Devin managed. "The words…did something. Woke…something. The blade, it's…" He looked down at the gleaming metal in his hand with no little wonder, realizing it then. "It's afraid."

Natalie took a deep breath, held it for a long moment…looked away and then back again, catching him with the determination of her gaze. "Can you ask it?"

He gasped a curse through half a laugh, and clung to the chair—not wanting to go down—all the way down—in enemy territory. "I've spent all this time trying to keep it *out*—"

"I know," she said, just as determined. "But it's *afraid,* Devin. Maybe that means it knows what's going on."

It was afraid. But *it* had nothing on Devin, on the hard cold of deep horror at the thought of opening up to the deadly allure of it—at the thought of doing anything but fighting it with everything he could muster. Building walls, holding them.

"I *know,*" Natalie said again. As determined as she was, the fear still reflected in her own eyes, as clearly as a mirror. "I *know.*"

Of course she did.

Because she knew exactly what the blade could do. She'd seen it years ago in the alley; she'd seen his brother's mad features, his distorted death mask. She'd seen it in the parking lot weeks earlier; she'd seen Devin fighting it ever since—she'd seen it strip his sanity.

And she was trapped in here with him.

With it.

Chapter 21

Natalie didn't push. Not at the raw emotion on Devin's face—facing his worst nightmare, facing his brother's fate. Not a slow decline if he couldn't handle it, but a cataclysmic failure.

"Not yet," she muttered fiercely. "Here we are, with all these books…all these notes…" She swung away from him, back to the shelves that had struck her as so out of place on her first pass around the room.

The travel books.

She touched the spines. *Brazil. Africa. The Balkans.*

The alley where Leo had died, turned into the seed of a humanitarian project that had grown and spread…

Wells. Latrines. Clinics.

The blade and death, turned by Compton's dark

humor, by some twisted impulse, into life and affirma-
tion. Here, and…

There? And *there?*

"Oh, my God," she said. "What if there are *more?*"
She spun away from the books, her back against the
shelves—pressed up against them as if that could hold
back the very thought of it.

"Do you hear it?" Devin asked, head bent, weight
shifted to favor his leg and favor his back, a visible
tremor running through all. His voice came distant and
strained—only the chair held him up. "Do you hear
them?"

"Did you hear *me?*" She pushed right back at him, ag-
gressive in fear—more from what she saw in him than
what she'd found here.

After all, Compton had already done his worst—already manipulated her, already controlled her. She was
so over him—over working here, over his neat little
faux life—

A faint whisper rasped against her ear, sandpaper
and grit; she glanced around, suddenly wary. "Devin,"
she said, and crossed to him, hand closing around his
arm—muscle beneath tense unto trembling. "*Listen.*
You have to hear this! If there's more than one blade…
it explains everything!"

He lifted his head just enough to look at her, but his
eyes held no comprehension—the blue of them lost in
darkened gray, bleary with struggle.

"*Everything,*" she repeated. "Why you felt the threat
at my place that night—why you killed a man who disap-

peared. Why your brother reacted as he did that night—
why you reacted as you did the night Compton drugged
you. Why the blade would turn territorial and take you
with it." She took a deep breath. "How he even knows
about them in the first place. Why he wants you. Why
he used *me*—he probably thought I knew you, because
Ajay always believed it—that I was seeing someone.
That night he intended to show me what a mistake it
was. I always thought his big plan had been interrupted
by what happened there, but now...I think his big plan
was what happened there. Except I think he was supposed to come away with that knife."

Devin snorted, swaying slightly. "The blade chooses,"
he said, tipping his head against some irritation of
sound—*whispers gone loud, buzzing into a sharp
burr.* The skin between Natalie's shoulder blades tightened—she felt the change in him as he straightened to
look at her more fully. "Don't hesitate," he said, clearly
enough—if with a voice gone strangely thick. "Run if
you get the chance. Don't stop running. Hit the canal
path. Find that rottie yard. Turn 'em loose if you have
to. And then *don't stop running.*"

She shook her head, abandoned by words. "You don't
mean to leave you—"

"I *do*," he said fiercely, and coughed. Coughed again,
surprised by it, turning his face to his arm. Inexplicable
wind brushed her face, the sharp sting of barely audible
sound plucked her ears—all forgotten in the horror of
it when he looked at her, faintly puzzled...bright blood
staining his mouth and smudging his chin.

She couldn't hold back the gasp of it. On horrified impulse, she stepped back, tugging at his jacket—pushing it off his shoulders and dragging it down his back.

Disbelief warred with the horror. *"No,"* she said, stepping back to look at him. To see it.

Fresh blood blooming through his shirt over once-healed skin. She couldn't help herself—she touched it. Warm and wet, smearing thinly over her fingers. Another step back and she could see his leg, the dark stain over worn blue denim. And now she could hear it—his breathing, the sickening liquid sound of it in his throat.

She thought he said something; she couldn't be sure over the sudden roaring in her ears. She spoke over it— urgent words, in a voice that sounded like it came from somewhere other than her own throat. "Ask it!"

If he'd spoken before, he was beyond words now— but his expression was eloquent enough. Incredulous. And there, in his eyes, a hint of dark fear.

"Ask it," she urged him, moving back to his side. "I *know* what it means—what it *could* mean. To both of us. But, Devin—it's taking back what it gave you. It knows something we don't! If we don't get a clue right *now,* we're going to die! Both of us—and then Compton will have the blade!"

The fear didn't fade. But it made room for resignation…for acquiescence. "You," he said, barely audible now, "got my back?"

Impatience sparked. "I stayed with you that first night, and I never knew you," she said with no little asperity. "Now that I love you, I'm damned staying with you through this!"

He grinned, bloodstained and wan, and yet still struck her with his honesty—the direct connection to all that was Devin. "I heard that," he said, wiping futilely at the fresh blood on chin, smearing it everywhere—holding himself still when she reached out with the cuff of her borrowed shirt folded over her palm to do it for him. "You love me. I heard that."

"You heard it," she muttered, all too aware that fresh blood welled at the corner of his mouth; she rested her hand against his face. "Silly boy. Now ask that thing what's going on!"

"Yes," he said, still grinning, no little amount of that heartfelt response still lingering, *"ma'am."*

And then his eyes rolled back in his head and he folded to the floor, all his strings cut…all his questions unasked after all.

Sawyer Compton resisted the urge to clap. Resisting rhetoric commentary, however, was beyond his means. "Oh, very well played, Natalie, well played indeed. But I'm afraid you're right. You're both going to die—and very soon."

Not that they'd paid any attention when he'd opened the door, or that Natalie now did anything more than flip her hair back and scowl at him from where she knelt over the failing body of her lover.

"Compton," she said, and he hadn't expected the cold nature of her voice. He'd not even thought she had it in her—so carefully nurtured into being his very own creature as she was. "What have you done? What are you *doing?*"

He scoffed. "Surely you don't think I'm going to play that game where I now tell you everything."

"Surely I do!" she snapped. "You damned well owe me!"

He pondered that. She had, after all, brought him to this moment, if not through the exact path he'd expected. "Perhaps I do," he conceded. "But I'd also have to *care.*"

"Bastard," she muttered. "I already know enough. I know the attacks have nothing to do with the restaurants and everything to do with you. I know you have one of these blades—that you probably have more than one. What I don't understand is how you're still sane."

He smiled at her. "That's easy, my dear. I know better than to fight it. I went looking for what the blades can give me—so what fool would I be to deny the full power of them?" He lifted his gaze to the shallow closed cabinets that held his blades—minors, both of them, just waiting for a major to pull them together in a Triad—and felt the song of them. Inhaled it, opening his lungs to draw in the influence, the taste of hot metal on the air and the power brushing up against his skin. "This is what two of them can do," he said, trancelike. "Two of them, given full freedom, given full feeding. Can you imagine what I can do with a Triad?" And he snapped his eyes open to catch the realization on her face, the dread…the utter terror.

Through him, the blades drank. Greedy, as ever. Hungry, as ever. Quivering with restraint.

He shook his head—once, sharply. "Not yet, lovelies." And spoke the words to end their influence over Devin James's blade. Precise words with glottal stops and tangling consonants, rhythmic and surging.

For the major blade could only be absorbed while not in direct conflict with the other members of the intended Triad. Only while in its classic, fierce acquisition mode. Only while on the hunt, or in the fight.

And an opponent down was no opponent at all.

What the fu—? Devin rolled over on a groan, and repeated himself out loud—opening his eyes to find Natalie leaning over him—upside down, at that.

She said instantly, "Compton's here."

Oh, yeah, pretty much all he needed to know. Devin wrenched himself to his side, up to his knees. Didn't really matter what had happened, or why it had stopped happening.

More or less. For a ferocity of pain still twisted through his chest, still left his leg wavering beneath him. His breath came hot in his throat, a spongy sound to his breathing.

Not as bad as he'd been. But not healed. Not *re*-healed. He cursed again, pushing the heel of his hand against his brow. If he pushed hard enough, maybe it would all just make sense....

"Talk to it," Natalie whispered, daring to lean in close...her urgency gone beyond any mere disagreement over how they might proceed. Her face had drained of color; her eyes shone, a hint of red at the rims. Then she said, much more conversationally, "Mr. Compton was just telling me about his plans to rule the world. Or something like that."

"Big surprise," Devin grunted, finally finding the man—there, over at the wall—by one of the display cabinets, now open. Anticipation brought his schooled features alive—revealed a faint glint of something beyond it in his eyes.

Instead of his ubiquitous suit, he wore loose slacks and a black turtleneck, setting off the impeccable silver of his hair. The blade in his grip gleamed an impossible dull black matte—a knife that shouldn't have gleamed at all. A tactical knife with a tanto blade, rear hook and rip teeth in front of a deep forefinger groove.

It fit Compton's hand most perfectly.

"He's got a blade," Natalie said, and if her voice sounded a little high and carried the faintest of tremors, she nonetheless kept her words matter-of-fact. "Devin, he's got *two* blades. And he wants yours."

Devin stared blankly at her. It was, for the moment, all he had in him to do. *Two?* And he wanted a third?

How did he even still have his mind? How had he gotten *two?* How did he even know—what was he even— The blank look gave way to stunned and nearly incoherent reaction. "What the *fuck?*"

"Brilliant," Compton said dryly. "I am bested before we even begin."

"Works for me," Devin said. "Natalie, let's go." And

he got one leg under him, ready to push off—as if he thought they could do just that.

"Indeed," Compton said. "Walk away from the man who arranged the circumstances of your brother's death? Who has repeatedly attempted to end your own life, as well as your new lover's?" He made a derisive noise at Natalie's surprise. "Yes, of course, my dear—it does show."

Devin's eyes narrowed. "That old man," he said. "Outside the architectural firm."

"Oh, certainly," Compton said. "He would have killed Natalie. Killed her and been gone while you held her dying in your arms, blaming yourself. He is a consummate professional."

"Devin," Natalie said, her voice broken. "I'm sorry. I'm *sorry.*"

"Don't blame yourself, my dear," Compton told her. "You reacted as you were meant to. It was a no-lose scenario for me."

"Breaking him down. All of it…the things that happened here," Natalie said. "So you could come after the blade."

"Hey," Devin said, straightening ever so slightly. *"Trying* to break me down."

Natalie's mouth twitched in the barest smile.

"Two blades," Devin said, and this time he did make it to his feet, looking pointedly at the wall cabinet and the custom-made holder for the unique throwing knife there—a wooden handle fitting into its asymmetrical wheel of blades. "What the hell are you even thinking?"

"That," Compton said, inclining his head ever so slightly, "is mine to think."

"Oh, *now* you're just playing with your food," Devin snapped. He didn't allow himself to think that Compton had plenty of reason for such confidence—didn't allow himself to acknowledge the weakness that pain and blood loss and new shock had wrought in him.

The blade would only keep him alive, and only keep him fighting, as long as it was *his*.

Except the blade was afraid.

Affected by whatever Compton had done. And afraid.

Maybe, just maybe, for the moment, they were in this together.

For Compton moved away from the shelves, and that glint was back in his eye, and in his movement showed every moment of his discipline in the gym and the influence of a blade. "I *played*," he said. "I'm done playing now. Now, I need a good fight. A *hard* fight, to cement the new bond." He held out his blade—not a threat, but a presentation, formally done. *"Baitlia."*

Devin stared in silence—suddenly aware of protocol unknown. Not posturing, here—or at least, not *all* posturing. But a Thing Done.

An introduction.

It has a name?

He didn't miss Natalie's desperate glance; he had no illusions his contrast with Compton—smooth and suave and confident, standing in opposition to a man battered and leaking blood and barely on his feet.

A man holding an unnamed blade.

"Well, hell," he said. "How about I kick your ass, and then we'll talk?"

The blade's heat warned him—Compton's harsh word, the sharp scent of hot metal and the spark of *change*—

Devin followed instinct, throwing himself aside—landing heavily, rolling awkwardly...tangling with the side table. His arm stung, in the manner of a paper cut; metal and wood sliced cleanly through the air, embedding in the wall opposite Compton. *Lance.*

"Devin," Natalie said, as urgent as she'd ever been. "He called them *minors*—his blade! He called yours a *major*. It's stronger than you think!"

And it's scared witless.

Nothing of the hunter in his mind, only the hunted. Nothing of its predatory ferocity, only an awareness of vulnerability.

Another harsh word from Compton, his hand out-stretched—and the lance returned to him, a molten flow finding final form in a strong Roman blade...gladiator's blade. *Gladius Hispanus,* his own blade whispered at him, wanting nothing to do with it.

Wanting nothing to do with *Compton.*

Because Compton had control. Compton and his gut-turally harsh words—commanding shape, commanding the moment. Commanding, in some ways, Devin's own blade. Taking from it, and forcing it to take from Devin.

Natalie was no slouch. She ducked in to snatch up the little table—moving it out of Devin's way, even as she flung it directly at Compton.

It shattered harmlessly against his outthrust sword, earning a snarl of annoyance, words spoken through gritted teeth. "This is not your fight, Natalie."

"You are so wrong," she said, standing braced. "This has been my fight for *years!*"

"Natalie," Devin said, coming to his feet—his blade's favored saber in hand, dread in his heart. "No—"

"Then," Compton said precisely, "it is not your fight anymore."

"Natalie—" And Devin saw it coming, and he wasn't close enough, or fast enough, or strong enough, to do anything other than watch the cold annoyance on Compton's face—

As he took that Spanish-Roman blade and ran her through.

Not a clean wound, not an instant kill. Battlefield death, slow and grueling. Devin knew it, crying out in anguished denial as Natalie staggered back, hands clutched over blood spilling low on her slender torso.

Compton yanked the sword back and watched with a smug satisfaction as the leaf-shaped blade drank in dark blood, cleaning itself…clearing metal unto gleaming, a spiking flash of lucent movement along its edge.

It was the look he sent Devin that did it. *Was that enough to bring out the fight in you?*

Devin choked on grief and fear and fury, forgot he was barely on his feet, forgot his pain and his blade's reluctance, leaping forward with the saber held just so, balanced in his grip, over Compton's guard and ready for the strike—

A harsh word, and the blade beneath his own glared hot and flung itself at his ribs, a flanged mace. No power behind the swing—no room for it, no time for it—but heavy metal that thumped into his side and sent the floor up to slam him in the face.

Chapter 22

The laugh came low and in his ear. "Come, Devin. Must I torture her through her last moments to bring you into this fight with your whole heart? Or didn't you ever realize—the fiercer the battle, the deeper the new bond?"

What—?

Words, only words, making no impact against the only driving force left within him. Not the blade. *Natalie.* He retched blood on the intricate carpet, pattern swimming before his eyes, and caught a glimpse of her—fallen against the wall of shelves, clutching the deep wound low in her side, her gaze catching his. *Terror. Understanding.*

Resignation.

Damned well *not*.

Talk to it, she'd told him, and he'd flinched from

the thought. A coward, losing the moment. The *only* moment.

But resignation?

Damned well *not*.

He focused bleary eyes long enough to find her gaze, eyes huge and heartbreaking where light pooled down on her from the skylight. "Come and get me if I get lost," he told her, and waited just long enough to see those eyes widen with understanding before he sank back down into darkness.

Talk to me, he told it, clawing to hold on to thought, far too aware that while the blade now kept him alive, it did little else. Silent. Retreating.

It knew what they were up against.

It knew so much more than he did.

Talk to me.

Tell me your name.

Denial. Refusal. Scorn. Its name was not for him.

It *blamed* him, he realized—for the position they were in. For the shackles it feared.

What shackles?

Denial! It struck back, drawing fire through his bones—making that fragile human body arch with pain.

But answers... The shackles would come from the Triad—that which Compton had every intention of creating. That the major blade would not dominate the two minor blades, but be dominated and controlled by them—and they, in turn, by the single man who wielded them.

A single man who would then wield the combined power of all three.

A man's only got two hands—

A slap of irritation, an excruciating rake of pain—a body crying out of its own volition—and whispers of awareness, thoughts rising as though they'd been his all along. With a Triad, a man had more than physical weapons. He had subtle influence. He could instill fear; he could incite lust. He could control and manipulate and own, and he could see to it that no one had the means to stop him.

Tell me your name.

Bracing himself for the response did no good. He was dimly aware of his head thumping against the carpet, his body seizing—Compton, frustrated, kicking him—demanding battle. *Craving* it. Natalie's cry of protest in the background, weak and filtered by veils of reality.

A temper tantrum, held by an entity with power and bitter resentment, acted out on his body. Flailing away at his thoughts, his being…his very awareness of self. It was someone else choking for breath, someone else spitting blood, someone else clawing at the expensive silk carpet with one hand and clutching a preternaturally sharp blade in the other.

Just enough presence of mind left to ask…

What do you want?

Silence. Startled cessation.

And then a flood.

It didn't want to be in the Triad. It didn't want to be with Compton. It hadn't seemed to have cared if Leo lived or died, but now Devin wasn't even sure of that, now knowing how much Compton had interfered with Leo...how much he'd incited the blade, had turned Leo against his own nature.

And then, in a whisper...an answer. Direct and clear in his mind.

Redemption.

He didn't understand. Denied it.

Death, he told it, snarling back. *You want death. You want me to find it for you. You want to corrupt my soul until I do. That's what you've* always *wanted.*

The punishing pain was more of a caress, as the blade measured such things. A wash of dull coals, welling up from within, sweeping past the worst of the injuries... stopping the blood. And the words, again, very clear.

I change you. Or *you change me.*

His breath caught on sudden understanding.

Redemption.

A bully of a blade, captured up in itself...nuances he didn't yet understand, origins he didn't yet understand...

Waiting for someone to change it for the better, instead of being changed themselves—for the worse.

Even possible?

Faint and haughty negation.

The blade thought not.

But there was a first step. There was the human resisting *being changed.*

Devin clung to persistence, to the faint and familiar signs of healing, the blade exhausted, the human exhausted but at least not dying. He gathered his will and he gathered his words and he punched through that final fog. *Tell me your name.*

Silence from within. Only the sound of Natalie's soft, uneven breathing, her faint gasp of pain. Of Compton, hovering, growling with frustration…wanting his fierce, climactic fight, wanting the blade's ownership sunk deep.

Of Devin's own harsh breath, his heart hammering out a galloping and unsteady beat, the rush of it through his body.

Until, finally…

Anheriel.

Relief made him as weak as the pain had done. A foothold…*a chance.*

Because he now knew enough. He knew what the blade wanted. He knew neither of them wanted Compton to prevail. Neither wanted Devin to die. He could work with that—

And the blade, whispering in his mind. *I am what I am.*

Threat without malice. Threat as fact. *Threat as reality.*

But someone had him, if not by the throat, by the front of his shirt, there at the base of his throat—lifting him, a gust of rude breath against the side of his face, no little amount of spittle with the vehemence of it. "Fight, damn you! I expected more from you than this! Or do you truly want to hear her agony before she dies? Before *you* die?"

And the blade in his hand, warming, changing…

the little brass knuckle knife. *Perfect.* He slammed a
blow into the side of Compton's face, heard the crack
of bone—thumped back down to the floor as Compton
shouted in surprise and fell away.

First things first. He wrenched himself to his side,
rolled up from there—hands and knee, one leg dragging,
over to Natalie. Seeing that even the fear and adrenaline
wasn't keeping away shock—skin gone pale, a fine sheen
of sweat dampening the tendrils of hair at her temple, the
rest of it fallen loose from its clip, highlights as bright
as ever beneath the skylight.

"Triad," he said. "Gotta stop him, sweetheart. Even
this blade knows better."

"I know," she said, without any sound behind it—
reaching out just long enough to brush him with the
ends of her fingers before her hand fell.

God, he wanted to gather her up and kiss the tremble out of those lips and the fear out of those eyes. He
wanted—

Compton cursed behind him. Devin closed his eyes;
he turned away. And he barely made it to his feet before
Compton staggered back to his own, the elegant lines
of his face distorted.

Devin's saber had returned. He looked at Compton,
gave him a grim little smile, and said, *"Anheriel."*

Compton took a sharp breath. Through his teeth, he
said, "Congratulations. I hadn't expected that much of
you."

"Get over it. I haven't joined you on the dark side of
the force. And Anheriel doesn't want to, either."

"Anheriel," Compton breathed. He smiled. "Anheriel won't have a choice."

Just as Natalie had never had a choice. Nor Leo. Nor all those others who died in the alleys.

Devin found the strength. He stole it from the blade, he stole it from himself. He closed in on Compton with speed and sparks and flashing light—found Compton, too, had reverted his blade to something long and sweeping, heavier, bearing a wicked trailing point and a sharp swage. A blade that would only need to bite deeply once to finish this fight.

But a slower blade.

And Compton bled.

And Compton tired.

If Devin felt his own energy bleeding away, his good leg growing leaden and his bad stuttering beneath him, he also felt the fire of Anheriel behind him. And Natalie—pulling herself straighter, managing to crouch against the wall—getting out of his way; she was behind him, too.

Swift blows, a parry barely there in time, a beat against Compton's blade and a quick faltering bind and that broad, heavier sweep reached out to tap him, nicking out flesh from his arm.

Devin blew sweat from his upper lip. *Anheriel—*

But the blade, as much as it fought for them, still sought his weak points. Twisted against him, turning him. Yearning for the wild animalistic retribution it had brought out in Leo, those years ago—

Bringing in the fog.

Devin snarled against it, battering Compton back—and the blade surged within him.

I am what I am.

The blade's nature. As if it could stop itself no more than he could.

"Devin," Natalie whispered, seeing it. "Oh, God, Devin, fight it!"

But for that, he needed Natalie. And he was losing Natalie. Even in this moment, even as she tried to stay out of his way—

His hand drooped—knuckles clenching white, the fog closing in.

"Devin!" Natalie cried, a thin sound.

I am what I am—

And Compton smiled within that ruined face, streaming blood from a dozen deep wounds, tattered and worn and—

Victorious.

He smiled, and he lifted his blade, and he came on.

"*My* choice!" Natalie cried.

Her hand coming around his waist from behind, that electrifying touch, crystal clear.

Spreading its clarity...fingers firm against his skin, sliding up to rest on his ribs—coming up from beneath his sword arm from behind, reaching out—

Snapping reality back in place, her hand over his on the blade as he raised it, lifting it—a high guard position to slip beneath Compton's strike as they stepped aside together, thrusting out with the saber—

Parting muscle, cleaving bone...

Stopping a beating heart.
Stopping the world.

Compton's blades wailed in denial—grieving, howl-ing banshee mad in the strident, rising voice of an-guished metal, circling the room to clash and echo and intertwine—

And slap them down.

Natalie hadn't expected to open her eyes at all.

Not with the blood spilling out of her body, internally rent and torn and far too much time had passed to do anything about it.

But open her eyes she did.

For a long moment, she did nothing more than that—sorting out the tangle of Devin's arm beneath her, the sprawl of his body beside her—the sound of his con-fused groan in her ears.

Alive.

As she was, somehow, alive. Her wound throbbed with an increasing intensity—a burn, and a sudden twitch that made her gasp.

And then, like that, it eased. She found herself breath-ing again. She found herself thinking again.

She found herself with the urge to close her grip around the cool, textured handle resting loosely within her fingers, and frowned.

That wasn't right.

She didn't have Devin's knife.

She found herself belly-down on the intricate Persian carpet, looking at her own hand where it lay before her face, resting across an unfamiliar knife—strong, straight spine joining directly to the handle of polished antler, no thumb rise over the flat top guard, the long drop quillon brushing her forefinger. Five inches of blade, a drop point and Damascus steel...

Brazilian knife. Hard-working knife for hard-working llama and alpaca herders.

How?

And her belly burned from the inside out, hot whiskey flames firing her mind, and she knew.

"Oh, no," she said, panic rising as she pushed herself away from the floor and yet somehow couldn't bring herself to let go of the knife even as she recoiled. "No, no, no. Not me. *Please* not me—"

Baitlia.

Compton's blade.

Devin groaned, a heartfelt sound, and followed it with a curse—extricating the hand on which she'd been lying, grunting as he sorted himself out...panting there on his back, a regular if pained rhythm.

And then his breath caught, and she knew he'd seen. Knew he understood. "Natalie—"

"*Please* not me!" she repeated, holding the blade out...looking at it, feeling some nameless urge...unable to understand at all.

"Compton," Devin said gently. "It wants...*Compton.*"

To absorb him, just as Devin's blade had absorbed every sign of the men in the parking lot.

"That's just *sick!*" She glanced at Compton's crumpled form, so very near, so very dead; she wanted to fling the blade away. *Don't even touch me, blade!*

She didn't.

Instead, she sobbed—half a sob, a choked sound. "It belonged to him, and now it would *feed* on— Oh, *God.*"

"It never belonged to him," Devin said. "Not in that way. And…" he hesitated, spoke with new assurance. "It is what it is."

She yanked Devin's red shirt from her waistband, pulling the soft material up until it cleared the gaping wound in her belly.

Gaping, but not bleeding.

And above it, the edge of a brand-new tattoo—more than a tattoo, really. Slightly raised whorls of a sinuous design that might have been Celtic, might have been a Middle-Eastern glyph—and wasn't truly either. *Just like Devin's.*

She couldn't help the noise that escaped her—panic and horror and understanding.

"Natalie." He moved up close behind her, his arm encircling her—a comfortable enclosure, resting over one shoulder, brushing her collarbone…drawing her back to him. "This is us. We can do this."

She drew a deep, shuddering breath. "My choice," she said, and laughed, low and bitter. "No one to blame but myself."

He pressed his lips against her neck. "We know more than we did. Look around—we know how to *learn* more. We can do this." He eased his hand down her arm, to her wrist—led it, unresisting, to place the blade by Compton. "Let it recharge. It'll be easier if you do."

She did, then, finally drop the blade, leaning back against him. "My choice," she whispered.

Chapter 23

Natalie pushed the legal papers across Devin's kitchen bar counter, riddled as they were with terms and phrases that only a lawyer could parse.

Didn't matter. She'd gotten the gist of it. She'd understood it as it was explained by Compton's lawyer; she'd understood it as the bone-deep awareness of Compton's history trickled in through Baitlia.

Demon blade.

She understood, these weeks after Compton's death, that the estate belonged to Devin now.

Typical of Compton's dark humor, she was beginning to understand. Build humanitarian efforts in those places where he'd acquired blades. Give his wealth not to some distant relative, but to the very man who'd killed him. Mocking humor.

And they'd learned something else, too: the lawyer knew. About the blades, about the gist of what had happened in that private little study. Although the disposition of the estate had been a long-standing arrangement, Compton had left his lawyer a letter with Devin's name. *In case.*

Too bad he hadn't left a body.

And that was something else they'd learned about his lawyer. He was a man who could arrange things. Bribes, a predeceased John Doe playing the role of Sawyer Compton, now declared dead of natural causes—a body ready for cremation; ashes to be buried beneath a stone with Compton's name. All done before they'd even known the terms of the will. While they still huddled together at Devin's small home, healing and holding, and letting the rest of the world wonder what had happened.

Not a man they particularly trusted.

Natalie spread her hand out over the papers, shaking her head. In the little living room, Devin's television muttered away over an old Western; he lay sprawled on the couch, his eyes half closed. Or probably closed now. It was, she'd learned, the one way he shut out the murmur of his own blade. Not enough, in the long run—not even enough any longer—but a habit in which he still retreated when he had something to absorb.

And ohh, there was plenty of that.

The estate…now Devin's. Not that it wouldn't take a while to straighten things out—a time during which the brutish security teams had been dismissed, Jimena had been assured of her position, and Devin had gone through Natalie's little home, clearing it of invasive hidden cameras.

She still didn't feel welcome there. Small Devin's home might be, but…

It held two of them. For now.

Besides, she had a lot to learn about wielding a blade.

It sat small and warm in her pocket, a sheathed Spanish blade: antler-handled, a short palm knife with a straight spine and an upswept curve—meant for rabbit-skinning, and all around utilitarian.

Maybe one of these days she'd get used to knowing so much about any given knife at a glance, and more than that when she took it in hand. Or maybe she'd get used to the idea that she quite suddenly had a tattoo over her heart, curving over the swell of her breast…both beautiful and horrifying.

Baitlia.

She glanced at Devin, found him still sleeping—or not—his sock-clad foot twitching slightly where it hung over the end of the couch. Self-consciously—forever self-conscious about *this*—she lifted the hem of her soft cotton sweater, pushing down slightly on the waistband of casual slacks.

It was still there. The healing scar of the wound that should have killed her, only a week or so earlier.

She tested it, stretching her arms overhead, twisting from side to side. Only a twinge. She couldn't help a guilty glance at Devin—he'd been so deeply battered, so embattled with his blade…the healing hadn't been clean. He'd finally returned to Enrique's for careful weights and treadmill work, but Enrique would have to find another sparring crash test dummy for a while.

She smiled. Enrique, irascible and still without any clear notion of how to use a cell phone, but back at the gym.

For the moment, Natalie didn't see the kitchen or the papers. She didn't see Devin dozing out in the other room, trusting her...his foot twitching and his breathing just slightly uneven, as if in response to those things going through his subconscious mind.

She saw him as he'd been, two days after Compton's death, bringing Enrique home—but stopping at the gym first, of course. Just to check on it.

Enrique had looked terrible, barely able to stand straight enough to walk, his face swollen and misshapen—but his eye sharp between bouts of fatigue.

Devin had looked little better. Limping, still coughing...weight and muscle lost in the process of healing. But fiercely protective of Enrique—enough so the young men at the gym quickly faded back as Devin settled Enrique behind his desk. Just a visit...just long enough to see that all was well, and then straight home to bed, where his teenage grandniece would be spending half days with him until he healed.

Natalie herself was still tender, still tentative...still dazed by her new association with Baitlia.

None of them had been expecting Ajay Dudek. Leo's old friend, and Natalie's former fiancé. The man Compton had used in his quest for the blade—and the man who'd been happy to comply for what he'd hoped to gain.

"Nat," he'd said.

And Enrique had narrowed his eyes and reached for a certain desk drawer, and Devin had straightened his shoulders no matter the cost, taking a step that put him between Ajay and the other two.

Ajay had shaken his head. He looked older than Natalie expected—his features, instead of maturing into definition, had thickened at his neck, his nose; added flesh to his cheeks. His broken hand had been swaddled in casting. "No, no," he'd said. "I'm not Compton's any longer."

"What makes you the hell think I care?" Devin growled.

Ajay lifted one shoulder in a shrug. "I came here knowing you might kill me. That you could. And that no one would ever be the wiser." He gave Devin's hand a meaningful glance, where it had slipped into his vest pocket. *Anheriel.*

"Then why come at all?" The growl hadn't left Devin's voice—the glower hadn't left his eyes. Natalie put a hand on the small of his back—quietly, from behind. Being with him. Letting him know she was all right.

Ajay shifted back a step. "Because I need to know whether or not you're coming after me. Now, later... whenever. And if I run, is it going to make a difference."

Enrique suggested kindly, "I think you just kill him now, *hijo.* Put him out of that misery."

Devin grinned, and Ajay—not a man of much color to begin with—paled, but for harsh red spots on his cheeks from the outdoor cold. "Nat," he said, and stopped to swallow visibly. "Nat, you might say something."

She moved up closer to Devin; she found her hand slipping into the pocket that held Baitlia. "What do you want me to say, Ajay? You want me to stop them from playing with you? I think you deserve that. You want me to stop them from killing you?" Her voice grew harder; her eyes narrowed. "You almost killed Enrique. You almost killed the man I love. And why—because you thought there was some faint chance that you could still come out of all this, all these many years later, with one of those blades? What exactly do you want me to say?"

His lips thinned. "You loved *me* once. We had a good thing, once. That oughta be worth something."

Natalie stiffened; Devin glanced back at her. To her surprise, his glower had changed to something of grim satisfaction. She gripped the back of his vest. "No, Ajay. We *didn't*." Was it her imagination, or had Devin leaned back ever so slightly into her touch? Subtle support. "*You* had a good thing once. I grew out of it, and now I know I'm better than anything you ever offered me."

The conviction in her voice startled Ajay—widened eyes, and that unpleasant expression he got when things weren't going his way.

It was Devin who added, so casually, "You wouldn't be looking for this, would you?" as he guided Natalie's hand out of her pocket—there, where Baitlia sat—first the little palm-sized Spanish skinning blade it liked so much—and then, under Ajay's scrutiny, shedding its snug, minimal sheath to flare bright blue-white, singeing hot metal flowing to the Brazilian knife it also favored.

Ajay cursed...but his gaze stayed riveted. Not horrified, not frightened...

Lusting.

"Kinda gets you, doesn't it?" Devin said. "All the years you've waited, all the trouble you've gone to... even the way you used Natalie back then. Or thought you were using her, you dumbass. She never had anything going with my brother—never even knew him. Hanging out with people who hang out with each other...not even *close*." He tipped Natalie's blade; light stroked along the glimmering Damascus steel. "Now she has one."

"Son of a bitch," Ajay muttered.

"No, seriously," Natalie said. "I think *dumbass* is closer to the truth. Maybe even double dumbass."

And there was Anheriel in Devin's hand, the agate handle polished bright, the metal reflecting sharply. "By the way, Ajay," he said, so gently, "the third blade—" The one left bereft of bonding at Compton's death, never part of the action at all— "Don't come looking for it."

And Ajay, his lust fading visibly into defeat, had said, "But...we're good. You're not going to let me walk away now and mess me up later?"

"*We're* good," Devin had observed—in total command of the blade, now. In total command of himself. "You pretty much suck. But go suck on your own time."

Natalie hadn't been able to help it—the twitch of a smile.

Ajay had taken a step back; Devin had taken a step

forward. "Maybe you might want to move on out of this area anyway. Just for your own sake. Because, dude— check it out. What's this city got to offer you now? Except maybe the constant reminder that Natalie has what you always wanted…and I've got *her*."

Natalie smiled, there at Devin's kitchen bar, her eyes closed and her mind's eye leaving memory to replace it with now, *here*.

So many things left to sort out. Details about the estate…details about the knives, about how she and Devin would move forward from here. Some of it was obvious—the research, the need to understand what the knives were—where they came from, whether they could be controlled without completely succumbing to the dark path Compton had taken, whether Natalie's methods would keep their souls intact after all.

Not to mention that Compton had chronicled visits to three countries. Started humanitarian projects in three countries, establishing his philanthropy even as he sought the power that made him a danger to all. *His cover.* And in that private study, they'd found hand-crafted mounts for three blades.

But Compton had had only two.

So many things left to sort out.

For now, it was enough to know that they had lived through the previous days; they were healing—together. They would learn—together. They would get through this—together.

Their choice.

Natalie gathered the papers and padded quietly past

the back of the couch, returning them to the little table by the door. She thought she'd do some yoga stretching…maybe some of the Tai Chi he'd begun to teach her.

Quiet activities, done quietly. Healing, focusing.

Except as she padded back past the couch, his arm snaked up, snagged her—and just that fast, dragged her over the back of it to slide down on him—a shriek of surprise, a laugh of delight, limbs already tangling. "I thought you were asleep!"

"Big mistake," he said, inhaling deeply of the hair behind her ear and tickling her mightily in the process.

"Or incredibly clever ploy," she shot back at him, her hand slipping unerringly down the flat of his belly and under his belt.

"Wuh…" he said, quite obviously forgetting how to breathe, his hands closing around her arm, her waist— and then gone demanding, one hand down her pants to knead her bottom. He pulled her close, pushing up against her as the other found its way up under her sweater.

Natalie laughed, stroking him; his head tipped back, his eyes closed. She soaked in his groan through the sudden skin-on-skin contact, belly to belly, chest to chest. Here, then, was another sort of focusing activity.

And she didn't think it would be quiet at all.

* * * * *

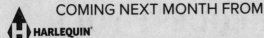
#161 DARKEST DESIRE OF THE VAMPIRE
by Rhyannon Byrd and Lauren Hawkeye

A highly sensual collection of stories from Rhyannon Byrd and Lauren Hawkeye. In "Wicked in Moonlight," Lainey Maxwell poses as a vacationing tourist in hopes of uncovering the truth about her brother's death. She's stunned when help comes from the last place she ever expected it: Nick Santos, the dark, intimidating vampire who owns a private beach where a string of recent murders has occurred. Then, in "Vampire Island," all Isla Miller wants is one exciting week in the midst of her boring life. When she meets Sloane Goldhawk, a vampire employed at a tropical island, she gets far more than she bargained for.

#162 PHANTOM WOLF
Phoenix Force • by Bonnie Vanak

U.S. Navy SEAL and powerful shape-shifter Sam Shaymore's assignment is clear: defeat the Dark Lord. Until, that is, a former lover he hasn't seen since he was a teenager becomes involved. The moment Kelly Denning learns that the Dark Lord is kidnapping children from the orphanage she manages, she insists on accompanying Sam on his dangerous mission. Fearful for her life, Sam insists on Kelly staying behind, but he can't deny the powerful passion rekindling between them or the strong woman she has become.

REQUEST YOUR FREE BOOKS!

2 FREE NOVELS FROM THE PARANORMAL ROMANCE COLLECTION PLUS 2 FREE GIFTS!

YES! Please send me 2 FREE novels from the Paranormal Romance Collection and my 2 FREE gifts (gifts are worth about $10). After receiving them, if I don't wish to receive any more books, I can return the shipping statement marked "cancel." If I don't cancel, I will receive 4 brand-new novels every month and be billed just $22.76 in the U.S. or $23.96 in Canada. That's a savings of at least 17% off the cover price of all 4 books. It's quite a bargain! Shipping and handling is just 50¢ per book in the U.S. and 75¢ per book in Canada.* I understand that accepting the 2 free books and gifts places me under no obligation to buy anything. I can always return a shipment and cancel at any time. Even if I never buy another book, the two free books and gifts are mine to keep forever.

237/337 HDN F4YC

Name	(PLEASE PRINT)	
Address		Apt. #
City	State/Prov.	Zip/Postal Code

Signature (if under 18, a parent or guardian must sign)

Mail to the **Harlequin®** Reader Service:
IN U.S.A.: P.O. Box 1867, Buffalo, NY 14240-1867
IN CANADA: P.O. Box 609, Fort Erie, Ontario L2A 5X3

Want to try two free books from another line?
Call 1-800-873-8635 or visit www.ReaderService.com.

* Terms and prices subject to change without notice. Prices do not include applicable taxes. Sales tax applicable in N.Y. Canadian residents will be charged applicable taxes. Offer not valid in Quebec. This offer is limited to one order per household. Not valid for current subscribers to Paranormal Romance Collection or Harlequin® Nocturne™ books. All orders subject to credit approval. Credit or debit balances in a customer's account(s) may be offset by any other outstanding balance owed by or to the customer. Please allow 4 to 6 weeks for delivery. Offer available while quantities last.

Your Privacy—The Harlequin® Reader Service is committed to protecting your privacy. Our Privacy Policy is available online at www.ReaderService.com or upon request from the Harlequin Reader Service.

We make a portion of our mailing list available to reputable third parties that offer products we believe may interest you. If you prefer that we not exchange your name with third parties, or if you wish to clarify or modify your communication preferences, please visit us at www.ReaderService.com/consumerschoice or write to us at Harlequin Reader Service Preference Service, P.O. Box 9062, Buffalo, NY 14269. Include your complete name and address.

PARA13R

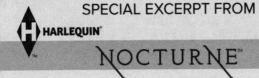
WICKED IN MOONLIGHT

by Rhyannon Byrd

"So now you're no longer afraid of me?" Nick asked, that in-
scrutable expression back on his face.

"Why should I be?"

His voice went eerily soft again. "There's a hell of a lot I
could do to you without killing you, Lainey."

"True. But you wouldn't."

"Yeah?" His blue eyes were shadowed…dark. "And why's
that?"

"I can just…tell."

"Christ, I don't believe what I'm hearing," he muttered, the
moment of teasing over as he shoved to his feet. Suddenly she
found herself staring up at almost six and a half feet of pissed-
off vampire. "You can just *tell?*"

Her chin went up a notch. "That's right."

"The way I see it," he bit out, glaring down at her, "you
should be screaming bloody murder right about now."

She would have explained if she could, but she barely understood her own mind at the moment. All she knew was that she
felt safe with this man…or vampire…or whatever he wanted

to call himself. Safer than she had in…a really long time.

Locking her gaze hard on his, Lainey looked him right in the eye and said, "I'm not afraid of you, Nick. So why would I scream?"

"Take off the goddamn blinders," he snarled, swiping one of those large hands through the air. "You saw what happened to your brother. You shouldn't trust me. Hell, you shouldn't trust *any* man."

"Yeah, well, you know what I think? I think you need a woman who can help you learn to lighten up a little."

He went completely still. "Is that right?" he finally asked, his voice doing that soft, raspy thing again that made her feel like the words were stroking her skin.

"Yes," she breathed out, trying not to shiver.

"You mean a woman like *you?*" He moved even closer to the side of the bed, the look in his eyes both dark and bright, as if the midnight sky had been spread out over a hot, molten glow. "Is that what I need, Lainey?"

Find out if Lainey is exactly what Nick needs in WICKED IN MOONLIGHT by Rhyannon Byrd, featured in *DARKEST DESIRE OF THE VAMPIRE*. Available June 4, 2013, from Harlequin® Nocturne™.

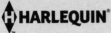
NOCTURNE™

They're on a collision course with danger and destiny…

Powerful mage and navy SEAL Sam Shaymore teams up with his former lover Kelly Denning to stop a deadly assassination plot. Although he has every reason to distrust her, Sam knows he must rely on his instincts— and his heart—before it's too late.

PHANTOM WOLF,

**a suspenseful new tale in
The Phoenix Force miniseries from**

BONNIE VANAK

**Available June 4, 2013,
from Harlequin® Nocturne™.**

HARLEQUIN®

A *Romance* FOR EVERY MOOD™

**Stay up-to-date on all your
romance-reading news with the
Harlequin Shopping Guide,
featuring bestselling authors, exciting new
miniseries, books to watch and more!**

The newest issue will be delivered right to you
with our compliments! There are 4 each year.

Signing up is easy.

EMAIL

ShoppingGuide@Harlequin.ca

WRITE TO US

HARLEQUIN BOOKS
Attention: Customer Service Department
P.O. Box 9057, Buffalo, NY 14269-9057

OR PHONE

1-800-873-8635 in the United States
1-888-343-9777 in Canada

Please allow 4-6 weeks for delivery of the first issue by mail.

HSGSIGNUP